Praise for

the Seems
the split second

A Kidsreads.com Best Book

"This sequel continues to develop a truly ingenious setting while proving every bit as much of a nail-biter as the first." —*Booklist*

"Hilarious wordplay, capitalized idiomatic expressions, puns, and figures of speech propel the plot along at a manic pace. . . . Advise readers to approach this book with a Grain of Salt and with Tongue firmly in Cheek for a wild ride." —*SLJ*

Praise for

the Seems
the glitch in sleep

A Book Sense Pick
A Kidsreads.com Best Book
A Teenreads.com Best Book
A New York Public Library 100 Titles
for Reading and Sharing Selection

★ "This is a rollicking tale, with great world-building and likable characters and a strong setup for further adventures. Unlike Garth Nix's conceptually similar The Keys to the Kingdom series, this story is upbeat and full of humor, seeming to draw a novel from David Wiesner's *Sector 7* template." —*SLJ*, starred review

"The high sense of adventure and an abundance of goofball humor should appeal especially to boys." —*Publishers Weekly*

"Offbeat exploration of a universe-tilting idea." —*Booklist*

Books by John Hulme and Michael Wexler

the Seems
the split second

John Hulme and Michael Wexler

illustrations by Gideon Kendall

BLOOMSBURY

NEW YORK BERLIN LONDON

Published by Bloomsbury U.S.A. Children's Books
175 Fifth Avenue, New York, New York 10010

The Library of Congress has cataloged the hardcover edition as follows:
Hulme, John.
The split second / by John Hulme and Michael Wexler ;
illustrations by Gideon Kendall.—1st U.S. ed.
p. cm.—(The Seems)
Summary: Now thirteen years old and still a Fixer in the parallel universe called
The Seems, Becker Drane is called upon to repair the damage caused by an
enormous bomb planted in the Department of Time, an act of terrorism perpetrated
by the evil members of The Tide, a group that is trying to destroy The World.
ISBN-13: 978-1-59990-130-5 • ISBN-10: 1-59990-130-7 (hardcover)
[1. Terrorism—Fiction. 2. Space and time—Fiction. 3. Technology—Fiction.]
I. Wexler, Michael. II. Kendall, Gideon, ill. III. Title.
PZ7.H8844Sp 2008   [Fic]—dc22   2008012241

ISBN-13: 978-1-59990-299-9 • ISBN-10: 1-59990-299-0 (paperback)

Typeset by Westchester Book Composition
Printed in the U.S.A. by Quebecor World Fairfield
1 3 5 7 9 10 8 6 4 2

All papers used by Bloomsbury U.S.A. are natural, recyclable products
made from wood grown in well-managed forests. The manufacturing processes
conform to the environmental regulations of the country of origin.

To John O. Morisano, who finally got his "O," and to Liz Schonhorst, the best editor in The World (or The Seems)

Contents

the seems

the split second

the Seems

Human Resources

MEMORANDUM

From: The Powers That Be
To: All Seems Employees
Re: The Tide

EFFECTIVE IMMEDIATELY:

Due to recent events and information regarding a specific and credible threat, it has become necessary to elevate security measures Seemswide.

Employees are advised that valid Badges must be displayed at all times and all individuals, regardless of Clearance, are subject to random inspection. Personal effects should not be left unattended and any/all suspicious activities should be reported to departmental administrators.

We regret any inconvenience this may cause, but only through our combined efforts can The World, as we know it, be protected.

Yours truly,

Eve Hightower
Second in Command, The Seems

Masterpiece Theatre

Los Angeles, California

"What am I, a speed bump?"

Albie Kellar slammed his hand on the trunk of the fancy white car as it screeched to a halt only inches from his toes.

"No!" screamed the driver. "You're a stupid moron!"

Crossing against the light probably wasn't the best idea, especially at the back end of rush hour, but pedestrians had the right-of-way in this state, and Albie planned on exercising that right whenever he darn well pleased. "*You're* the stupid moron!"

The driver flashed him a hand signal that strangely resembled a bird, then turned onto Marengo and disappeared onto the 10.

Albie shook his head. He honestly couldn't remember if people had always been this bad or if they had gotten worse lately, but it seemed as if today they were particularly offensive. The smog didn't help either. It hung low and thick and he could feel it collecting around his lungs with every breath.

"Oh no." Albie began to run down the sidewalk. "No. No. No, no, no, no, no . . ."

A block and a half away, a packed bus was leaving the curb, and Albie raced after it, trying to get the driver's attention— but the man behind the wheel seemed to purposely pull away.

"Thanks a lot, pal! Really appreciate the kindness to your fellow man!"

Over by the weather-beaten bus stop, a small Mexican woman watched as Albie kicked his briefcase against a wall. Anna secretly referred to him as *el tirano* ("the tyrant") because every time she saw him, he seemed to be in such a bad mood. Not that her mood was so much better . . .

Anna Morales had come to the City of Angels for a better life, but this better life was not without a cost. Though she could earn enough money here to support herself and send some back to her family, her days were spent mostly alone. Riding the bus only seemed to make it worse, for she could barely understand the language, and people seemed to look right through her. At least in Chapala, even a stranger was a friend.

"'Scuse me. Anyone sittin' here?"

She looked up to see a tall, skinny black kid stepping beneath the overhang. He was dressed in hospital scrubs and looked no better off than she did, oversized headphones tuning him out from the rest of the world. Anna quickly moved over, but there wasn't very far she could go, because *el tirano* had already grabbed the seat to her right.

"When the hell is this thing gonna show up already?" Albie Kellar muttered, angrily checking his watch. "I don't even know why I bother anymore."

As the sun began its daily descent, Anna tried to make

herself even more invisible than usual. The kid in the scrubs just turned up his music and said to no one in particular, "Tell me 'bout it, yo."

Sunset Strip, Department of Public Works, The Seems

Becker Drane had barely stepped off the monorail when an Assistant Scenic was already in his face.

"Thank the Plan you're here!" The young artist's smock was covered in paint and sweat beaded off his brow. "It's a total disaster!"

Becker couldn't help laughing. Every Mission seemed to start the same way, but now that he had nine of them under his belt, it didn't faze him anymore.

"Just stay calm and take me to my Briefer."

"He's over by Easel #4, inspecting the replacement. Follow me!"

As they jogged over to the strip, Becker could hear the *click-clacking* of his cleats against the hard concrete. He had been in the middle of a Little League game—Park Deli vs. Bagel Dish—and it was no easy task to slip from the on-deck circle, duck into the outhouse to deploy his Me-2™[1], then sneak away from Donaldson Park as the other Becker cranked a double to right-center, tying the score with two outs in the bottom of the sixth.

---

1. All Tools copyright © the Toolshed, the Institute for Fixing & Repair (IFR), The Seems, XVUIVVI. For more information, please see: "Appendix C: Tools of the Trade."

The Assistant Scenic led Becker down the street marked "Glorious Boulevard," then turned onto the back lot that served as the deluxe design studio for all The World's sunsets. Enormous canvases were lined up, row upon row, with no less than twelve artists per panorama, each supervised by a Master Scenic whose vision and keen sense of color would soon supply The World with a priceless and never before (or again) seen tapestry of light and Emotion.

"Fixer Drane—over here!"

Over by Easel #4 stood a short, stout man with a laminated "B" proudly affixed to his uniform. Becker had to admit he was slightly disappointed that he hadn't been assigned his favorite dorky, Tool-obsessed, Coke-bottle-glasses-wearing Seemsian, but Briefers worked on a rotation basis too. There were over three hundred of them, each as capable and distinctive as the next, and though very few of them still wore the official dress blues (which had once been mandatory), "the Sarge" always wore his.

"Talk to me, Sarge . . ."

"It ain't good." The Sarge rubbed his grizzled chin. "This Set was under construction for three weeks—some sort of fancy one they sent down from upstairs. By all accounts it was a masterpiece, but then the guy just snapped—threw a can of primer all over it, tore the thing to shreds, then completely went over the Edge."

"Who was the painter?"

"Master Scenic #32"—the Sarge looked down at the Mission Report on his Blinker™—"Figarro Mastrioni."

"The Maestro?"

"That's the one." The Sarge knew what else his Fixer was wondering, because everyone in The Seems had received the same memo in the mailbox this morning. "Too early to tell if our 'friends' were involved."

"What about the replacement Sunset?" Becker looked up at the huge canvas that had been cobbled together as a backup for the original painting. "Anything we can use in there?"

"The light and texture are fine, but the clouds are rushed, and the Memory Triggers are all over the place . . ." The Sarge spoke under his breath, so as not to offend the anxious Scenics who toiled on ladders and scaffolds. "If you ask me, it's a wash."

The beauty of the Sarge—#1 on the Briefing Roster—was that having him on board was like working with a second Fixer. His Tool recommendations were impeccable, and his Mission Log read like a history book at the Institute for Fixing & Repair. Becker didn't have to look at the canvas twice to know it wasn't gonna cut it.

"How much time we got?"

"Rotating Dusk begins in fifty minutes."

Fixer Drane did the calculations in his mind. Rotating Dusk meant that the same exact Sunset would be seen all across the globe, as opposed to the usual practice of giving each Sector its own individual painting. This was a rare event—much like an Eclipse or Meteor Shower—and intended for billions of viewers worldwide. But even a Scenic as talented as the legendary Maestro would be hard-pressed to craft a new Sunset in that amount of time.

"Take me to the Edge."

Sunset Strip, a sub-department of the Department of Public Works, had been built overlooking the Stream of Consciousness, and for good reason. The Seemsian sun set in the north, casting a warm glow over the tranquil back lot, while a pleasant hike down the Path of Least Resistance led to the Stream itself. But perhaps its most eye-catching spot was the Edge of Sanity—a jagged outcropping high above the weaving canyon—which attracted many a Scenic looking for a never-before-imagined shade or hue. But it also drew a different sort of visitor.

"How the heck did he get all the way down there?"

Becker lay flat on his stomach and peeked over the Edge. Far below him, a lone figure was huddled on a narrow sill jutting from the face of the cliff.

"No idea," said his Briefer, kneeling beside him. "But that rock he's sitting on isn't gonna hold for long."

A queasy feeling was working its way into Becker's stomach. He'd once had a Glimmer of Hope in mind for just such an occasion, but he'd been forced to blow it on his very first Mission, so now he had to suck it up.

"Recommendation?"

"Sticky Feet™."

"Agreed." Becker pulled the rubber soles from his Toolkit, careful not to touch the bottoms with his hand lest he would have to go to the Department of Health and have them surgically removed. "But set me up a Safety Net™ just in case."

Many feet below, a tortured artist wearing a thin mustache sat with his arms around his knees. He rocked back and forth, muttering to himself, until his attention was drawn by a handful of silt that trickled down from above. Gazing up, he was amazed to see a lanky thirteen-year-old boy with shaggy hair standing at a ninety-degree angle and looking straight down the face of the cliff.

"Stop right zere!" screamed the Maestro in his thick North-Seemsany accent. This picturesque region of The Seems was famed for cultivating persons of a certain artistic flair—painters, musicians, and especially masters of culinary delights like Twists of Fate or the Snooze—but the rolling hills also engendered a particularly fiery temperament. "You no come closer or I jump!"

"I just want to talk," said Becker, dangling over the Edge of Sanity.

"Zere nothing to talk about! It is done. Over. Finis!"

The painter punctuated the statement by slamming his fist to the ground, knocking pebbles and baseball-sized rocks out from beneath the ledge. Becker could see that the Sarge was right . . . it wouldn't hold for long.

"Is it okay if I join you?"

The Maestro ignored him, gazing toward the water with despair. Becker took that as a yes, and found his way to a small crevice that the centuries had carved from the wall. It wasn't much of a sitting place, so Becker kept his Feet firmly planted on the rock.

"I don't know about you, but I'm not a big fan of high places." The Fixer knew the key to talking him down was establishing a rapport. "It's not that I'm afraid to fall, it's just that there's always this little voice in my head saying 'jump, jump, jump'—and someday I'm afraid I'm gonna listen to it."

"It is probably just ze Mischievous Imp," said the Maestro without looking up.

"Nah. We caught that guy a couple years ago. He's up in Seemsberia knitting pot holders and singing 'Kumbaya.'"

Down below, the slightest of chuckles was just audible above the wind.

"Mind if I call you Figarro?"

"You can do whatever you want."

At least he was talking now, so Becker figured this was the time to strike.

"What happened out there today?"

The Maestro shook his head angrily, but was too filled with disgust to even speak.

"Look at zem over zere." He pointed bitterly to the other side of the canyon, where a gated community and its lavish clubhouse was perched even higher than they. "Yuppie scum in fancy houses."

"This isn't about Crestview." Becker made a harsh transition to tough love because time was running out. "This is about a very important Sunset that you were supposed to paint tonight but decided to rip into a million pieces instead."

The Maestro flinched at the implication, and Becker knew that he was starting to get through.

"I can't help you, Figarro. Not unless you tell me what's wrong."

The Maestro sat and stewed for a moment before finally speaking up.

"My entire life I work to make Sunsets zat will remind

people of ze beauty of Ze World, bring zem a precious little moment at the end of another hard day. But everything I do—it is for nothing!"

Far down below, the waves in the Stream crashed against the rocks, and Becker again resisted the urge to see what would happen if he . . .

"I brush Hope in ze clouds for people of ze Philippines, and next day, zey are hit by Typhoon. I hide beautiful Memory in shade of pink, but ze person it is meant for is too sick to even look up and see!"

"The Plan works in mysterious ways," said the Fixer.

"But why must zere be so much suffering?" The Maestro seemed to be asking himself as much as Becker. "Why cannot Ze World be a better place?"

This type of rhetoric sounded awfully familiar to Becker and it forced him to ask a very uncomfortable question.

"This wouldn't have anything to do with a certain . . . organization . . . would it?"

"How *dare* you accuse me of being in Ze Tide! I pour my heart and soul on ze canvas each and every day!" Figarro slid another inch forward. If this didn't turn around in a hurry, not only would there be no Sunset, but there would be no Figarro. "But what is ze point? Ze Maestro makes no difference at all . . ."

And that's when Becker knew what was really wrong in the Department of Public Works and how he was going to Fix it.

"Au contraire, Figarro." Becker carefully unclipped his Blinker from his belt. Dotting the view screen of the rubber-buttoned communication device were a host of folders—individual Case Files of those who would be affected by the

Sunset (or lack thereof). "With one look at this Sunset, lives can be changed forever . . ."

Down below, the man with the thin mustache slowly turned to listen.

". . . and it's not just people struggling. I can't even count how many are on beaches or on hikes through a mountain pass or lying in a meadow with their best friend and don't know they're about to enjoy one of the greatest moments of their lives."

"But one Sunset, my friend? What can one Sunset do against ze troubles of ze entire World?"

"Maybe nothing. Maybe everything." Becker flipped over to one case in which he was personally involved. "A good friend of mine's future may depend on him getting a little dose of Confidence tonight. But even if he looks away at just the wrong moment or something awful happens tomorrow it doesn't really matter. All that matters is that we try."

The Maestro looked Becker directly in the eye.

"Do you really believe zis?"

"If I didn't, I wouldn't be here."

There was a long silence, and from the way Figarro peered down at the rocks below, Becker wasn't sure whether he had won him over or lost him.

"All right, Fixer-man. Maybe ze Plan is out of our control. But if only one person in zose Files of yours stops to look . . ." He rose and proudly faced Becker. "Then I shall give zat person the greatest Sunset Ze World has ever—"

But before he could finish his sentence, the entire ledge the Maestro was standing on broke off and went plummeting down toward the Stream.

"Figarro!"

This time, Becker *did* listen to the voice in his head screaming "Jump!" Detaching from his Sticky Feet, he plummeted straight toward the Maestro, who was screaming in abject horror. It was a second or two before he caught up to the flailing painter, which only brought a small modicum of satisfaction, because it would only be a second or two more before they both smashed headlong into the rapidly approaching rocks below. But Becker knew something that Figarro didn't. At least he hoped he did . . .

"Sarge, please tell me you set up the—"

Thwap.

The Fixer and the Maestro found themselves encircled in a ball of nylon twine, which stretched uncomfortably close to the water before recoiling back up toward the top of the cliff. Thankfully, it was connected to the twin firing mechanisms that the Sarge had undoubtedly anchored to the Edge of Sanity, and whose retractable crank was now reeling the two survivors of a near-death experience back to the top.

"How you doin' down there, boss?" barked the Sarge over his Receiver.

"Hangin' in there."

The best part about a Safety Net was the safety. The whole net thing Becker could have done without, because at the moment it was imprinting a familiar waffle-shaped tattoo on their faces.

But better to be a waffle than a pancake.

Sunset Strip, Department of Public Works, The Seems

They say the most frightening thing for any artist is a blank canvas, but for a Master Scenic with his heart in the right place, it is but a playground for the imagination. The Maestro stood before a tower of white, surrounded by the materials of his ancient craft. To his left were cans containing indigo, lapis lazuli, violet, and cadmium yellow. To his right, jars of Emotion—Joy, Gratitude, even Bittersweet—which, when painted across the surface of the sky, could literally be experienced by anyone who took the time to view it.

"The way I see it," said Fixer Drane as he looked over the Maestro's shoulder, "it takes three minutes for the paint to dry, seven to roll the canvas for shipment, and six to get across the In-Between to Realization.[2] That leaves you only thirteen minutes to paint the whole thing."

Becker looked back over his shoulder where Set Dressers and Junior Scenics eagerly awaited their master's commands.

"Can it be done?"

"I am Figarro Mastrioni." The Maestro licked his fingers and began to twirl his mustache into a handlebar. "Zere is nothing I cannot do!"

With a single snap of his fingers, his minions were in action. They grabbed their brushes and cans while Figarro himself picked up a roller and began to lay a base of disappearing blue.

"Fixer Drane," the Maestro stepped onto a scaffold that was slowly raised into the sky, "this friend of yours—ze one who needs ze Confidence . . ."

"Yeah, he's a Briefer. Back when we were at the IFR, I was going through a very hard time because I was only ten and I

---

2. The process by which Goods & Services produced in The Seems are converted by the Fabric of Reality into aspects of The World.

was a lot smaller than everybody else. But there was this one guy, Harold—they called him 'C-Note'—who was always telling me 'BD, you got the skills to pay the bills!' Things are tough for him right now, and his Case Worker wants to tell him the same thing."

"Well, considering the issue of Time, not to mention what you have done for me this day . . ." Figarro flipped him a fat paintbrush, then pointed to a squeeze bottle of Confidence itself.

"Perhaps you would like to get your hands dirty as well?"

Los Angeles, California

Inexplicably, the bus had still not arrived at the corner of Marengo and Clement, where now over a dozen seething passengers waited for their ride. The only bonus was that the smog had lifted, clearing both the air and the sky above.

"Finally!" shouted Albie Kellar, as the local "E" slowly rounded the bend at last. A mock cheer went up, and people started to gather their things, but Anna stayed seated. She was hoping *el tirano* would get on the bus first, so she could make sure to be sitting as far away from him as possible. But as Albie started to get in line, his eyes accidentally drifted upward . . .

"Wow, look at that." Painted across the horizon were the beginnings of a spectacularly setting sun. Streaks of blue, yellow, and purple wove in and out of a drifting web of clouds, seeming to bathe both the heavens and the earth below in a shade of magic pink. "Do you see what I'm seeing?"

Albie turned to the lady on his left, but she had beaten him to the punch. Anna's eyes were already filled with tears, for if she tilted her head just right, the sky no longer looked like a sunset, but like waves crashing upon a shore. The sand stretched across the horizon and the foaming water looked so real you could almost smell the salt and hear the gulls squawking overhead.

"Es hermoso . . ."

On a shore just like this one, she had spent many a day with her grandfather, when she was only a child. Her *abuelo* and she would play hooky from work and school, collecting shells and talking about her dreams for the future.

"It is a big world out there," the old man would say, pulling Anna close. "And it can be frightening too. But you must explore as much of it as you can, if you are to find out what is inside you."

All these years later, Anna had forgotten what had inspired her to leave all she knew behind. But as the orange disc of the sun slowly dipped toward the west, she realized just how much she had already discovered—and that the adventure had just begun.

"I remember, Grandfather," she whispered aloud. "I remember."

"Remember what?"

Anna turned to see *el tirano*, Albie Kellar, staring down at her with a smile on his face and tears in his own eyes.

"Qué?"

"You said you remembered something . . . ," Albie said to her in perfect Spanish, which he hadn't spoken in years. "I remembered something too."

She asked him what it was and Albie started to tell her, but the lump in his throat caught hard, and he found himself unable to speak. So he only pointed to the spot on the horizon where the last vestige of smog had somehow shaped itself into—

"It looks like a sign," said Anna.

"Doesn't it?" Albie whispered, finally able to choke out some words. "Just like this old road sign in the town where I used to live."

Albie tried to explain that he'd spent his twenties traveling the world, and how on the day he returned home to take a so-called real job, he'd scribbled "I'll be back" on that road sign. But the fact that he'd never fulfilled that promise overwhelmed him with sadness and regret. Anna pulled out a small plastic bag stuffed with Kleenex, and was handing one to Albie when the local bus pulled to a stop.

"It's about time!" grumbled several of the other passengers as they filed onto the bus. But for Albie Kellar, who normally would have been one of those grumblers, the anger that had marked his day had faded. All he wanted to do now was share his story with someone—if only to remember every last detail of the man he used to be, and could still become again.

"Thank you for the tissue," Albie said to Anna as he followed her up the steps.

"No problemo, señor."

Anna took a spot in the middle of the bus. She looked down at the empty seat next to her, then back up to the man she had once known as *el tirano*.

"Would you like to sit here?"

As the bus pulled away and disappeared into the night, one passenger remained seated on the bench. It was the kid with the hospital scrubs and the headphones—and even though the music was turned up as loud as it could go, he couldn't hear a single note.

"Someone's on their game today," whispered Harold "C-Note" Carmichael, eyes glued to the sky. "Big-time."

Only one trained in the inner workings would have been able to recognize that Rotating Dusk had begun, and Cases like Anna's and Albie's were playing out all across The World. But as he studied the Strokes of Genius that stood out like ornaments on a Christmas tree, Briefer Carmichael never considered that one of those Cases might be him.

Not only was med school a mighty challenge but Frau Von Schroëder—his closest friend from the IFR—had leapfrogged him and been unexpectedly promoted to Fixer. Though he was happy for the Frau, he couldn't help but think that everybody in Fixing circles took it as a sign that he wasn't good enough for "the best job in The World," and he was starting to believe it himself. Until he saw something in the upper-right corner of the sky . . .

It was a sloppy dollop of a cloud, malformed and with not nearly enough Fluff. But what it did have was a massive burst of Confidence, all of which surged through his mind and body at once.

"I'm Harold C-Note Carmichael!" The Briefer rose to his feet and shouted to no one in particular. "Second-highest score on the Practical of all time!"

As C-Note remembered that triumphant day when he'd been granted his Briefer's badge, he also reflected on the tenuous state The World was in. Whatever the words "specific and credible threat" referred to, it was definitely not good. But even though he wasn't one of the thirty-eight who held the title of Fixer, thanks to this glorious Sunset, the pride of Baldwin Hills would be ready if duty called.

"39, baby! Your magic number is 39!"

C-Note was looking around for somebody to give a high-five to when he noticed something else in the sky, just below and to the right of his Confidence. It didn't look like clouds, though. It looked more like letters . . .

"BD."

A new feeling surged through C-Note. He reached down onto his belt and pulled off a small black device known as a Blinker. It came with a host of functionalities, one of the best of which was real-time messaging to anyone in the crew. He toggled down the Duty Roster to Fixer #37 and began to type in a text, "Thx! I needed tht."

Harold Carmichael smiled and waited patiently for a response, which came only a few seconds later.

"No sweat," texted back the Fixer known as Becker Drane. "Catch u on the Flip Side."

The Golden Rule

Becker Drane's life was pretty much always this exciting.

Not only did he have "the best job in The World," but on the day he turned thirteen, Becker's allowance doubled, his bedtime was pushed to "it's up to you," and his need to sneak into PG-13 movies was rendered obsolete. Best of all, he had finally hit a growth spurt, transforming him from a small kid with old-school corduroys and shaggy hair to a medium kid with old-school corduroys and shaggy hair. But although his newfound lank granted him an extra gear on the soccer field and an added measure of respect from the Melvin Sharps[3] of the world, it didn't mean that all was well.

The stresses of leading a double life had definitely begun to wear on him. Becker's grades had continued to suffer—

---

3. The undisputed toughest/scariest kid at Lafayette Middle School. Bryan Lockwood used to be the toughest/scariest kid at Lafayette until Mel unseated him at the infamous "fight by the bike rack." That was awesome.

dropping precipitously close to a C-plus average—while the pressure of having to save The World every six weeks or so had caused him to drop a few pounds and have noticeable bags under his eyes. His parents and teachers constantly asked him if everything was okay and he knew the unspoken suspicion centered around a host of possible maladies, including but not limited to: the Internet, video-game addiction, male anorexia, and clinical depression.

Much harder to deal with was the strong sense of disconnect that had slowly wormed its way into the Fixer's life. When Chudnick and the Crozier boys wanted to trade MP3s or talk about girls, it was like he just couldn't join in the fun. He tried to confide in his co-workers from The Seems, but even though they were cool and interesting, they were all much older than he. In fact, the only regular kid that Becker could be honest with was his brother, Benjamin. But even that was tainted, since the seven-year-old believed The Seems was just an intricate fantasy world that his brother had dreamed up.

Sooner or later, Becker needed to find someone to talk to— and he knew who he wanted that someone to be.

The Atrium, The Big Building, The Seems

"Five minutes, mates!" A voice with a familiar Australian accent echoed over the loudspeaker. "Five minutes till we're back!"

Becker polished off his Dazzleberry muffin and admired the glass-enclosed atrium. This was the lightest and airiest part of the Big Building, used for conventions and cocktail parties, and it was filled with all sorts of custom-designed flora that the Department of Nature had been kind enough to donate. Intermission was almost over and Becker was preparing to head back for the Monthly Briefing when a voice whispered from behind the Zen rock garden.

"Drane—over here!"

Becker turned to see a scraggly janitor, casually mopping an already clean spot on the marble floor. He was wearing a Big Building jumpsuit with a Blue Collar around his neck—signifying that he was a master of the custodial arts—but anyone who knew would know that Brooks was in The Know.[4]

"I thought I said *after* the meeting," Becker replied, peeking over his shoulder to make sure no one else was looking.

"Sorry, kid." Brooks dipped his mop back in the slop. "You're not my only customer."

Becker strolled over to the rock garden as if he'd just noticed a diamond wedged between two stalks of bamboo.

"Did you get it?" he asked.

"The question is, did *you* get it?"

Becker took another cautious peek over his shoulder, then reached into his Toolkit. But instead of producing one of the Toolshed's finest innovations, he pulled out a white bag with an onion-heavy smell emanating from somewhere within. "Of course I got it. The System's open 24/7."

Inside the bag was a California Cheeseburger and an order of fries (salt, pepper, ketchup) from the White Rose System, the

---

4. A secret society that trades in Plan-sensitive information. Though technically considered a criminal organization, they are often a Fixer's ace in the hole when normal channels just won't do.

best fast-food establishment in central New Jersey and arguably the entire World.[5] Brooks tore off the tissue paper wrapping and inhaled half of the burger in a single bite.

"Ahh . . . that's what I'm talkin' about . . ." A look of sheer bliss was covering the janitor's face. "SeemsBurger just doesn't have that extra . . . *umph.*"

This was the truth. Though the Seemsian Food & Drink Administration had done its best to replicate fast food—one of the few creations that The World can call its own—it had never quite perfected the ratio of grease to Love. And while the Fixer hangout known as "The Flip Side" produced a mouth-watering burger, it was more of a gourmet experience.

"I held up my end of the bargain," Becker reminded his contact. "Now you hold up yours."

"Take a Chill Pill, Drane." Brooks cleansed his palette with a swig of vanilla shake, then pulled something from his pocket. "I got what you need."

It was a small circular cartridge, with the letters "JK" written on them in white Sharpie marker.

"How is it?" asked the nervous Fixer.

"Don't worry. You'll be happy with the merchandise."

Becker already was, and couldn't wait to pop the cartridge into his Blinker. But before he could find a quiet corner, an eighty-three-year-old South African woman cheerily waved from across the room.

"Come, dear," said the Fixer known as the Octogenarian. "Time to finish up."

On the other side of the atrium, the rest of the Duty Roster

---

5. Though some believe it has gone downhill ever since Frank sold the place.

were filing back toward Central Command for the second half of the Briefing.

"Thanks, man," whispered Becker to his shady cohort. "Same time next month?"

"Bet," replied Brooks, polishing off the rest of the Cali Cheese. "And next time grab me a pork roll too."

The two confidants shook hands on the deal, and Becker was about to rejoin his fellows, when his growling stomach forced a final request . . .

"Lemme get a fry."

Central Command, The Big Building, The Seems

In the basement of the Big Building, some five hundred floors below the Powers That Be, was the fortified ops center known as Central Command. Here, highly trained personnel monitored the health and well-being of The World on a moment-by-moment basis, making the final determination of whether or not to send in a Fixer (and Briefer) when a problem arose. And it was also here that each month the entire Roster gathered in the Conference Room to discuss any new or pressing developments.

This month's meeting had been pretty much business as usual, concentrating on a recap of last month's Missions and the ongoing transition from the Door system to the newly ratified Skeleton Key™, which had revolutionized how commuters traveled back and forth between the worlds. Instead of searching for a series of scattered portals, they could now insert the handy Tool anywhere in the Fabric of Reality and open a seam directly into the In-Between. The only problem was, the group charged with phasing out the antiquated Doors was the same group who used them most often.

"I don't know about you guys," chirped No-Hands Phil, Fixer #36 on the Rotation. "But if I have to seal up another one of these Doors, I'm gonna apply for a job at Home Depot!" Phil's feet were kicked up on the conference table and his eye patch barely hid his prickly attitude.

"They would never hire you, Phil," retorted Tony the Plumber, #22, hands resting on his generous belly. "You have to not be a jerk."

Becker cracked up at Tony's diss on Phil. Though #36 was undeniably one of the most talented Fixers on the duty roster, his personality left a lot to be desired.

"Now, now, gentlemen," the Octogenarian soothed the warring factions with her always sunny disposition. "We're all on the same team here."

The side door to the conference room abruptly swung open and in walked a Fixer in her twenties, with double-braided pigtails and flip-flops on her feet.

"All right, mates," said Cassiopeia Lake, "the meeting is back in session."

For three years now, Casey had been the bearer of the Torch—an eternally lit flame that symbolized the unofficial leader of the Fixers—and thus it was her job to run the monthly Briefings.

"We only have one item left up on the docket, but it's probably the most important, so please pay attention."

Frau Von Schroëder, at #38 the newest of the Fixers, whipped out an old-fashioned Briefing pad, but Becker leaned over and whispered in her ear.

"Don't worry about taking notes, Frau." He and the German mother of three had been Candidates together at the IFR and had become pretty tight. "They'll send you the minutes over your Blinker, so you're better off just tuning in."

"*Danke*, Becker," said the Frau, feeling like a freshman on her first day of class. "Lucky I am sitting next to you."[6] She tucked the pad back into her Toolkit, then quietly waited for Fixer Lake to continue.

"As all of you undoubtedly know, a certain 'underground organization' has been sticking a poison-tipped thorn in our sides for some time now."

A murmur of agreement ran through the crowd, for all of them at some point or another had faced acts of sabotage perpetrated by the shadowy movement known as "The Tide." Fixer Lake flipped over a white grease board on which was ominously drawn the image of a black cresting wave—foaming and ready to crash upon the shore.

"Jammed-up fans in the Wind Tunnels. Locusts in the Color Fields. A corked and blown-up Rain Tower." One at a time, she removed photographs depicting these Tide assaults and tacked them on the board. "With increasing audacity, this insurgency has sought to undermine operations in The Seems in ways that have continually threatened the integrity of The World. And yet, their agenda remains unclear."

"What's unclear?" shouted Tony the Plumber. "They're terrorists who want to destroy The World!"

---

6. All Fixers and Briefers make regular use of the Tool known as the Sprecheneinfaches™—a thin sheath attached to the tongue that allows them to speak in a language that everyone can understand (while still maintaining ethnic and regional flair).

27

"It's a little more complex than that, Anthony," said Lisa Simms, who, in her other life, traveled The World as a violinist for the London Philharmonic. "My experience with The Tide suggests they actually think they're trying to save it."

"She's right. T. Thibadeau Freck joined The Tide and he truly believes the Plan is broken." Becker was referring to the French teenager who had been his best friend during Training, until the day he was lost in a Well of Emotion. But on #37's first Mission he found Thib very much alive, and a fervent believer in The Tide's cause. "Judging from my last job, a lot of Seemsians are feeling the same way."

"Regardless of The Tide's ideology, the danger caused by their acts is very real." Arguably the best surfer in southern Australia resumed control of the meeting. "In the last three months, however, these attacks have suddenly ceased."

The table full of Fixers nodded, for they too had noticed the unsettling silence.

"I would like to think this is partially due to increased security throughout The Seems, but we must consider the obvious alternative . . ." Casey twisted one of her pigtails and leaned forward on the podium. "They are planning something big."

Becker had a feeling this was coming, especially after the memo from the Powers That Be and double especially when Fixer Lake pulled out a padded yellow envelope.

"Today at 9:30 a.m., this package was found in the mail room of the Big Building, addressed only to the Powers That Be." She held up a small circular cartridge that was the standard platform for all audio, video, and textual content in The Seems. "It contained the following message . . ."

As she inserted the cartridge into the clunky-looking player, Becker flushed red for a moment, because just such a cartridge was burning a hole in his pocket right now. But his guilty conscience quickly faded due to what was being projected in the center of the room.

"Allow me to introduce myself." The player had cast a three-dimensional hologram of a person, whose features and voice were obscured by the garbled fuzz of the transmission. "My name is Triton."

The figure sat on the table as if he or she was actually in the room.

"You might call me the leader of The Tide, if there was a leader of The Tide. For The Tide is not an organization, but an idea."

The Siberian Fixer who called himself Greg the Journeyman swept his massive hand across the image. "Has anybody tried to clean this kaplunsky up?"

Casey nodded her head. "Kevin, our AV guy, is working on it right now, but we think it was recorded this way intentionally."

The image of Triton casually leaned back upon the table and continued.

"The World is irreparably broken and a new one must be created from the ashes of the old. But before this can happen, those who are responsible for the perversion of what the Plan originally intended must be held accountable. Hence, we issue the following demands . . ."

Triton's voice gained in fervor and even though Becker couldn't see a face, something about the tone got under his skin.

"One, the wholesale resignation of the existing members of

the Powers That Be. Two, The World itself must be put on immediate hold, until a referendum can be held to determine both new leadership and a revision to the Plan. And lastly, the Second in Command must be placed on trial in the Court of Public Opinion, for crimes against humanity."

"Is that all?" joked the Octogenarian, but even she wasn't laughing.

"If these demands are not met within seven days, all necessary action will be taken to accomplish these goals unilaterally." The figure fritzed for a second before fading off into digital fuzz. But though the image had vanished, Triton's last words continued to ring. "We anxiously await your response."

A somber mood fell over the room, prompting even No-Hands Phil to take his feet off the table.

"Do we have any idea of what they might be planning?" inquired Becker.

"Chatter's been low and most of our field operatives report little or no activity." Casey seemed to pause for a second, as if in possession of some news that she didn't want to deliver. "But new intelligence suggests they may have successfully completed the construction of a Time Bomb."

Becker felt like he'd been punched in the stomach, and the looks on his peers' faces said they all felt the same. Almost a year ago, fifty trays of Frozen Moments had been stolen from the Daylight Savings Bank in the Department of Time, and they were still unaccounted for. On their own, that was small cause for alarm, but if combined with enough fertilizer and a highly unstable Split Second, a weapon of almost unimaginable consequences would be in the hands of the wrong people.

"How is this possible?" asked Mr. Chiappa, who hailed from the isle of Corsica. More than anyone else in the room, the fifty-year-old high school teacher seemed weighed down by the report. "I thought we had Time on lockdown."

"We do," responded the bearer of the Torch. "But this information comes from a very reliable source."

Becker wondered who that reliable source was, but Fixer Lake was privy to information that only a handful of others were cleared to know.

"At this point, there's really not much we can do, except keep our 7th Senses bingolocked on Time. Po, is there anything you'd like to add?"

Everyone turned to Fixer Li Po, #1 on the Duty Roster and the acknowledged master of the 7th Sense. Po's vow of silence kept him from answering aloud, so he produced a pouch of Olde Seemsian characters instead, and his fellows waited as he patiently spelled out the words:

Time is of the Essence

"Ah c'mon, Po," cried No-Hands Phil. "Can't you just give us a straight answer for once?"

The table cracked up, on Phil's side of an argument for a change, but Po just shrugged and returned the chuckle.

"All right, people. I guess that's a wrap." The Fixers rose from the table as one and waited for Casey Lake to give her trademark parting shot. "Now let's Live to Fix out there . . ."

"Fix to Live!"

And with that, the meeting was adjourned.

With the Briefing spilling over into lunchtime, the hungry Fixers said their good-byes and split off in various directions—some heading to Mickey's Deli for a whole New Perspective (or a half, for those watching their weight), others to The Flip Side, and the rest back to their homes and families and "real jobs" in The World.

"Becker, I'm gonna let my Me-2 take the kids today," offered Frau Von Schroëder. "Would you like to grab a piece of strudel at the FDA commissary?"

"Thanks, Frau," Becker apologized. "But I've only got a little while before I have to get home, so I think I'll just grab a pretzel on the Field of Play."

Fixer #38 had a fourteen-year-old of her own, so she could recognize when a teenager needed to be alone with his or her thoughts.

"No problem. Catch you on the Flip Side then."

"On the Flip Side." Becker still felt a little bad for blowing her off. "And congratulations, Frau. You're gonna be great!"

Ilsa Von Schroëder smiled and gave a half-wave, then headed for the monorail. Becker went in the opposite direction, toward the huge recreational facility known as the Field of Play.

As he stepped through the flower-garnished entryway, his brain was still buzzing from the Briefing. He hadn't personally encountered The Tide since that first Mission in Sleep, and all attempts since then to track down his old friend Thibadeau had failed. It was as if the Frenchman had gone completely underground again, and considering how they'd parted ways,

Becker wasn't looking forward to the day when he came up for air. But he pushed those thoughts aside, for there was something much more pleasant on his mind.

Fixer #37 rummaged through his pocket and pulled out the contraband that he'd scored from Brooks. Recorded on the tiny cartridge were excerpts from the Case File of a person in The World—transcripts of conversations, deposit slips from the Memory Bank, even Helpful Hints sent by Clara Manning, Case Worker #423006. None of this information required a particularly high Clearance—in fact, it was quite mundane—but to Becker Drane it was like gold, because all of it pertained to a certain girl who lived in a certain small town in Ontario, Canada.

On the same Mission when he had squared off against Thibadeau and fixed a nasty Glitch in Sleep, Becker had also made a friend named Jennifer Kaley. She had been scheduled to receive a Dream that night—a Dream to help her cope with a difficult time in her life—but Becker had accidentally destroyed it. Given the chance to build her a new one, he was able to deliver the intended message of hope himself, and though the day they spent together was all too brief, it was one of the best he ever had.

Unfortunately, by entering into Jennifer's Dreamworld, Becker had invoked the "Golden Rule," one of the primary directives in the Seemsian Rulebook. This rule stated that:

No employee, agent, or advocate of The Seems having access (or with access) to the confidential Case File of a person in The World may engage in contact, communication, and/or relationship with said person, romantic or otherwise.

When Becker took his Fixer oath, he swore to uphold every one of those Rules, no matter how difficult some of them were to follow, and he hadn't broken any as of yet.[7] But over the course of the past year, he'd begun to tread on some dangerously thin ice.

It began professionally enough. Becker checking in with Jennifer's Case Worker now and again to see how she was doing. But these updates only piqued his curiosity, and he found it difficult to shake the memory of the time they'd spent together at the Point of View. He soon found himself googling her on the Internet, perusing her online photo album, and seriously contemplating sending her an e-mail—but his respect for the Rules (and desire to keep his job) kept him from pressing the "send" button. Everything he found out, however, only confirmed the impression he'd had the first time he'd seen Jennifer—that there was just something about her.

"Passing on your right!"

Becker was yanked from his thoughts by a group of bike-riding Case Workers out for a lunchtime spin around the Field. He watched them disappear, then scanned the park for a more secluded place in which to sequester himself. His first choice was to take a long walk down the Short Pier, but Becker was disappointed to see that someone had already scarfed his favorite spot. He was about to retreat to the Grassy Knoll when he realized that someone was a tall African man, with blue-tinted shades and a sweat suit from the Institute for Fixing & Repair.

---

7. Though accused of violating the Rule of Thumb on his first Mission, Fixer Drane was ultimately cleared of all charges by the Court of Public Opinion.

"Fixer Blaque!" Becker was always happy to see his old Instructor. "What are you doing here?"

"I might ask you the same thing." Jelani Blaque smiled and rose from the bench that overlooked the still water. These days, he was carrying a traditional Igbo walking stick, partially because his leg was bothering him again and partially because it made him look even more mackadocious[8] than he already did.

"We just finished the monthly Briefing," said Becker as they shook each other's hand. "I was just gonna unwind for a while before making the Leap back home."

Becker hated to lie, even a lie of omission, because outside of his mom and dad, Fixer Blaque was the one person in The World (or The Seems) who had taught him the most about life and how to live it. But he knew the retired Fixer would never approve of what Becker had concealed in his back pocket.

"I assume they showed you the message from Triton?" asked the IFR's head instructor.

"Yeah, pretty freaky, huh?" Becker was glad the conversation had turned back toward business. "It's gonna be a long seven days."

"With people like you on the job, The World is in safe hands."

"Thank you, sir. I hope so."

"I, too, had a meeting at the Big Building today."

"Really, sir?"

"With the Second in Command herself."

That was surprising, because the leading voice of the Powers That Be rarely had time for face-to-faces.

---

8. Suave, cool, all that.

"I've never met her personally," said Fixer Drane. "But I hear she's quite a woman."

"To say the least. And she had some very interesting things to report this morning."

"About what, sir?"

"About *you.*"

Becker's heart almost skipped a beat. Maybe two.

"Excuse me, sir?" Becker scanned Fixer Blaque's face for any trace of a smile—for he was known to enjoy pulling his old Candidates' legs—but the trademark blue shades concealed all.

"I was quite surprised myself. Especially when she informed me that one of the best students I've ever trained was on the verge of breaking the Golden Rule . . . and, in fact, may have already done so."

Becker's mind raced for some kind of excuse, but he didn't want to tell another lie.

"I assured her," Blaque continued, "that this was just a phase my former student was going through—perhaps due to his age and the difficulties of maintaining a secret life. I also assured her that this phase would immediately be ending, and would in no way compromise his ability to carry out his duties in the field."

Becker could read between the lines as well as anyone, and there was no wiggle room whatsoever. But that didn't make this moment any easier.

"I wasn't trying to break any Rules, sir. Or even pry. It's just . . ."

Fixer Blaque's face softened and for a moment he returned to being Becker's mentor and friend.

"I know how it is, son. I've even been there myself, many

36

years ago. But the Golden Rule is golden for a reason." Blaque bent down and picked up a thin skipping stone from the ground. "As emissaries of The Seems, we are in a position of great power when it comes to the private details of people's lives, and this power cannot be abused. Even when it seems like the right thing to do."

Blaque flung the rock and it skipped across the glassy surface of the pond.

"That was at least nine," the Instructor mused.

"I counted ten, sir." As Becker looked around for a rock of his own, he felt a heaviness in his chest. "I just wanted to make sure she was doing okay, y'know? Because things were so hard for a while."

"I know, son. And I know how hard it's been for you as well."

Becker shrugged. "It's not that bad."

"You haven't even been at this job for a year, Mr. Drane. You can't expect to have figured out the balance between work and personal life in that short a time." Blaque watched Becker's rock fail to skip at all. "And sometimes I think you forget you're only thirteen years old."

"Yes, sir." Becker forced a grin, remembering his Elevation Ceremony, when Blaque admitted to the same mistake. "Sometimes I do."

"Regardless, I expect you to cease all activities relating to this Case. That includes World-based communications, and especially your relationship with certain people in The Know."

Becker didn't know how Fixer Blaque knew about Brooks, but then again, Becker didn't know how Fixer Blaque knew about a lot of things.

"Understood, sir."

"Good." Jelani Blaque gripped the brass handle of his walking stick with one hand and gave Becker the IFR secret handshake with the other. "I'll leave it up to you whether you want to take one last look at the piece of information in your pocket. Or not."

Their hands were still clasped and Blaque gave him an extra squeeze, which Becker interpreted to mean "It's gonna be okay." And he surely hoped it would.

"Live to Fix, sir."

"Fix to Live."

As Becker's instructor slowly vanished into the woods, probably on his way back to grade papers at the IFR, the boy from Highland Park pulled out the small circular cartridge that contained the most recent data about the life of a thirteen-year-old girl. All he really wanted was someone to hang with or talk to on the phone about stupid stuff, but the most important thing in Becker's life was the job that he had as Fixer. And if he wanted to keep that job, he had no choice but to do one thing: forget that he'd ever heard the name of Jennifer Kaley.

"It was nice knowing you."

Without taking another look, Becker chucked the cartridge into the pond. It skipped three times, then fell beneath the water.

Time to Make the Zeppole

12 Grant Avenue, Highland Park, New Jersey

Exactly seven days later, Becker lay in what might be described as a mild coma beneath the covers of his bed.

"Becks, are you ready to go?" Dr. Natalie Drane's voice reverberated through the floorboards of the house and into the room of her eldest son. "We're hitting the road in five minutes!"

"Almost ready!"

That wasn't quite consistent with the facts. It was nearly eleven in the morning, and while the rest of the Drane clan was packed and ready for their annual vacation to Cape Cod, Becker could not bring himself to move. This was one of the telltale signs of depression, as was an overwhelming sense of sadness—both of which he was exhibiting today.

Knock, knock.

Becker's mother appeared at his bedroom door, sunglasses on and car keys in her hand.

"What are you doing?"

"Lying in bed."

"I can see that." Natalie pulled off her shades and did not look amused. "I mean, why aren't you ready to go?"

"Why? That's a very complicated question."

Indeed it was. Not only had Becker been forced to toss the info regarding Jennifer Kaley, but during the upcoming week, he would be missing Connell Hutkin's pool party and the Highland Park Street Fair. Instead, he'd spend the foreseeable future frequenting crab shacks, playing Parcheesi, and suffering through long days at the beach with the lovable yet longwinded Dranes of New England.

"Ferdinand!" Becker's mom called downstairs to her husband. "Your son is having some sort of existential crisis up here and since I deal with this every single day of the year *except* my vacation, you'd better come up here *now!*"

Natalie flashed her son an angry look before turning and starting to hum the song "Vacation" by the Go-Go's, which Becker only knew because she forced the family to listen to the same song every year as they pulled out of Highland Park. The music faded down the hallway, replaced by the pounding of his father's footsteps up the stairs.

"Let's go, sleepyhead."

Becker could feel his father standing in the doorway, and he knew that Professor F. B. Drane was probably fiddling with his beard or adjusting his glasses, which is what he always did when he was perturbed.

"Listen, I don't know whether it's girls, grades—which you *should* be depressed about—or a touch of the bird flu. And to be honest, I really don't care. But we have an eight-hour drive

42

ahead of us and if your mother is in a bad mood, that means I'm gonna be in a bad mood, which means everyone is gonna be in a bad mood. And nobody wants that, do they?"

"No," Becker managed to mumble.

"Good. So I expect you downstairs and packed and in the back of the car in the five minutes your mother just gave you."

"Fine."

Becker heard his father take a few steps into the hallway before turning back to the bedroom.

"Seriously, buddy. Are you okay?"

"I'm fine, Dad. I'll be down in a minute."

Becker waited for the Rutgers University professor of mathematics to leave, then finally managed to swing both of his legs onto the floor and drag out his backpack from under his bed. He was just starting to stuff in his bathing suit and aqua-socks when—

"You have issues, dude." It was his little brother, Benjamin, seven years of precociousness all crammed into one little body. "Maybe you should see a shrink, and I don't mean Mom."

Becker's answer was to huck a Nerf basketball straight at Benjamin's head, nearly decapitating him.

"Mom! Becker just tried to kill me!"

Becker flinched again, sending Benjamin hurtling out of his room and back down the carpeted stairs. The Fixer took a deep breath, mentally calculating how to pack, shower, and grab his Toolkit all in the remaining three minutes and 12 . . . 11 . . . 10 . . . 9 . . . seconds, but he couldn't stop himself from thinking about Jennifer Kaley. Where was she? What was she doing now?

And was she okay?

30 Custer Drive, Caledon, Ontario

"And make sure the OJ is fresh squeezed!" Steven Kaley shouted to his daughter as she headed for the door.

"Anything else, Dad?" Jenny chided her father. "This is the third time I've been to Norm's in the last two days!"

Jennifer Kaley's parents had been stressed out all week about the partners brunch that would be taking place in roughly an hour, but the fact that she'd been able to keep the change on every shopping trip more than made up for the tension in the house. This time her father had given her a Jefferson, which, if she spent wisely, would leave her enough to purchase some supplies for her own big day.

"Pick up six jumbo eggs while you're there." Her mother already had over a dozen, but better safe than sorry. "I promise, sweetheart, this'll be the last time."

Jennifer skipped outside and began the pleasant jaunt to Norm's Great Grocery. When she had first moved to Caledon, these streets had seemed like the worst kind of suburban wasteland, filled with tasteless McMansions and the shallow people inside. But in the months that followed, she began to realize that a lot of those first impressions were judgments she had placed upon the town, and weren't necessarily the way it really was.

"Hey, Mr. Krakower!" Jennifer waved to a heavy-set man on a riding lawnmower. "Need anything from Norm's?"

"How 'bout a winning lottery ticket!"

"Join the club!"

Getting to know the neighbors had been a piece of cake for

the easygoing thirteen-year-old, but the transition to life at her new school had been much rockier. Not only did she have to leave all her best friends behind, but a few of the meaner kids had singled her out because she didn't wear makeup and had patches from bands that no one had ever heard of all over her knapsack. Pretty soon she didn't even want to get out of bed, let alone walk the halls while everyone snickered behind her back.

All that started to change, however, on the night she had this really weird dream. A boy claiming to be a Fixer had invited her to a place called "The Seems" and given her the grand tour. According to Becker (she couldn't for the life of her remember his last name), the world she lived in wasn't what she thought it was, but actually something much, much better. It wasn't like she actually believed it, but imagining all these people dedicated to "The World" made the real one a pretty fun and sparkly place to be.

Not to mention that whole thing about "the Plan."

"Hey, JK!" A short Indian kid in glasses was shouting at her from the driveway of his parents' house. "We still on for today?"

"You bet," Jennifer answered, whipping past the boy on her three-speed Schwinn. "I'm pickin' up supplies right now."

Vikram Pemundi was also relatively new to the neighborhood, and had endured a similar fate upon his entrance to Gary Middle School, which is probably why he and Jennifer had become such fast friends. "Don't forget the carpenter's glue!"

"I won't!" Jennifer yelled over her shoulder, then kicked her bike into a higher gear. "And tell everyone else to meet me at the woods!"

Today was gonna be a really good day.

Though Becker made it out of the house just before his mother had a conniption, the Drane family wagon had still not left the borough of Highland Park. While the gas tank was being filled, Benjamin had been sent inside to take a pee (so they wouldn't have to stop at the Grover Cleveland rest area like last year), and their dad was completing his checklist of water, Sun Chips, and a book called *Car Games for the Entire Family*, which Becker dreaded like the plague.

"It's noon and I'm *still* not on vacation," complained his mom, frustration coming out of her in waves.

As that awful feeling of not being able to get out of Dodge permeated the car, Benjamin hid inside a sketch pad, while Becker took out his Blinker and jacked in his headphones and Transport Goggles™—necessary plug-ins for Mission Simulator mode.[9]

"Is it just me," Professor Drane was starting to come apart at the seams, "or is that guy moving in slow motion?"

Becker looked up from his Blinker to see the turbaned gas-station attendant not pulling the nozzle out of their already-full tank. He seemed to be lost in thought, or caught in a daydream, but when Becker looked closer, his hand was slowly moving. Very slowly.

"Rafik!" Becker rolled down the window and yelled at the attendant, who he knew from late-night Slim Jim and Chip-which runs to the twenty-four-hour Racemart. "Rise and shine!"

---

9. Allows users to engage in fully immersive, first-person POV practice Missions.

Rafik slowly turned to reply to Becker. Very slowly. So slowly that it reminded him of "super slo-mo" on the DVD player at 12 Grant Avenue.

"Dude, my mom is gonna blow a gasket if you don't—"

Suddenly, Rafik seemed to kick back to regular speed, topping off the gas tank, hanging it up on its holder, and rescrewing the cap back onto the car.

"$52.93, please. Thank you, sir."

"$52.93!" As Professor Drane handed Rafik his credit card, his face began to turn a darker shade of red. "I knew we should've gotten the hybrid!"

"I thought you said hybrids were ugly and riddled with technical problems." His mom was *still* not on vacation.

"It was the guy at the Saturn dealer who said that!"

As his parents exchanged looks that only people who've been married fifteen years can understand, Benjamin tunneled deeper into his drawing of "Shanty Town," the name of the broken-down beach house that had been in the Drane family for generations. Meanwhile, his older brother reaffixed his headphones and tried to shake off the weird little moment with Rafik.

In all truth, Becker should have seen it coming. Yes, he remembered Casey Lake's admonition to tune his 7th Sense to Time, and no, he didn't forget that the Powers That Be had refused to grant Triton's demands in the week that ensued— but his ability to put the pieces together properly was blocked by the stress level in the car.

So he just put on his headphones, cued up "Mission: Eye of the Storm," and forgot the whole thing.

Alton Forest, Caledon, Ontario

After dropping off the eggs and the OJ at home, Jennifer pedaled out to the Alton Forest Conservation Area and parked her bike by the edge of the hiking trail. She slipped onto the red path, which led to the yellow path, which led to the unmarked path, which Jennifer had marked with a blue splotch of paint. These woods had been a refuge for her during those early days in Caledon, and she would never forget the afternoons where the trickling brook and the wind-blown leaves had been her only companions. Today, however, she was expecting company.

"Marco!" yelled Jennifer into the woods.

No response except the wind and the chattering of squirrels in the trees.

"Marco!" she yelled again, and waited for the other half of the password, but it never came.

Seeing that she was the first one there, Jennifer snuck past the waterfall, climbed up the shale staircase, and slipped beyond the pricker forest to find a fallen pine tree, which now lay at a forty-five-degree angle against a towering elm. Using the pine as a slanted roof, she had built a kind of clubhouse for herself with plywood and sticks, and spent most of her time here—even when she had been the only member of the club.

Since the night she'd had that Dream, however, not only had The World begun to look different, but she'd also managed to make a few friends. Part of that was because the bullies had backed off, seeing that they weren't going to be able to break her—while at the same time, she'd been approached by a handful of the other outcasts from the seventh grade. They were certainly a motley crew, but one by one, she had brought them out here to form the underground insurgency whose name was chipped onto the massive elm:

Les Resistance

Most of their HQ had been built in the cool, cavelike environment beneath the dangling pine needles—but now that summer had arrived, Jennifer had been struck by the idea to build a *Swiss Family Robinson*–style addition to the clubhouse, complete with observatory deck, drink holders, and telescope that would allow them to scope out the surrounding terrain.

All they'd constructed so far was a circular platform about ten feet off the ground, and she quickly pulled herself up the rope ladder. Climbing had always come easily to Jennifer, which was why she was lead architect on this project, and in charge of constructing the second floor. She was just about to hammer some more nails into the frame when she heard an unusual sound . . .

Thunk.

Thunk.

Thunk.

The noise was coming from the other side of the elm tree, every three seconds or so. Jennifer carefully swiveled around on the platform, because the support beams were still loose—but when she finally made her way over, she couldn't believe what she saw.

It was a woodpecker, with red and black feathers, only a few feet over her head. But unlike every other woodpecker she'd ever seen, this one was pecking the wood so slowly it looked like a wind-up toy whose batteries were dying.

"Marco!" A familiar voice with an Indian accent called out in the distance, but Jennifer was too amazed by what she was looking at to answer. The bird was still pecking, but appeared to be slowing down even further.

Thunk.

Thunk.

Thunk.

She tentatively reached up to touch it, to see if it was even real, but right before her hand stroked the feathers, the "battery" suddenly kicked into overdrive. The woodpecker not only went back to regular speed but shot far past it, slamming against the tree like a miniature jackhammer. Jennifer jumped back in shock and nearly fell off the platform, but not before watching *Picus canadensis* zip into the sky and disappear at an astonishing rate.

"Marco!" That same voice was louder the second time—the voice of her friend Vikram Pemundi. Jennifer looked out over the forest to see Vik and the other three members of Les Resistance emerging from the pricker patch, each with their own bag of construction materials.

Part of her wanted to shout for them to look to the sky or tell them all about the crazy woodpecker, but to be honest, the whole incident had her a little spooked. So Jennifer decided to keep it to herself.

"Polo!"

Grover Cleveland Rest Area, New Jersey Turnpike, New Jersey

Despite having relieved himself at the Raceway in Highland Park, Benjamin had again complained upon passing Exit 11 that he needed to go. Professor Drane pulled off the turnpike only fifteen minutes after starting out and gruffly escorted Benjamin inside the men's room to take care of his business. Becker now sat on the hood of the aging Volvo station wagon that his father refused to part with, watching The World go by.

"I'm only gonna be gone a week," reassured Dr. Natalie Drane over her cell phone, pacing back and forth by the picnic area. "If you have an emergency, page Dr. Rosetti and he'll be more than happy to help you."

Becker's mom was just turning off her cell when one of her clients had called in a panic over the fact that there would be no session this week. Natalie saw an average of twenty-five clients a week, but only a few were raving lunatics like the unnamed person on the phone.

"Yes, Dr. Rosetti is licensed to practice in New Jersey, and no, I cannot meet you in Connecticut for a mini-session."

Becker shook his head and turned his attention back to the front doors of the rest area. Though his experiences in The Seems had taught him to appreciate The World and all the people who lived there, he was still in a foul mood, and couldn't help but notice that everyone who exited the building was carrying either a huge bag from Roy Roger's or putting the finishing touches on a heaping mound of Carvel ice cream.

"This is the beauty of The World?" whispered Becker to the

ghost of Grover Cleveland, but his father answered back instead.

"Becks! Get the heck back in the car!"

"Huh?"

Becker turned over his shoulder to see that his whole family was looking at him through the windshield.

"I know you're working on your tan, but we really need to start making some time . . ."

Becker hopped off the hood, completely befuddled. Just a second ago his mom was on the phone with "unnamed client" and Benjamin and his dad hadn't even emerged from the bathroom. But there they were, his father at the wheel and Benjamin buckled in and knocking back a Nathan's footlong.

"When did you guys get back in the car?" asked Becker.

"What are you talking about?" his mother responded.

The Dranes looked at each other as if this strange query only confirmed their worst fears: that their son was, in fact, becoming a troubled youth.

"Hey, Mom?" Benjamin stoked the fire with an evil grin on his face. "If Becker has to go away for a while, can I have his room?"

As he got back in the car, Fixer #37 was too consumed with what had just happened to care about the little monstrosity and his barbs. He knew he wasn't crazy—or at least he was 99 percent sure he wasn't—but he couldn't shake the feeling that Time itself had just skipped forw—

And that's when it happened.

One by one, the hairs on the back of Becker's neck began to slowly rise, like people standing up in line. That line then began to march down the curvature of his spine and straight into his stomach, where #37 knew from experience they would soon be causing a mild set of chills. This was the progression of the 7th Sense—that feeling that all Fixers use to determine if something has gone wrong in The Seems (and hence The World)—and the fact that Becker had now broken out into a cold sweat meant that it was probably something severe.

"Mom!" cried Benjamin. "Becker's breaking into a cold sweat back here!"

"I am not!"

Natalie examined her older son closely, who was definitely shivering in mid-July.

"It must be the video game I was playing." Becker tried to throw his mother off the scent. "In Japan, it gave kids epileptic fits."

"Then why are you playing it?" His mom was more than a little bit horrified.

"You're right. I'm gonna read a book instead."

"Don't read a book. That'll only make you more carsick! Why don't you just rest your eyes for a little while?"

"Good idea, Mom. Thanks."

Satisfied that she had exercised the proper amount of parental control, Natalie Drane went back to her book on tape. Becker, on the other hand, only half closed his eyes, concentrating most of his attention on his Blinker, which was set on vibrate mode and clipped to the side of his belt.

In years past, Fixers worked on a rotation—so everyone knew when they were next in line to receive a job—but recently, that process had changed. After many complaints and long discussions, the Powers That Be decided that Fixers would now be called in via a matching system. In other words, when a request came in to Central Command, the Dispatcher would decide whose individual skills best corresponded to the needs of the Mission—which meant that every Fixer had to be ready every time his or her 7th Sense went off.

The youngest Fixer opened one eye, and seeing that everyone in the car had fallen back into their routines, covertly slid one of the headphone buds into his ear. Based on what he'd seen today (combined with the monthly Briefing), Becker had a pretty good idea which department was in the midst of a crisis big enough to be causing hives to break out all along his ankles and feet.

The only question now was who would get the call?

Gandan Monastery, Sühbaatar Province, Outer Mongolia

Precisely sixteen seconds earlier, the inimitable Li Po's eyes opened upon the sacred temple that he called home. He'd been deep in the process of training a new Initiate—perhaps his greatest student yet—when hives of his own had broken out, and now he waited serenely for Central Command to make its decision.

"Suvahhh."

As the chanting of the monks rose in celebration of the celestial and unseen, Fixer #1 on the rotation rubbed the bottoms of his sockless feet. Whatever was happening in The Seems during the infinite space of the present, he was surely the first to feel it.

And tonight, he knew exactly who the Powers That Be were going to call.

Staten Island, New York

"Ma! I told you not to wash the cat in the freakin' sink!"

As his mother muttered something about "Smokey needs to look pretty," Tony the Plumber shook his head and yanked the massive furball from the pipe. He was about to pull himself out from under the sink when a nasty set of chills shot down his left leg.

"Ahh. They're never gonna call me anyway."

Ever since the new matching system had been put in place, Tony had only been summoned on one Mission. He wasn't happy about this, especially because his ability to practically talk to machines had once been considered priceless. But even though he was miffed at the lack of respect, Fixer #26 pulled out his Blinker anyway.

So did Casey Lake, the Belgian in the White Tuxedo, Sweet Lou, and thirtysome other Fixers around The World (and hopefully Tom Jackal), all of whom at this exact moment had stepped away from their motorcycle rally, laboratory experiment, morning mass, or lifelong search for an ancient artifact and waited for the shrill beeping of their Blinker to go off.

But only one Fixer heard it.

Sarténe, Isle of Corsica, France

BLINK! BLINK! BLINK! BLINK! BLINK!

In the middle of his sweaty palm, Mr. Chiappa's Blinker was flashing off the hook. He couldn't believe this was actually happening. And it was actually happening now!

"Not again!" cried Mrs. Chiappa. She and her husband had just sat down to dinner, their modest wooden table filled with fresh-baked breads and fruit. "You haven't even had a bite to eat!"

"I'm sorry, *tesorina*," Mr. Chiappa apologized. "This will surely be the last one."

Many years ago, Lucien Chiappa had received a special exemption to the "Keep Your Mouth Shut" Rule, for he had promised his wife on the day of their wedding that he would never keep a single secret from her. That didn't make it any easier, however, for she was sick to her stomach with worry every time he went on a Mission.

"Don't they know you're supposed to retire in four days?"

"Of course they know," Lucien answered. "I'm sure it's just a broken Window or a Foible."

He hated to fudge the truth to Ombretta, but as he kissed her on the forehead and adjourned to his office in the attic, he knew he couldn't tell her what was really going on. Pushing aside the schoolbooks and lesson plans, the high-school English teacher unclipped the Blinker from his belt and placed it atop his desk. It was still flashing vehemently, and in his heart of hearts he sensed what had happened in The Seems and why they had chosen him. Part of him was proud to have that responsibility, but another part just wanted to turn in his Badge, attend the farewell gathering at Flip's, and ride off into the Sunset. The Plan had other ideas, though.

Fixer #12 pressed the yellow Accept button and his Blinker began to transform. Audio would come first—a high whine settling to a low hum—which would soon be followed by the image of a double-sided wrench. As he waited for the Dispatcher to tell him what he already knew, Mr. Chiappa softly whispered in his native Corsican, "Time to make the *zeppole*."

The Time Bomb

Lucien Chiappa's career as a Fixer was solid but largely undistinguished. He was generally known for being a workmanlike presence, with no grand disasters on his record, and also for his hobby regarding Time. Ever since he'd tasted his first Déjà Vu and felt like he'd had one before, the English teacher was fascinated by this Department and the way in which it aged The World to perfection.

Perhaps this is why he was called in on the Day That Time Stood Still, when a Glitch overwhelmed legendary Fixer Tom Jackal and caused the entire World to grind to a halt. Mr. Chiappa's remarkable stratagem was to create a device that could generate enough force to get the whole thing moving again.

He called it a "Time Bomb."

"Now arriving, Department of Time, where it's always now. Please watch the gap between the train and the platform."

The computerized voice of the monorail echoed through the empty car and the doors whisked open, sending Fixer #12 onto the concrete platform that overlooked Time Square.

The main hub of this Department was a quaint village, like one would find tucked away in the mountains or nestled by the shore. There was a small park in the center and the cobblestone streets were lined with shops and stores. Daylight Savings Bank (FDIC) was the most dominant feature, with its marble columns and massive sundial, but the Second-Hand Store, Time in Memoriam, and the Around the Clock Diner were institutions in their own right and attracted visitors from all across The Seems.

"Where is everybody?" Mr. Chiappa whispered to himself, unable to shake the awful sense of foreboding. On most days, this place would be jammed with street vendors or customers sipping lattes at Magic Hour—the always crowded coffee shop on the southwest corner of Memory Lane. But today the streets were empty and all the stores shuttered up tight. "Hello?"

As if in response, he heard a creak, and turned to see someone stepping from a door in one of the alleys. It was a Chinese girl, no more than nineteen, with jet black hair and a laminated Badge on her chest.

"Briefer #375, Shan Mei-Lin, reporting for duty, sir!"

"At ease, Shan," said Chiappa to his Briefer. "I know who you are."

Indeed he did. Shan Mei-Lin was known in IFR circles as the

fastest Candidate ever to make it to Briefer, and she showed no sign of letting up. Her gear was immaculate—the newest jumpsuit from the Catalog, a red voice-activated Briefcase G5—and her wiry frame conditioned like a long-distance runner. There was one other thing that Chiappa also knew about Briefer Shan—she was decidedly type A. Her strict professionalism and adherence to the Rules sometimes made her an exhausting presence.

"What's the skinny?" he said.

"I've evacuated all nonessential personnel and Administrator Neverlåethe is awaiting your arrival."

"Well done. Are the Minutemen here yet?"

"Affirmative. Their best man went in for a look, but says he's way out of his league."

Chiappa shook his head, still in shock that this Mission had come only four days before his retirement. He had almost allowed himself the fantasy of the next school year, when he would finally have time to revise his lesson plans and watch bad TV and eat popcorn with his wife. But here he was, in a very different sort of Time and place.

"They're waiting for you, sir."

Chiappa snapped back to the present moment, resolving that to fight what was so was pointless. Not only that, it could cost The World dearly.

"Then let us not keep them."

Time Management, Department of Time, The Seems

Back down the alley and through the door with the faded grandfather clock was a long, dimly lit hallway with public restrooms on the side and an ordinary black swipe pad at the end. Anyone with clearance of eight or above could gain access to a second corridor, which led to a spiral staircase that had another black swipe pad at the bottom, which demanded clearance of nine to gain entrance to the sprawling underground bunker where the machinery of Time Management was housed.

"Clear a path," shouted Briefer Shan, a little louder than necessary. "Fixer coming through."

The first corridor had been empty, but the second was lined with Minutemen, whose job it was to handle the very Essence of Time. This was one of the most dangerous positions in the entire Seems, given to only the most sturdy of souls. But today they looked ashen-faced and shaken, and very few could muster up the courage to look Chiappa in the eye as he passed.

"Go get 'em, chief," said the obvious leader of the group, his visor popped open to reveal a sweat-soaked face. "This one's got your name written all over it."

"I'll do my best, Millsy."

A few others offered words of encouragement, but for the most part the stricken employees just chewed their Trouble Gum™. Like Chiappa, they had dreaded this day, but had never believed it would actually come.

"Thank the Plan you're here!"

At the bottom of the spiral staircase was a man of light complexion, with bright blue eyes and wispy blond hair . . . also known as Permin Neverlåethe, Administrator of the Department of Time. Like all of his rank, Permin wore a three-piece suit and a pocket watch, but his Time Piece™ was unique in that it showed World Time in all four thousand and twelve Sectors.

"Good to see you again," said Fixer Chiappa, shaking the Administrator's hand. "If only it were under better circumstances."

"Lucien, how could this have happened?" If Permin had been any whiter, he would have been transparent. "I thought we destroyed the blueprints!"

"We did," said Fixer #12. "Yet here we are again."

On that terrible Day That Time Stood Still, it was Permin Neverlåethe, then a manager at Daylight Savings, who assisted Chiappa in constructing the mechanism that restarted The World. But though their Mission had been successful, it had not come without a price.

"I knew this would come back to haunt us." Permin was on the verge of tears. "We should have never built it in the first place!"

"Of course we should have, Permin." Chiappa put his hand on his old friend's shoulder. "Now, just calm down and tell me what happened."

Though the gears of Time were quite a sight to behold, they were largely ceremonial. This system of towering cycloids, dangling weights, and brass pinions no longer pumped the Essence of Time. Yet, for obviously symbolic reasons, The Tide had chosen this hallowed ground on which to strike their latest blow.

"The first anomaly caught us completely off guard," said Administrator Neverlåethe over the roar of the spinning gears. "It looked like just a Slowdown in a few of the Sectors, but then it happened again—followed by a couple Speedups."

Slowdowns and Speedups were malfunctions that involved elements of The World moving through Time at wildly different rates. They were usually caused by flow-management issues in the pipeline that pumped Time over to Reality, but were typically resolved before anyone in The World would notice.

"We thought we had things under control," Permin continued. "But then there was a Timeout for four minutes and twenty seconds!"

"I thought that was weird," added Briefer Shan. "I was rereading *Ulysses* and the next thing I knew I was lying in bed. I didn't even know how I got there."

Chiappa had had a similar experience. He'd been peeling potatoes at the kitchen sink and suddenly found himself seated at the dinner table—but he had written it off as daydreaming or a "senior moment."

"A skippage of that magnitude is no accident," said the Fixer. "The Tide must have infiltrated the department and blocked the flow of Time."

Permin dropped his head in a mix of sadness and disgust, for this was a very proud department, as the sign above the entrance to Time Management declared:

3,650 DAYS WITHOUT MISSING A BEAT

"Now I realize it was all just a distraction," Neverlåethe pointed to a crawl space between three of the largest gears. "One of the tour guides spotted it when he was dusting up for today's show."

Tucked in between the whirring clockworks was a complex device that bore an eerie similarity to Chiappa's original invention. The timer was a simple alarm clock, which was duct taped to a titanium freezer caked with ice and frost. Inside were no doubt those missing trays of Frozen Moments, and the freezer itself was surrounded by several bags of fertilizer, stamped with the logo of the Department of Nature. Last but not least, there was a long black cylinder wired to the entire contraption.

"What's up with the tube?" shouted Briefer Shan above the din.

"It's a different kind of casing than the one we used," Chiappa observed. "But it looks like a Second Splitter to me."

"I could be wrong, my friends," Permin pointed to the smallest hand on the alarm clock, which sat stationary just above the number three. "But I think it's set to go off in twenty-seven minutes."

"Twenty-six minutes and forty-seven seconds, by my calculations," corrected Briefer Shan.

"Either way, we'd better get in there," Chiappa announced, resisting the impulse to shoot Shan a look of annoyance. "And we'd better shut down these gears."

As Permin instructed his managers to bring the ancient mechanism to a halt, Fixer and Briefer gathered their respective equipment.

"Lucien!" Administrator Neverlåethe was still shouting even though the gears had gone quiet. "I don't think I can . . ."

"It's okay, Permin," Chiappa let him off the hook. "I didn't expect you to come."

"It's just . . . Heidi and the children, they depend upon me . . ."

"I know that. You've done all you can here."

Permin nodded and looked like he was trying to say something, maybe an effort to save face or just a warning to his old friend. But before he could come up with the words—

"Get out of here, you old sandman," Chiappa interjected with a twinkle in his eye. "We've got work to do."

As Shan Mei-Lin began to unfold her Tool Table™, she was anxious to get cracking. Being the fastest Candidate ever to make it to Briefer, she fully expected to be the fastest Briefer ever to make it to Fixer as well. Sure, there had been younger Fixers than her, like Casey Lake and Becker Drane, but never had anyone moved up the ranks with such meteoric speed. And though she was stuck working with an old fart like Chiappa, this was the perfect opportunity to distinguish herself on a high-profile Mission.

"Give me Those Things That Look a Lot Like Tweezers That You Use to Cut Wires With™," requested Mr. Chiappa.

The entire chamber had been cleared of all personnel (as had the corridors above), and with the gears turned off, the only sounds left were the clanking of Tools and the ticking of the alarm clock. Briefer Shan handed over Those Things and watched as her Fixer snipped a blue wire that connected the freezer to the fertilizer. The bomb itself was covered with a host of such wires, in many different colors.

"How do you know which one to cut?" asked Briefer Shan.

"Most of these are just dummy wires meant to throw us off the trail," Chiappa explained. "But we've gotta clear them out before I can figure which ones are important."

Briefer Shan couldn't help but notice Chiappa's hand trembling as he cut the excess cords. Though she had studied the Mission Report from the Day That Time Stood Still at length, the specific blueprints of the device had been stricken from the record, and there were still a few things she didn't understand.

"How did you know the original bomb would restart Time again?" she asked.

"ICU™, please." Chiappa ignored her question and reached for the monoclelike Tool that allowed him to see through the freezer walls and onto the racks where the Moments were arrayed. "I didn't."

"Excuse me, sir?"

"I didn't know that it would work. I only had a hunch." Chiappa snipped another dummy wire, then continued. "I knew it would take a tremendous shock to get The World going again. And the only way I could think of creating that kind of energy was cracking open a Second."

"Why not a First?" inquired the Briefer.

"Not enough Essence inside," Chiappa explained. "No . . . it had to be a Second or a Third."[10]

Shan knew why he hadn't chosen a Third—cracking open one of those might destroy both sides of the In-Between in one fell swoop.

"The real key, though, was the Frozen Moments."

As if to illustrate that point, Chiappa picked the lock on the freezer with his Finger Nail™, and the door slowly swung open. Inside were fifty trays, each containing sixteen pristinely frozen cubes of ice. And inside each of those sixteen pristinely frozen cubes of ice was a moment of someone's life, captured and preserved for all eternity—or as long as they didn't melt.

"Frozen Moments are the one thing in The World that flow

---

10. Firsts, Seconds, and Thirds are the three naturally occurring geological phenomena from which the Essence of Time is distilled. For more on the science and nature of Time, please consult appendix B: "Time Is of the Essence."

backward to The Seems. Hence, it stood to reason that if we sent an explosion back in the opposite direction, it might be able to jump-start The World."

"Huh." For the first time, Briefer Shan was beginning to gain a little respect for Mr. Chiappa. "That's pretty genius."

"Hardly. By cracking the Second, we put the entire Seems at risk. It was only by the grace of the Plan that we didn't blow up the whole kit and kaboodle."

Chiappa winked at Briefer Shan, who was beginning to feel like so many of his kids at Sartene High. He may have seemed over the hill, but his combination of humility and old-world charm made it hard not to smile in his presence.

"There's one thing I can't figure out, though . . ." Chiappa had a perplexed look on his face as he studied the inner workings of the Bomb. "Where's the Containment Field?"

"Containment Field, sir?"

Chiappa pointed her attention to the black cylinder that he had referred to as the Second Splitter.

"When Permin and I built ours, we made sure to make only a tiny incision in the Second. But just in case it split in two, we surrounded the whole thing in a Time-resistant glass enclosure so the Essence couldn't escape."

"It's The Tide we're talking about, sir. Maybe they want it to escape."

At that moment it all started to get very real for both Fixer and Briefer. Immediately, their minds raced to friends and family and all the things they would never see again if they were unable to successfully deactivate the Bomb.

"What's your Mission Inside the Mission, Briefer Shan?" Chiappa was referring to something small in The World that

Fixers and Briefers were trained to wrap their hearts around when fear threatened to overwhelm them. He knew this was a personal question, but when would be a better time to ask?

"I'm not much of a believer in the MIM," Shan confessed without much hesitation. "I rely upon my skills and hard work at all times."

Chiappa wasn't surprised. Young Briefers were often seduced by the illusion of pride.

"What about you, sir?"

"It's always the same for me, regardless of the Mission," Chiappa smiled and pulled a photo out of his wallet. "And she'll kill me if I don't make it home for dinner."

Briefer Shan felt a flash of shame at the purity of the Fixer's love for his wife, but she quickly had to snap back on beam, because Chiappa had turned his attention back to the Time Bomb. There were now only fourteen minutes left on the alarm clock.

"The way I see it, all we have to do is disconnect the Second Splitter from the rest of the components."

"How can I help?"

"Look for any Booby Traps™."

Shan scanned the entire face of the machine, but found no evidence of the snares, snags, or sniggles invented by John Booby.[11]

"All clear, sir."

"Good. Then let's do this thing."

Chiappa returned Those Things, then requested a pair of

---

11. An ex-employee of the Toolshed who turned his talents toward darker purposes and is rumored to be a founding member of The Tide.

Oven Mitts™. Donning the protective gloves, he placed both hands under the black cylinder.

"I need you to cut that wire . . . that wire . . . and that wire." He was pointing to the ones that connected the alarm clock to the Splitter, and the Splitter to the freezer and the fertilizer. "And I need you to do it at the exact same time."

"When?"

"Now."

"Now?" Shan was flabbergasted. "I thought there would be more time to prepare."

"Well, we could wait till it gets down to 5, 4, 3, 2, 1 . . . but by then my lasagna will be cold." Chiappa winked again, then rolled up his sleeves to prepare for the operation. "Seriously, Shan—don't think too much about it. Just cut when I say so and this will all be over."

The calmness in Chiappa's voice relaxed the Briefer, but the ticking of the alarm clock seemed to get louder and louder. It was the same kind of alarm clock Shan had by her bedside in Beijing, which was always set to four a.m. But when it went off it only meant another day at university . . .

Briefer #375 took a deep breath to steady her nerves, then bundled the three crucial wires in her hand.

"Ready when you are, sir."

Chiappa bent his back to give him more leverage to lift the Splitter, then gave her the nod.

"May you live in interesting times," she whispered, then squeezed the handle of Those Things That Look a Lot Like Tweezers That You Cut Wires With and snipped the final three.

The clock stopped.

The wires fell to the floor.

And that was it.

Nothing else happened.

Briefer and Fixer looked at each other like, "It couldn't really be that easy, could it?" But apparently it was. Chiappa wiped the sweat from his eyes and waited for his heart to return to its normal speed.

"Update Central Command that the Time Bomb has been diffused and we will be delivering the Second back to the Minutemen." As the Briefer pulled her Receiver™ off her belt, Chiappa had one last thing to add. "And well done, Shan."

"Thank you, sir."

Briefer Shan was already mentally adding this to her list of successful Missions as the Fixer slowly lifted the cylinder into the air. He had handled many a Second in his time (not to mention Thirds) and despite its natural volatility, he was quite confident in his ability to contain it. As he freed the Splitter from the wires, Chiappa could almost taste the retirement ceremony at Flip's and the popcorn (with butter and salt) that lay just on the other side of this final task. "Now, if you could just open that doo—"

Rinnnggg!

Suddenly, the bell on the top of the alarm clock began to ring—as loud and grating as the sound that jolts unfortunate dreamers from the pleasure of a Good Night's Sleep. It was also rattling on top of the freezer, and by the way the many wires attached to it danced lifelessly about like tentacles, Chiappa knew that he had made a terrible mistake.

For *all* the wires were dummies.

"What's happening, sir?" cried Briefer Shan, the coppery taste of panic soaking her tongue. What was once seven minutes was now six, now five, now four, as the arms of the clock whipped wildly toward zero.

"It's a wireless detonator!" Chiappa screamed at his Briefer over the shrill ring of the alarm clock. "Look for a transmitter!"

"What's it look like?" Shan frantically scoured the Bomb up and down.

"A small box with a little rubber antenna!" Chiappa wanted to help her look for it but he was stuck holding the Second Splitter, and by the time he put it down it would already be too late.

"I can't find it, sir!" shouted the Briefer. "I can't find it!"

As the minute hand passed two on its way to one, a strange peace descended over Mr. Chiappa. He knew that wherever the wireless was, it would soon be activating a guillotine-like device inside the cylinder that would cut the Second neatly in two, sending one half hurtling through the trays of Frozen Moments. Where it would go from there was unclear, but the one thing he knew for certain was that anyone trapped inside the blast radius would be exposed to the Essence of Time.

"Get out of here, Shan!"

"No way, sir. A Briefer never leaves her Fixer!"

"That's a direct order!"

"But sir—"

"Go! Now!"

Briefer Shan hesitated before bolting back through the gears and to the door that led to the spiral staircase. With tears in her eyes, she took one last look at her Fixer—who was gently easing the Second Splitter to the ground—then closed the door behind her.

Lucien Chiappa released the long black cylinder and took off his Mitts.

"Four days," he whispered aloud.

Some would have spent their final ten seconds lamenting the Plan's twisted sense of humor, or cursing the Powers That Be for not cutting him a little slack. Yet Fixer #12 only felt blessed that he had been lucky enough to have a job such as this, a wife such as Ombretta, and a World such as the one in which he was privileged to live. The last thing he thought was, "I knew I should have added *For Whom the Bell Tolls* to the lesson plan."

And then the Time Bomb exploded.

Merritt Parkway, Bridgeport, Connecticut

"Ahhh!"

Becker Drane didn't realize he was screaming until his mom shook him by the arm. "Becker! What's wrong?"

It took the boy a few more shakes to snap out of it and quiet down. He'd been following along on Mr. Chiappa's Mission via the "Missions in Progress" function on his Blinker, when he'd been overwhelmed with the physical sensation of a terrible wrongness in The Seems. Not only did it hurt, but he felt as if he was about to ralph all over the car.

"I think I'm getting carsick."

"Can you wait till the next rest stop?" said Professor Drane, pointing to a sign that said, "Service Area, Three Miles."

"I don't think so," replied his son, turning a deeper shade of green.

Even Benjamin kept his mouth shut, because he was starting to worry about Becker too. The professor pulled to the side of the Merritt Parkway and up onto the grass. "Go over there by the woods."

Becker opened the door and stumbled out of the car.

"Go with him, Ferdinand!"

"It's okay, Mom. I'll be right back. I'm just—" But before he even got five steps past the shoulder, Becker and his family witnessed what half a turkey and provolone from Highland Pizza looks like after it's been in a stomach for forty-five minutes. (Note: It don't look good.)

"Dude, that's so gnarly," Benjamin said admiringly.

"Thanks . . . a lot . . . nimrod," answered Becker, before upchucking again.

"He's right, son," their father chimed in. "That is pretty gnarly."

Becker rose to his feet and wiped his mouth on the edge of his sleeve. He was starting to feel a little better, though that was small comfort, for never before had his 7th Sense screamed in this way. It told him that the last update he'd received on "Missions in Progress"—"Time Bomb successfully diffused"—had been somewhat premature.

The Fixer raised a finger to his family as if to say "give me a minute," then staggered over by the woods. Once he was sure that he was safely out of view, he pulled his Blinker off his belt and was about to check on the status of Mr. Chiappa, when—

BLINK! BLINK! BLINK! BLINK! BLINK!

He covertly pressed the yellow Accept button, holding it down an extra second so it wouldn't go through its transformation to a keyboard with oversized viewscreen.

"Stand by for transmission."

Becker pretended to dry-heave again just in case his family was watching, then turned the volume on the Blinker up just loud enough to hear.

"Fixer #37, F. Becker Drane. Please report. Over."

The Dispatcher usually wore a headset, a uniform, and a perfectly manicured buzz cut. But this time his hair was disheveled and dark bags had formed beneath his eyes.

"#37 present and accounted for!"

The Fixer prepared to wait for verification but the Dispatcher uncharacteristically skipped the formalities. He was fraught with emotion in a way that Becker had never seen before.

"What happened?"

The Dispatcher pulled his headset off and wiped the cold sweat from his eyes.

"We need you, kid. We need you real bad."

Fallout

Customs, Department of Transportation, The Seems

By the time Becker arrived in Customs, a state of emergency had already been declared by the Powers That Be. All departmental employees were instructed to remain at their posts until further notice and only authorized personnel were allowed to board the monorail. But as Fixer Drane boarded the express and headed toward one of the greatest disasters in Seemsian history, his head was still spinning from the mess he'd left behind.

Shortly after the haggard Dispatcher had disappeared from his screen, Becker had grabbed his Toolkit from the trunk of his parents' car and returned to the woods under the guise of walking off a final bout of nausea. From there, it only took a minute to inflate his Me-2, insert his shiny Skeleton Key into the base of a maple tree, and open a portal directly into the In-Between. But just as he was stepping inside—

"Becker?"

The ever-present Benjamin rounded the bend to take another whiz. From the horrified look on his face, the seven-year-old must have thought he was carsick too, for standing next to his older brother was . . . his older brother.

"You're dreaming, B." Becker and his Me-2 tried to cover for each other in perfect harmony. "Go back to the car and when you wake up you won't remember any of this."

"Yes, I will."

"No, you won't."

"Yes, I will. Because I'm *not dreaming*!"

The last thing the Fixer needed was another Rule violation, but seeing that the boy was on the verge of hysterics, he had little choice but to kneel down beside him and come clean.

"I know this is gonna be hard to believe, B," Becker waited for an eighteen-wheeler to rumble by, "but um . . . everything I told you about The Seems—it's real."

The fact that there was a blue tunnel apparently extending into infinity (as opposed to the inside of a maple tree) backed up Becker's claim.

"I have to take off for a little while, so you hang out with Me. But whatever you do, don't say anything to Mom or Dad or you're gonna get the worst flying wedgie of your life."

As if to punctuate the threat, the inflatable Becker put its hands together and made a violent upward yanking motion.

"I swear I won't say anything. I *swear*."

Becker slung his Toolkit over his shoulder and gave his little brother a hug.

"Take good care of him, okay, Me?"

"Affirmative," answered Becker's alter ego. "Now get going!"

"Now arriving, Department of Time, where it's always Now. Please watch the gap between the train and the platform."

Even before the monorail pulled to a stop, Becker had a feeling it was going to be bad. He was the only passenger on a train normally packed with commuters, and the closer he got to the station the more the Fixer could hear the sound of sirens through the plate-glass windows. But he never expected it would be quite as bad as this.

Scattered across the platform were hundreds of people—employees and visitors alike—laid out on stretchers or huddled on the floor in blankets, crying out for medical attention. Emergency Care Givers from the Department of Health were scrambling to help everyone they could, but the sheer numbers of those who'd been caught in the blast had them overwhelmed.

"Help me! Somebody help me!" A girl Becker recognized as one of the baristas from Magic Hour was clutching her leg in agony. "My leg . . . it's getting older!"

Seeing that no one was answering her cries, Becker ran over to see what he could do.

"It's okay! It's gonna be o—"

But it wasn't gonna be okay—for on closer inspection, the skin right below the girl's knee had rapidly begun to age, wrinkling like Saran Wrap right before Becker's eyes. Even worse, the bones beneath the skin were gnarling and warping into those of an old woman.

"Help!" Becker called out at the top of his lungs. "We need a medic over here!"

"In one second!" cried a sweat-soaked Care Giver. "We have to deal with the most serious cases first!"

As Becker tried to comfort the anguished girl, he realized that as bad as what was happening to her, what was happening around them was much, much worse. Two paramedics were treating a teller from Daylight Savings, but their Anti-Aging Cream had failed to stop his teeth from falling out of his head. Everywhere Becker looked, blonds and redheads were turning gray and white, spines were hunching, and years of life were rapidly draining away.

"We need more dustpans over here!" shrieked a nurse to no one in particular. "We need more dustpans *stat*!"

True horror, it is said, lies in what remains unseen—but that is only said by those who have never truly seen it. Becker was now witnessing it firsthand, as Seemsians who only a half-hour ago had bright futures ahead of them were following the aging process to its logical conclusion—their lives cut short as they literally crumbled into piles of dust. Weeping Care Givers were delicately sweeping up the remains and pouring them into ceramic urns so friends and family could someday honor their loved ones.

"Somebody do something!" he shouted, noticing how fear had made his voice sound high pitched and shrill.

Becker had never seen a dead person before, except for a girl named Amy Lannin. Amy grew up around the corner from Becker and was by far his best friend, but she was stricken with leukemia when she was only ten years old. On the day of her funeral, the sight of her made up and lying in the coffin had been almost too much for Becker to bear. And even after a year of service as a Fixer, to be in the presence of death again shook him to the very core.

"Fixer Drane! Over here!"

Becker looked up to see the Dispatcher himself emerging from a makeshift ops center.

"One second, sir!" Becker was still holding the hand of the terrified barista, who was finally having a tourniquet applied to her leg. "I need to make sure she's—"

"That's an order, Fixer Drane!" Even the Dispatcher's famously gruff voice got caught inside his throat. "The needs of the many outweigh the needs of the one."

Reluctantly, Becker pulled his hand out of the grasp of the barista.

"Please . . . don't leave me!" implored the girl.

"I have to," answered Becker. "After I Fix this thing, I promise I'll come back and make sure you're all right."

But that brought the young woman small comfort as she was lifted onto a stretcher and loaded onto the monorail with the rest of the victims. Becker still hoped that he could find her at the Department of Health when all of this was over, but then he realized . . . he never even had the chance to get her name.

"Here's what we know so far . . ."

The Dispatcher pulled Becker inside the curtains that had been hung around the kiosk to keep it separate from triage. Behind them were a host of Time Keepers, Central Command personnel, and even a few off-duty Night Watchmen who had come down from the Department of Sleep to help monitor the effects of the Bomb on both The Seems and The World.

"As soon as the Second was split, it caused a massive release of the Essence of Time. The bulk of it went through the Frozen Moments as planned, but since there was no containment field in the basic design, there was a large degree of spillover into the department itself." The Dispatcher took a quick look outside, as another load of victims was lifted onto the train. "Which explains what you see out there . . ."

"Any word on Chiappa?" asked Becker, still a bit rattled from what he'd seen on the platform. And he wasn't alone.

"Negative. We can only assume the worst."

"What about his Briefer?"

"Shan made it out of there before it detonated and thank the Plan, she had the wherewithal to set up a Fallout Shelter™."

Becker stepped to the opposite side of the booth and pulled the curtain aside. Normally, this would have given him a perfect view of the quaint little village known as Time Square, but today all he could see was a giant blue tent that covered all eight blocks of downtown.

"Nice work," admired Fixer Drane, appreciating Briefer Shan's quick thinking. The Fallout Shelter had been invented by Al Penske to protect a Fixer in the midst of cataclysmic events, but recognizing that it was air, water, and fire tight, Shan had inverted its purpose and used it to keep the Essence from spreading out even farther. Becker had never seen one quite this big though.

"Who knew the Double XL would ever come in handy?" the Dispatcher chuckled, marveling at the wizardry of the Toolshed's head designer. "But it's not gonna hold for long."

Becker did the quick calculations in his head and knew that with so many first responders on the scene, an alternate solution to the Fallout Shelter could probably be conceived. The World was another matter, though.

"For all intents and purposes, it should have been destroyed already," added Permin Neverlåethe, hands shaking and face seemingly drained of all blood by what had happened in his department. "With this level of exposure, the Fabric of Reality should have been soaked in the Essence and the entire World reduced to dust, much like my . . . ," the Administrator of Time tried to choke down the emotion, ". . . former employees."

"Then why hasn't it happened yet?" A cold wash of fear came over Becker as he thought of his family and Me-2, who were no doubt stuck in traffic on I-95 near New Haven right now. "Outside of a few minor anomalies I saw before the Bomb went off, there weren't any noticeable effects."

"That's what we've been trying to figure out." Neverlåethe whistled toward a crowd of Tickies who were still trying to rig up some servers to keep what was left of Time up and running. "But we do have one potential theory . . ."

"What's up, boss?" a young, shaggy programmer in a Rush[12] T-shirt appeared at Becker's side. "We're about to patch in the laptop Window so we can check the World's timing."

"Bochkay, show Fixer Drane what you showed me."

At the mention of the word "Fixer," the normally flippant Ticky suddenly found himself tongue-tied, until Becker gave him the peace sign, which seemed to mellow him out.

---

12. A popular World-based band from the 1980s whose chart-topping single "Tom Sawyer" became a crossover hit in The Seems.

"Well, a typical Second kind of looks like this, right?" He sheepishly reached into his pocket and pulled out an egg of what Becker recognized as Silly Putty. "I don't normally bring this to work with me, but uh . . ."

Seeing that nobody cared, he continued his explanation.

"Imagine the putty is the Essence inside the Second and the egg is the Second itself." Bochkay split the two pieces in half and removed the taffylike gunk. "Now, assuming this Bomb is relatively similar to the original, the moment the Second was split in two, all of the Essence would have gone into the Frozen Moments with this half of the egg."

He jammed the entire ball of putty into one half of the egg and flipped it over to Becker.

"The only reason I can think of to explain why what you're holding in your hands hasn't hit The World yet is that it somehow took a detour into one of the Frozen Moments themselves— or may even be ping-ponging between them."

"Does that mean it could still end up hitting The World?" Becker inquired.

"Absolutely. It's really not a matter of *if*, but *when*."

Becker wanted to ask, "Well, how do we stop it?" but then he remembered that that was *his* job.

"What if we were somehow able to get our hands on this piece," Fixer Drane held up the putty-filled half of the egg in his hand, then grabbed its empty partner from the Ticky. "And put it back together with *this* piece."

"That would be ideal," said Bochkay. "But how the heck are you gonna do that?"

Becker only smiled and flipped the Silly Putty back to its owner.

"You leave that up to me." He turned to the Dispatcher. "In the meantime, put the rest of the Roster on call. We don't know what we're gonna find inside that tent."

"There's one more thing, Drane." The Dispatcher pulled a piece of information out of his back pocket. "I didn't tell you why you were the one called in as the replacement for Chiappa."

Becker wanted to say, "Because I've been on a hot streak lately?" but it didn't seem appropriate, especially when the Dispatcher popped the piece into his own custom-designed Blinker.

"The Powers That Be only declassified this info ten minutes ago. I think you need to see it."

Onscreen was an MOS[14] image of the three largest spinning Gears of Time. Judging by the grainy black-and-white quality and the time stamp in the lower-left corner, it was shot by a security camera mounted on the wall of Time Management.

"This is only a few moments before the Bomb was discovered."

Nothing happened for a few seconds, then a masked figure entered the room and jammed a crowbar in between the spinning gears. Moments later, two similarly dressed accomplices came in, bearing the already-assembled device that would soon bring down the entire department. As they awkwardly managed to maneuver it between the jammed-up gears, the first figure took the time to pull out a black spray can—but instead of spraying the prototypical Tide symbol, he walked directly toward the security camera and unexpectedly pulled off his mask.

"Thibadeau," Becker whispered.

---

14. "Mit out sprechen," or "without sound."

The young Frenchman looked well enough, though his beard was significantly longer than it had been the last time they'd seen each other at The Slumber Party. He shouted some orders to his comrades before turning back to the camera and kissing it directly on the lens.

"I wonder why he took his mask off," asked Bochkay the Ticky.

"Because he wants us to know that it's him." Becker could feel the muscles tightening in his stomach. He would never forgive Thibadeau Freck for faking his own death and betraying everything the two of them had once stood for. And the sight of him orchestrating this destruction made his blood boil.

"We thought that your knowledge of Mr. Freck's methods might come in handy," said the Dispatcher.

"Understood, sir. You made the right decision."

Becker looked back at the Blinker, hoping to see what the Tide's operative would do next, but he had already painted the camera lens black.

On a bench on the far end of the platform, a girl wrapped in a wool blanket rocked back and forth as if she were shivering on a cold winter day. Her long hair, which had once been jet black, was now splashed with white—and the trembling fingers that covered her face were streaked with age. But thankfully the Anti-Aging Cream had stopped the process at about seventy years old.

"I have to be honest with you, #37," the Dispatcher whispered in Becker's ear. "I think she's cooked."

From where Becker stood, only twenty feet away, he couldn't

argue with this conclusion. Though Shan Mei-Lin had managed to contain the disaster in Time, she had remained inside the Fallout Shelter to pull out as many victims as she could. But the physical wounds she had sustained were nothing compared to the psychological ones.

"I know you like to work with Briefer #356, but he's on a leave of absence right now." The Dispatcher pulled out his Blinker. "Why don't you let me call in the Sarge?"

"With all due respect, if she doesn't get back on the horse right now, she probably never will."

"Understood," said the voice of Central Command. "But remember you have more important things to do than save the career of one Briefer."

Becker nodded, then quietly made his way over to the bench.

"On your feet, Briefer."

Shan parted two fingers and Becker saw one tear-stained eye.

"Excuse me?" she whispered.

"I said on your feet!"

The sound of a thirteen-year-old voice shouting like a drill sergeant at the top of his lungs snapped Briefer Shan out of her fugue state.

"Yes, sir!" She stood up and snapped into her salute. "Briefer #375, reporting for duty, sir!"

"That's better!" Becker was happy to see that her face had been spared injury. "Now I've read the Mission Report and I know what you've been through, but we still have a World to save and I need a Briefer on this Mission."

"Isn't there somebody el—"

"I don't want somebody else." Becker's voice softened. "I need *you*."

"I don't know, sir," said Shan. "I'm not sure I'm up to it."

"I'm not sure I'm up to it either," the Fixer confessed. "What do you say the two of us roll up our Sleeves™ and find out?"

Time Square, Department of Time, The Seems

Unlike Pajamas™ or Thick Skin™, the white spandex bodysuits known as Sleeves™ were lightweight, breathable, and did not require a bulky helmet. Instead, sleek Eyeglasses™ were woven directly into the fabric, which allowed the wearer to see through any Cloud of Suspicion or Rain of Terror. Fixer Drane and Briefer Shan pulled theirs on tight, then strode down the platform and into the "new" Time Square.

Just as with the wounded, the very infrastructure of the village had been partially aged to its logical conclusion. Halves of buildings had crumbled into dust, trees had devolved into lumps of coal, and even the Rock of Ages—the indestructible monument that had become a favorite climbing wall for Seemsian children—had been reduced to a solitary pebble. All of which gave a ghastly preview of what might happen in The World should Becker Drane fail in his Mission.

"It was the strangest thing, sir," said Shan, leading her Fixer back toward the door she and Chiappa had entered only a few hours before. "There was no sound when the Bomb exploded. Just a flash of white light, and then it was like being splashed across the face with water. Except I wasn't wet."

"The Essence of Time," Becker observed. "It's a miracle you made it out in one piece."

"I know that, sir."

Becker knew that Shan was dealing with a bad case of survivor's guilt, and for lack of a better phrase, only Time would heal the wound. But when she opened the door with the faded grandfather clock, it was apparent that much more Time would be required.

"Wuh de ma," she whispered in her native tongue.

Lining the hallways were neat little piles of dust—all that remained of the brave men and women of the Minutemen.

"I told them to run. I did. But they refused to leave their posts."

Shan bent over and picked up a half-melted ID Badge, upon which the name "Beaufort Mills, Captain" was still visible. It was Chiappa's old friend Millsey, whose Time had come all too soon, and she felt her eyes welling again.

"It wasn't your fault, Shan," Becker tried to keep his Briefer on beam. "With them . . . or with Mr. Chiappa."

At the mention of her late Fixer, the tears Shan had been fighting to hold back came easy. She was nowhere near ready to forgive herself—especially for thinking of him as a doddering old fool who might hold back her career.

"The best way you can honor his memory is to save the department he loved."

The Briefer nodded and wiped her cheeks dry.

Farther down the hallway the security doors were gone, and the spiral staircase down to Time Management had been reduced to a twisting metal frame. Becker and Shan deployed their Chutes & Ladders™ and quickly descended into the darkness below.

"What are you looking for, sir?"

"I'll let you know when I find it." The fluorescent lights that normally lit up Time Management had gone black, and Becker crawled on his hands and knees clutching a penlight. "Can you fire me up a Flash in the Pan™?"

"Affirmative."

Shan reached into her Briefcase and quickly sparked the one-thousand-candlepower skillet. Fully illuminated, the room showed remarkably little effects of being the epicenter of one of the greatest disasters in Seemsian history. In fact, the only remnant of the Time Bomb was the black cylinder that had once contained the Second Splitter . . . or what was left of it.

"There's something inside there," noticed Shan. "It looks like some kind of shell."

"That's half of the Split Second. Put it somewhere safe, 'cause we're definitely gonna need it."

While Becker continued scouring the underside of the gears, Shan managed to detach the Split Second from the clamp that held it in place. It indeed looked like half an eggshell, except with a reflective metal finish instead of nutrient-rich white. Shan was surprised at how hard the surface was and wondered what the guillotine could have been made of to so easily cut such a thing in two.

"Brrr!" she shivered, tucking the shell deep into her Brief-case. "Maybe I should unwrap a Hot Potato™ too?"

Due to the temperature-resistant properties of the Sleeve, it had taken her a while to notice just how cold it was down there.

Obviously, the same generator that powered the lights also handled climate control.

"Not yet," grunted Fixer Drane from beneath the largest of the gears. "We need it to stay below freezing."

"Why, sir?"

"Because we don't want *this* to melt."

In Becker's Sleeved hand was what at first glance appeared to be a shard of glass. But when Shan leaned in closer, it was actually a thin sliver of ice, with something frozen inside of it.

"It's a piece of a Frozen Moment." He held it up to the light and showed his Briefer what looked like a butterfly about to land on a human palm. "They were all shattered when the Bomb went off—but somewhere inside them is the *other* half of that Split Second."

Briefer Shan was about to ask, "How do we get it out of there?" when the method to Becker's madness began to dawn on her. Shan had gone through the same Training Becker did, and had seen the same simulation, when a legendary Fixer's Mission had gone terribly awry in front of an archaic ice machine. And for the first time since Mr. Chiappa had ordered her to leave the room, she knew exactly what to do.

"I'll start collecting the rest."

Half an hour later, Fixer Drane and Briefer Shan were staring down at fifty trays' worth of shattered ice. The Briefer had found the original freezer, broken in two pieces and embedded in the ceiling of Time Management, and had managed to extract the bulk of the Moment shards.

"No one's ever done this before, sir."

"No one who's ever lived to tell the tale." Becker Drane picked up his Receiver. "Fixer Drane to Central Command."

"Go ahead, Fixer Drane," the Dispatcher shouted over the sound of the monorail, which Becker hoped was pulling away with its final load.

"Initial survey finds power in Time Management down, but pipeline to Reality still intact." Becker could hear the audible sighs of relief from everyone who was listening in. "Only problem is, the shattering of the Frozen Moments has turned this place into an icebox. Recommend calling in Tony the Plumber to restore basic functionality."

"Why? Where are you gonna be, #37?"

"Briefer Shan and I are gonna melt what's left of the Frozen Moments and go looking for that Split Second."

The silence on the other end of the line informed Becker that his plan was just as crazy as he himself thought it might be.

"Say again, Fixer Drane?"

"It's the only way."

"But you'll never make it out of there, son."

"Yes, I will," said Becker, though he had no precedent to support his claim. "And besides, if we don't put that Second back together, there won't be any World for me to go home to."

Muffled voices came back over the line, and Becker had the distinct impression that the Dispatcher was covering up the microphone of his Receiver so neither he or Shan could hear what was being discussed.

"Understood," the Dispatcher relented. *"I'll handle the paperwork."*

"Thanks."

"And Fixer Drane? It's an honor to serve with you."

"Likewise." Becker tried his best (and failed) to hide from Shan how much the Dispatcher's compliment meant to him. "Drane over and out."

He hung up his Receiver and pulled the aforementioned Hot Potato from his Toolkit.

"Ready, Briefer Shan?"

"Ready, sir."

They looked at each other, knowing full well that there was a distinct possibility they might never return. But there was no greater feeling for one who had been trained at the Institute for Fixing & Repair under the auspices of Fixer Jelani Blaque than to put everything on the line for a cause higher than oneself. Which was why they smiled the smile they were smiling right now.

Becker ignited the spud and pointed the glowing skin down at the pile of Frozen Moments.

"Let's go for a swim."

Lost in Time

In the long history of the relationship between The Seems and The World, Frozen Moments are perhaps the only commodity that originate on the World side of the Fabric of Reality. When a human being's experience reaches a certain level of emotional intensity—be it happy or sad—that Moment, and the set of events surrounding it, are captured in a small cube of ice and sent careening back to The Seems. The hows and whys of this process are still under examination, but in the absence of scientific breakthrough, the focus of this department remains in keeping these precious artifacts secure.

—From *A Not-So-Brief History of Time*
by P. Neverlåethe (Copyright © Seemsbury Press,
MGBHII, The Seems), pages 4, 119.

Since few will ever have a vacation long enough to read Administrator Neverlåethe's infamous treatise, it is important to understand just what he means by secure. Each person's individual Moments are kept under lock and key in safety deposit boxes within the Daylight Savings Bank. Twenty-five-hour security surrounds the titanium vault, as does an alarm system complete with motion sensors, electric eyes, and Personality Scan technology. The contents therein are only removed when an individual account is closed and transferred to A Better Place, where they can be enjoyed at a person's leisure for all eternity. But for a living person to enter another's Frozen Moment is not only considered taboo . . . it is considered suicide.

"Sir—I highly recommend we roll down our Sleeves and don wetsuits instead," suggested Briefer Shan.

"We're not gonna be flowing through water, Shan." Becker stared down at the melted pool of experience. "We're gonna be flowing through people's lives."

Both of them circled the puddle, which looked much like the one that each had studied when reliving the Day That Time Stood Still, during the second semester of Training. Fixer Blaque counted on this simulation as a perfect example of the need for a "Mission Inside the Mission," but no former Candidate could ever forget the terrible sight of Fixer Tom Jackal drowning in a pool much like this one. Jackal had been a role model, if not hero, to many a Fixer, and his demise still weighed heavily on everyone at the IFR.

"Any more recommendations before we go in?" Becker asked his Briefer.

Shan bent down and stared at the blurry water. "The Moments were fragmented to start with and now that they've been melted, I don't know how stable they're gonna be. I suggest we use some Connective Tissue™ as an added safety measure."

"Agreed."

They unrolled six feet from the toilet paper–like spool, and attached one end to each of their belts. Down in the puddle, they could just make out a set of faces and places—even hear a distant voice—all blending together in a murky soup. Becker thought about giving one or two more words of advice, but the fact was there was nothing left to say except, "On my mark! 3 . . . 2 . . . 1 . . ."

And they jumped.

As soon as Becker's head dipped beneath the surface, he started to regret turning down the suggestion of wetsuits. They were sinking fast into cloudy, swamplike fluid, and the fear in Shan's eyes told him that she was thinking the same thing he was— "Let's break out our Iron Lungs™"—when the water suddenly vanished and their feet hit solid ground.

"Where . . . are . . . we?" coughed Briefer Shan, gasping for air.

"Looks like . . . the Sahara," replied Becker.

He had always stunk at geography, so it could it have been any desert—the Gobi, the Mojave, even the Rub' al-Khali, which he only knew from watching a documentary about meteor rocks on Nat Geo. The wind was whipping across their faces, but strangely enough, they were all alone.

"I wonder whose Frozen Moment this is," said Briefer Shan, scanning the burning white sands.

Becker shook his head, too carried away by the size and scope of the landscape to care. Much like a Dream (which the Fixer had visited in his first Mission to the Department of Sleep) the inside of a "Fro Mo" felt as real as The World itself. There was no telling how far it stretched and what, if any, boundaries there were. "I don't see anybody . . ."

Almost in response, a striped red and pink parachute rose above one of the nearby dunes. Attached to it were several taut ropes, and it kept on drifting higher and higher into the sky, until . . .

"*Sweet!*" shouted Becker at the top of his lungs, and it was.

Some adventurous soul with a board strapped to his feet crested the dune and shot into the air, propelled by a kite-surfing mechanism. Becker had never seen anything so radical in his life, and by the shout of exultation that echoed over the winds, neither had the kite-surfer himself. Fixer and Briefer were about to run down the hill and give the dude a high-five (or ten), when the sand beneath their feet turned to water.

"Whoaaa . . ."

It was like falling down a waterfall, although neither of them had ever fallen down a waterfall before. Their stomachs were stuck in their throats and their arms flailed to try to maintain balance. But this time, when they hit the ground, they hit it a lot harder.

"That sucked," said Becker, trying to untangle his legs from the Connective Tissue, which had twisted around them in the fall. "Maybe we need to cut each other some slack."

Briefer Shan extended the sturdy double-ply Tool a few extra feet, then they took in the sight of their new surroundings.

It was a wide meadow in the peak of spring—filled with daffodils and bees loading up on pollen. Once again, the owner of the Moment was not immediately apparent, but Becker kept his focus on the Mission at hand.

"We need to pick up the trail before we slip into another Moment." Becker dropped his Toolkit and shook the kinks out of his neck. "We may not be back this way again."

Shan recognized the Fixer's preparations as trying to clear his awareness for an extension of his 7th Sense. If he could gather some evidence left behind by the Split Second, they could potentially isolate which Moment it was bouncing around in now.

"Anything, sir?"

"Not yet," said Fixer #37, deep in meditation. "Let me concentrate."

The Briefer took that as a direct order to "shut up," and for the first time since she had lost Chiappa, Shan felt the sting of her old pride. "Who is this little kid to tell me how to do my job," she thought, "when I could do it just as well as he can?" She dropped her own Toolkit to the ground and was about to teach him a lesson, when a voice wafted through the pasture.

"Rufus! Stay!"

It sounded like an old man, but before Shan could see who was there, a squirrel shot past her feet—followed closely by a young Labrador retriever.

"Hey, boy," she said, immediately thinking of Xi Shi, her own Pekingese, who was no doubt sacked out on the couch back in her Beijing apartment right now. The dog stopped on a dime—perplexed to see a woman in a soaking-wet bodysuit and goggles—and was torn between its desire to sniff out a possible new friend or chase down that bushy-tailed rodent that was always sneaking into the yard and making off with its beloved rawhide chew toys.

"Rufus!" the voice cried again, closer this time. "Come back here, you little troublemaker!"

The old man emerged through the rye, dressed in a tweed vest and using a walking stick to bat away the grass. From the sound of his accent, Shan thought they were somewhere in the hills of New Zealand.

"Excuse me. I didn't know anyone else—" He stopped, just as confused as his dog to see the bizarrely outfitted strangers (not to mention the fact that they were tethered to each other by toilet paper).

"We didn't mean to startle you." Shan tried to cover for her boss. "We're just up here doing some . . . surveying."

"Very good then," the old man seemed to take her word on it. "Rufus and I will let you get back to work!"

Shan reached down and petted the dog, whose tongue was wagging in an effort to cool himself down.

"Seems like a good boy."

"The best. I haven't had one with this much pep since Barnegat, the dog I had when I was a lad."

Shan felt a tug on the Tissue at her waist and realized that Fixer Drane had started to wander off in the direction of a clearing in the glade. She knew she should probably say good-bye, but Rufus was intent on licking her shoes.

"Was Barnegat a chocolate lab too?"

The rope pulled tighter, forcing Shan to walk backward, but the old man seemed completely unperturbed and started to walk along.

"Ah, yes. It's the only breed I've ever owned. They may be a bit excitable, but they have so much love to give."

Behind Shan, Fixer Drane was picking up the pace, but she didn't want to interrupt his meditations to ask him if he'd found anything . . .

"If I could go back in time and do one last thing, it would be to wrestle with ol' Barney like we used to in the yard." The old man's eyes grew watery at the memory. "We would tumble head over heels, and I can't remember ever laughing so hard before or since. The kind where you feel like you might split apart at the seams."

Briefer Shan nodded her head, and petted Rufus, whose coat shone in the sun. She couldn't help but wonder what Frozen Moment this old man could still have, when life had already passed him by.

"Shan! I got something!"

She turned around to see Becker standing on a circular piece of grass that looked like it had been charred by a campfire.

"The Split Second came through this spot!" It was hard to argue with his assessment, especially since circles that perfect do not occur in Nature. "If we wait right here, maybe we can fall right along its trail . . ."

"Who did you say you work for again?" asked the old man, and Becker was surprised to see they had visitors.

"It's a company called The Seems." Shan figured that truth was stranger than fiction. "We're making sure that everything goes according to Plan."

The old man was about to pry further when Rufus jammed his nose inside the pocket of his vest. He had smelled the pepperoni treat the owner had been saving for when they got back to the house, but the pup was in no mood to wait any longer.

"Rufus! We're in the middle of a discussion. Wait until we get—"

But Rufus had already knocked the old man down to the ground, and in a blur of fur and tweed, man and dog began to tumble through the field. At first, Becker and Shan worried they would hear the sound of old bones crunching, but the only noise that drifted back to them was the sound of laughter. Though the person who was doing the laughing was at least seventy years old, something about the way it bubbled up from the grass made it sound like that of a child on one of those endless summer days when the idea of ever getting older seems impossible. The laughing got louder and louder and more uncontrollable until it seemed like the old man was literally about to split apart at the—

Then the ground began to fall away.

Again and again, this was how it happened: Becker and Shan tumbling down the waterfall of Time and landing in other people's experiences—experiences so rare or magical or moving that they were instantly frozen in ice. But since Becker had found the charred pathway of the Split Second, their tumble through an autumn hike in the woods and a Ferris wheel ride at the fair and a quiet afternoon reading comic books in a treehouse while Grandma sends up a basket of homemade cookies on a rope was not without purpose, for according to their 7th Senses, they were getting closer and closer to their quarry . . .

Until they landed in the hospital.

Robert Wood Johnson Hospital, New Brunswick, New Jersey

"Oh no."

The moment their feet hit the marble floor, Becker realized exactly where they were, and—even worse—when.

"What's wrong, sir?"

"I think I know whose Moment this is." There was a tremor in the boy's voice, and Shan could tell it had nothing to do with the severity of the Mission at hand. "It's mine."

The two of them were standing in a sterile waiting room with blue chairs, fluorescent lights, and nondescript carpeting. A few children were busy playing with puzzle toys on the floor, and they briefly looked up at the two figures in bodysuits, but soon wrote them off as surgeons or specialists called in to the Bristol Myers Squibb Pediatric Oncology unit.

Shan was about to ask Fixer Drane, "What are the odds The Tide would have stolen one of *your* moments?" but suddenly, he didn't look quite like Fixer Drane anymore.

"Sir, this may sound strange, but it appears you have . . . shrunk."

Indeed, Becker did appear to be a lot smaller than he had been only seconds before—several inches, in fact.

"What are you talk—," but when he saw himself in the *Freckleface Strawberry* mirror that someone had donated to the ward, he knew exactly what she was talking about.

The Fixer's Sleeve no longer hugged his body, but hung like a business suit on a child who tried to dress up like dad. Becker quickly uncovered his head and was stunned to see the face of an eleven-year-old boy staring back at him, with the same bad bowl haircut that his mom used to force him to wear squarely on top of his head. That was when he knew he wasn't just visiting his own Frozen Moment . . .

He was reliving it.

"Where are you going?" asked Briefer Shan, surprised to see her Fixer detaching himself from the Connective Tissue.

"There's something I need to do," answered the younger version of Becker.

"But sir!" Shan pointed to the ground beneath them, where a perfectly charred piece of rug indicated the place where the Split Second had burned through this Moment. "We can't leave this spot, or else we could lose the tra—"

"Wait here. I promise I'll be right back."

Briefer Shan was jarred by the noticeably higher voice of the eleven-year-old, and briefly considered whether or not she should invoke the Rule You Should Almost Never Invoke,[15] both because Becker had gotten younger and because of his clearly distressed emotional state.

"But sir?"

"That's an order!"

Becker peeled off the rest of his Sleeve to reveal different clothes underneath than he'd worn when he put the protective suit on. He knew Shan was right, that this Moment could end at any second and drop them into the next, but in the two years since this day had happened, he had thought over and over and

---

15. Used only three times in the history of modern Fixing, this clause allows a Briefer to relieve his or her Fixer of command based on mental incapacity or when their methods become "unsound."

over again about how he could have done things differently. He wasn't about to let this chance slip away . . .

"How can I help you, young man?" asked the receptionist, pushing aside the sliding window.

"I'm here to see a patient . . . ," answered the eleven-year-old boy in his OshKosh B'Gosh jeans.

"Which patient is that?"

Becker felt a lump gathering in his throat, but he coughed it away.

"Her name is Amy Lannin."

Since the age of five, Amy had been Becker's best friend in The World. She always wore overalls and a barrette and was pretty much game for anything he could dream up—from exploring the no-man's-land near Red's Boatyard to eating the Dusty Road at the Corner Confectionary. She was also the only girl allowed on the Slab—a square piece of concrete that overlooked the river behind Connell Hutkin's house—mostly because she had struck the "Con-man" out three times in the Little League playoffs. But even though they were too young to be boyfriend and girlfriend, Becker and Amy were about as close as you could get . . .

And then she got sick.

"Becks!" Amy sat up in her bed, stoked to see her best friend walking through the door. "I thought you would never get here."

Two years ago, Becker hated to see the girl with brown eyes and dirty blond hair strapped to tubes and pale as a ghost, and he hated to see it even more now.

"You look like the Bride of Frankenstein." Considering how everyone was always walking on pins and needles around her, he knew Amy would appreciate a good old-fashioned ragging contest. "She's alive! *Alive!*"

"I'd rather be the Bride of Frankenstein than have a head that looks like a salad bowl." Amy pointed to the disaster on top of Becker's skull. "Waiter, can you please bring me some extra dressing on the side?"

Amy laughed, and so did Becker, but underneath his laughter was a gnawing dread, because this was exactly how it happened back then. He didn't want to deviate from the script, though . . . at least not yet.

"Do you want to play something?" he asked. There was a stack of games sitting on a chair in the corner of the room. "Life? Sorry? Uno?"

"Uno. Maybe you'll finally be able to win a game!"

As Becker dealt the cards, knowing his only hope of victory was to get a plethora of "Pick 4 Wilds," he had to fight back the tears . . . and the knowledge of how unfair it was that this was written in the Plan. He wanted to yell at someone or walk right up to the top floor of the Big Building and demand a revision. But it was good to be with Amy again. So good that his anger fell away, along with his Mission, and it was just like old times—the two of them barraging each other with insults, jokes, and "Skip a Turns." Becker had almost forgotten how much he missed her, but there was no way to avoid the inevitable.

"When do you go in?" he asked, referring to the exploratory procedure that would judge her readiness for a bone marrow transplant.

"Tomorrow morning." Her face darkened. "They say it's gonna be a routine operation, but I just . . . I don't know."

In all the years he had known her, Becker had never really

seen Amy scared of anything, not even Micky Krooms, who lorded over the north side of Highland Park, extorting lunch money and pushing over little kids just for the fun of it. Amy had forced Krooms to give back little Benjamin Drane's box of Hot Wheels strictly by the look in her eyes—but here, in her hospital bed, that look was nowhere to be found.

"Becks." Amy turned to the window, where the city of New Brunswick was going about its day. "Do you think I'll be okay?"

Now, as then, he wasn't sure if she meant just surviving this operation or with the leukemia itself. On the day this Moment was frozen, Becker had answered that question by promising, "You're gonna be fine, Amy. I just know you will," even though he didn't know any such thing. The fact that twenty-four hours later the best friend he'd ever had passed away from "unexpected complications" broke his heart in two, and he'd thought of himself as a coward and a bold-faced liar ever since.

"Honestly?" Amy nodded, and this time Becker wasn't going to make the same mistake. "I kind of have a bad feeling."

"Me too."

As Amy began to face the fact that eleven years were all she was going to get on this earth, Becker reached across the bed and tried to hug her fear away.

"If something goes wrong," she said, "will you make me a promise?"

"Anything."

Both of them were crying, but it somehow felt okay.

"Promise you'll never forget me."

When Fixer Drane hit the ground, it took him quite a while to wipe the tears from his eyes. Though it was a terribly painful experience to relive Amy's dying day, that guilty feeling in his chest that had been there for so long was gone. It was only when his tears literally froze upon his cheeks that he lifted himself off the ground and took in the surroundings.

He had landed on some kind of frigid tundra, with a mammoth glacier behind him and an endless field of white in front. Wind-driven snow pelted his unprotected face, and his body was immediately sent into shivers—for though he had returned to his original age (and clothes), his Sleeve and Toolkit were back where he left him with Shan Mei-Lin. Wherever she was now . . .

"Briefer Shan?" The only Tools he still had were those that were clipped to his belt, and he shouted above the wind into his Receiver. "Briefer Shan, report!"

Despite the Powers That Be's approval of multiple new Towers to provide better reception in The World and The Seems, nothing came back over the line. For all Becker knew, Receivers didn't function inside Frozen Moments, and a quick check of his Blinker said that though its data was still intact, the communication functions were gone.

"Nice work, Einstein."

He angrily hung up the Receiver and cursed himself for committing a Fixer's cardinal sin—putting your own needs above those of the Mission. His only hope was that Briefer Shan was still on the trail of the Split Second, and he could somehow reconnect with her when this Moment led to another one and another one after that. His hands and feet were both beginning to go numb, though, so he hoped this one would end sooner rather than later.

"Hello?" Becker shouted into the wild. "Anybody there?"

Surely someone was about to arrive on the scene, for obviously this arctic wasteland had provided them with a peak experience. Any minute now, a cross-country skier or a boat bearing scientists on an arctic expedition would emerge through the snowy haze to have one of the most powerful Moments of their lives, and send Becker happily on his way.

Any minute now . . .

Two hours later, Becker stumbled across the ice, having lost all feeling in his body. The only thing that drove his rapidly clouding mind forward was the possibility that the dark line on the horizon was a forest where he could find shelter, maybe even some wood to start a fire. Not that he had anything to start a fire with.

This was not the first time #37 had been faced with the possibility of his own doom, but never had he been without his Toolkit and stuck in a Frozen Moment that for some reason refused to end. And with each step, he could feel the first stage of hypothermia setting in. Stage two would soon follow—typified by muscle miscoordination and the contraction of surface blood vessels to keep the vital organs warm—concluding with the terminal burrowing and stupor of stage three.

Becker knew none of these medical details as he tripped and fell into a bank of fresh snow. If he could have felt his face, he would have known he was smiling, for he was close enough now to see that those were indeed pine trees he was running toward. Once he got to his feet, Becker could easily cover the remaining ground and finally get the Mission back on track. But first, he just wanted to rest for a while. The cold wasn't really that bad once you got used to it—it was actually kind of warm—and this bank of snow was as comfortable as his bed back at 12 Grant Avenue.

"Twelve Grant Avenue?" he whispered hoarsely. "I wonder who lives there?"

As Becker curled himself into the fetal position and listened to the soft tones of WDOZ, he couldn't help but notice something emerging from the tree line. It was covered from head to toe in white fur, like a polar bear or the Abominable Snowman. Becker really hoped it was neither of those things, but the closer it got, the more he started to think it was a person.

"Help!" he tried to yell, but it came out more like, *"Uhh-hhh."*

Whatever it was, it was heading straight toward him, moving quickly across the ground with snowshoes on its feet. Moments later, the figure was taking off its jacket and wrapping Becker inside of it.

"Picked a helluva place to take a nap," said a gruff voice from beneath a frost-covered beard. "Try to stay awake."

Becker felt himself being thrown over a pair of strong shoulders, which began to carry him back toward the woods.

"Got a name?"

"B . . . B . . ." Becker licked what he thought may have been his lips. "Becker."

"Nice to meet you, Becker." The stranger carried the boy as easily as a bag of laundry, and as he turned into the wind, his powerful strides gobbled up the space between the tundra and the tree line.

"Call me Tom."

Tom Jackal

When Becker awoke, he was wearing nothing but a T-shirt and his IFR boxers. Heavy blankets covered his body, and as the waking world slowly crept into his mind, it was filled with confusion. The memory of a game of Uno with Amy Lannin came first, followed by the ugly reality of the Time Bomb. For a second, he hoped he was back in Highland Park and this was all a dream about his next Mission in The Seems, but then he realized he was lying in someone else's bed.

On the ceiling above were the slats of a log cabin, and the rest of his clothes were washed and folded on the dresser across from the bed. Becker looked around for a clock that would tell him how long he'd been sleeping, but the only thing he spotted was a small nightstand, upon which rested a medical kit and a pot of tea.

"Hello?" he called out. "Is anybody here?"

No one answered. Becker vaguely remembered the vast tundra and the figure of the Abominable Snowman, but he couldn't decide if where he was now was a Dream or a Frozen Moment or a Dream inside a Frozen Moment. Part of him worried that maybe he'd actually frozen to death out there, and now he was in A Better Place—an unpleasant thought that finally motivated him to leave the warm cocoon beneath the blanket.

"Ow!"

The moment his feet touched the floor, pain shot through Becker's legs and he immediately collapsed to the ground. It was only then that he noticed his hands and feet were heavily bandaged—by what was clearly an expert hand. After a few tentative steps, he found walking somewhat tolerable, and limped over to the table. Even though the chamomile tea had gone cold, the taste of honey and lemon was soothing on his tongue.

"Hellooo . . ."

Becker opened the room's single door, and found himself on the second floor of a mountain lodge. A quick investigation revealed three more bedrooms next to his—one a master, one with bunk beds and toys, and one with a wooden crib. Their owners, however, were nowhere to be found.

He crept down the wooden staircase and into a spacious den, where a fire was crackling in the cut stone hearth. Iron tools dangled from hooks on the walls and the fading light outside the diamond-shaped windows told Becker it was late afternoon. The only visual hint as to who called this place home was an oil painting that hung over the hearth. It depicted a young woman of half-Inuit, half-Nordic descent, her long black hair flowing from beneath a wool hat. She was standing in the snow-covered woods, smiling directly at the observer, as if surprised to meet him in such an out-of-the-way place.

"She's beautiful, isn't she?"

Becker whipped around to see the same bearded man who had pulled him from the snow standing at the door. He was wearing a red thermal shirt, with an ax in one hand, and a bag of freshly chopped wood in the other.

"Doesn't hold a candle to the real thing." The man shut the door behind him and tossed the wood on the floor. "But that's exactly what she looked like on the day we met."

The man noticed Becker take a few steps back from him, probably due to what he was still holding in his right hand. With a throaty chuckle, he hung the ax upon the wall, next to an old two-handed saw.

"Who are you?" asked Becker, cautiously watching the man sit down and pull off his snow-covered boots. Though "Tom" seemed friendly enough, the Fixer couldn't resist scanning about for weapons or avenues of escape.

"How are those hands and feet?" The man tossed his wet boots over by the front door. "A couple more minutes out there and you would have been a Popsicle."

Whoever he was, Becker couldn't place his accent. It wasn't quite English—maybe Gaelic or Scottish—but despite its coarseness, there was also a warmth that began to put him at ease.

"They don't seem so bad," Becker said, holding up his mummified hands. "But I'm afraid to look underneath."

"I warn you, they're a little worse for the wear—but I have a good bit of experience with frostbite, and I think I got to them in time."

That was a relief. There was already a No-Hands Phil, and Fixer #37 had no desire to become No-Hands Becker.

"Can I offer you anything?" Tom padded into the rustic kitchen, where the only sign of modern convenience, a stainless-steel fridge, was packed with food and drink. "Water? Or something to eat?"

"Got any Mountain Dew?" asked Becker.

"No, but you can have one of these . . ." He reached in and pulled out two brown, unlabeled bottles. "I call it Tom's Homebrew."

Becker had been in the presence of alcohol many times before—his dad liked to drink a beer while watching Mets/Jets/Nets/Rutgers games and his mom enjoyed the occasional glass of Merlot—but he had never tasted anything stronger than a Shirley Temple.[16]

"I don't know. Maybe just that glass of wat—"

"Don't worry, kid. It'll put some hair on your chest."

Becker had a hunch that this was the "peer pressure" that all the teachers and TV advertisements were referring to, but when he popped the top of the bottle, the joke was on him.

"Is that root beer?"

"Birch."

In fact, it was the best birch beer Becker had ever tasted in his life—red and not too bubbly, with just the right hints of juniper and clove.

"Excellent."

"I'm glad you like it. My children say it's too minty, but I say

---

16. Well, there was the one time that Becker's uncle Jimmy gave him a taste of Schlitz at the family picnic in Donaldson Park. But don't tell his mom or dad.

if it doesn't have a little bite, then what's the point?" While they talked, the man sifted through a wooden chest that looked like it had been salvaged from a shipwreck or something. "What kind of name is Becker, anyway?"

"My real first name is actually Ferdinand—which is why I go by my middle name."

"I see what you mean."

As the man continued to dig around in the chest, something about him seemed vaguely familiar. It wasn't the beard, and it wasn't the shaggy brown hair either, which was still dripping with snow. It was more just his body language, and the way he carried himself . . .

"You know, it was sheer luck I found you out there." Tom pulled a well-worn passport and an old rugby ball out of the chest and laid them on the floor to get them out of the way. "It was only because I couldn't catch a single bloody fish that I happened to look up and see something glinting in the sun."

He motioned to the mantel, where a small black box otherwise known as a Blinker sat beside an orange telephone Receiver.

"It must have been those," said Tom, raising an eyebrow.

"Yeah that's my . . . my pager."

"You decided to bring a pager to Greenland but not a jacket or gloves?"

Uh. That was a good question and Becker didn't have a good answer. Thankfully, the owner of the house seemed too preoccupied with his search to press the matter further.

"Ah! There you are." Whatever he had found, it brought a nostalgic twinge to his voice. "Long time, no see."

When Becker saw what Tom had pulled from the chest, a

chill shot down his spine, and all at once he knew why this man seemed so familiar.

In Tom's calloused hands—dusty and crumpled from being at the bottom of the pile—was a sheepskin bomber's jacket and a leather aviator helmet. And though it looked like they hadn't been worn in years, they were just as unforgettable as when Becker had first seen them—on photographs in his instructor's office or in the simulation of a fateful Mission known as the Day That Time Stood Still.

"You're . . . you're Tom Jackal."

"One and the same."

"But . . . how?"

Tom fell into in a well-worn recliner and a wry grin moved across his face.

"The Plan works in mysterious ways."

When Shan Mei-Lin watched Fixer Drane cut the Connective Tissue and leave the waiting room behind, she knew instinctively it was a bad idea. Trying to bury her uneasiness, she examined the white streaks in her hair, which she had to admit looked pleasantly punk. But it wasn't long before the wobbly sensation came again, the floor cracked apart, and Shan was falling through the Moment-filled stew.

As she bounced from experience to experience, stopping only long enough to witness a buzzer-beating jump shot or the birth of a child, the one thought that repeated itself in her mind was, "How could I have lost another?" If there was one responsibility that Briefers had above all things, it was to stand by their Fixers through thick and thin—especially when a Fixer was under extreme duress. Though a little voice inside her head whispered, "It was *their* fault, not yours!" a much louder voice shouted, "You blew it!"

The only consolation Shan could muster was the fact that each time she entered another Moment, the path of the Split Second was clear. Be it the shag carpet in a family's basement or the shattered tiles at the bottom of an empty pool, the tell-tale burned and perfect circle was easily located and the way the short hairs on her neck were raising, she knew she was getting closer . . .

"If I can just Fix the Split Second on my own," Shan resolved, "then maybe I can save face and The World at the same time."

But her search was picking up. When she finally caught a foothold in a Chilean apple orchard, the Briefer barely had time to smell the Jonagolds when the Moment fell apart. Shan once again had the distinct sensation of tumbling down a mighty waterfall, and though she didn't have the protection of a barrel, at least she was cloaked in her trusty Sleeve. It was a good thing too, for without the protective fabric, she may have been torn asunder by the rough edges of other people's lives.

Further and further she fell, no longer even stopping in the Moments anymore. She lost all touch with any sensation but the feeling of falling itself, until finally—

Splash!

Two long minutes later, Shan clawed her way to the surface and gasped to fill her lungs with air. The din of rushing water pounded in her ears and the pool she swam in churned with foam, forcing the Briefer to deploy a pair of Water Wings™ to keep herself afloat. Flapping desperately, she raised herself a few inches above the water and flew to the shore.

It was only when Shan allowed her bruised body to plop onto the black sand that she could see why she'd nearly drowned: there was indeed a waterfall that cascaded down from somewhere above and collected in a pool of swirling experiences. But where exactly she had landed was a mystery . . .

Shan knew she was no longer *in* a Frozen Moment, for this place lacked the heightened sense of reality and gauzy, romanticized glow. It was colder, bleaker, and only darkness was visible beyond the mist that surrounded the falls. The Briefer pulled the hair from her goggles, rolled down the soaked facemask of her Sleeve, and pondered the sheltered cove that perhaps had never seen a human visitor.

Except for the one whose footsteps were leading off through the sand.

Seemsian history is full of many myths and legends, but the tale of Tom Jackal holds a unique place. The Welsh-born Fixer came to prominence when he caught the Time Bandits on the "Night They Robbed the Memory Bank," and was one of three Roster members chosen to participate in "Hope Springs Eternal"—the classified Mission where he, Lisa Simms, and Jelani Blaque were sent to the Middle of Nowhere to bring back Hope for The World. But nearly eleven years ago to the day, his career had come to an unceremonious end.

"Ever face a Glitch, Drane?"

Fixers Drane and Jackal sat before the dwindling fire,

while outside the snow that had once been flurries was getting heavier.

"In the Department of Sleep, actually," Becker confessed. "On my very first Mission as a Fixer."

"Tough way to get your feet wet."

"Tell me about it."

Jackal lit himself a corn-cob pipe and deeply inhaled.

"On my last Mission, I faced the mother of all Glitches . . . and it didn't go so well." Jackal exhaled a thick plume of smoke, then leaned back in his chair. "They're probably using it at the IFR as the perfect example of what *not* to do on a Mission."

Becker flushed red, which only betrayed the truth.

"You're not serious?" Jackal seemed far more amused than annoyed. "Who came up with *that* lesson?"

"Fixer Blaque."

"Jelani Blaque?" Jackal burst into good-hearted laughter. His friendship with the IFR's head instructor was also the stuff of legend. "I can't believe the old lion sold me out."

Becker laughed too, glad to see that Jackal wasn't taking it personally.

"He claims that the reason things went wrong that day was that you didn't have a Mission Inside your Mission . . ."

"Jelani knows me well." An unmistakable shadow passed over Jackal's face. "He always did."

"It turned out okay, though." Becker tried to cheer Jackal up. "A backup Fixer figured a way to get things on schedule, and nobody in The World even realized what had happened."

"Good. That's good. I've often wondered what . . ." But Jackal's voice trailed off, and for the first time since Becker met him, his eyes grew sad and tired. "Toss a few more logs on there, will ya?"

"No problem."

Becker gingerly pushed aside the screen and used the brass tongs to rebuild the pile. The two Fixers were quiet for a time, listening to the crackle of burning wood, the tinkling of snowflakes against the windows. But #37 couldn't remain silent for long.

"What happened to you, Tom? I mean, the Powers That Be authorized a search party to go into the melted Moments and bring you back, but they never found a thing." Jackal's only response was to stare even deeper into the flames, so Becker kept pushing. "Eventually, the decision was made to refreeze them and put them back in Daylight Savings. They declared you Lost in Time."

"Not PIA[17]?"

Becker shook his head. "In fact, you're still #7 on the Duty Roster."

If this honor brought Jackal any belated sense of pride, his face didn't show it.

"When I first fell into the pool, I thought I was drowning," Jackal said, finally coming out of his daze. "But then suddenly I found myself on solid ground. This scientist in a laboratory was about to make the discovery of a lifetime, but before I could see what it was, the Moment fell apart. And me with it . . ."

"That's exactly how it happened with us." A sick feeling wormed its way into Becker's gut, as for the first time since he ended up at Jackal's cabin he remembered Shan Mei-Lin.

_____
17. Perished in Action.

"Every time a Frozen Moment was about to peak, the reality of the situation collapsed and we got kicked into another."

Becker wanted to ask Jackal why he thought *this* Moment had not similarly collapsed, but something told him this was not the proper time.

"I don't know how long I was falling. Months—maybe even years—felt as if I might be going mad. But then . . ." Jackal's eyes slowly rose to the picture above the fireplace. "I ended up here."

Becker's eyes followed Jackal's up to the painting.

"Who is she?"

"My wife."

Almost on cue, Becker heard the sound of voices outside the house and footsteps crunching in the snow. Seconds later, the door was thrust open and into the den piled a blur of fur, giggles, and toboggans. Two children—a boy of nine and a girl about seven—were trying to tell their father about how he'd never believe the run they had on "Dead Man's Fjord" but stopped short when they saw company in the den.

"Sander, Katia, I'd like you to meet a friend of mine." Jackal pulled his two suddenly shy children over by his chair. "This is Becker Drane."

"Pleased to meet you." Becker was only a few years older than them, but it felt like a lot more.

"Go on, it's okay." At the urging of their father, the kids dutifully shook Becker's bandaged hand. Sander looked just like his dad, right down to the square jaw and crystal blue eyes, but Katia was no doubt her mother's daughter, with the same dark hair and beauty. "Where's your mother and the Mistake?"

"They're wondering why someone forgot to put out the recyclables," said a woman's voice by the door.

Outside of the fact that there was a rosy-cheeked toddler in her arms, it looked as if Tom Jackal's wife had literally stepped from the painting above the fire. She was still wearing the same wool sweater and hat, and her hair was untouched by gray.

"More importantly," she placed the child in a highchair by the dining room table, "they're wondering what we're having for dinner?"

If there was any difference between a Frozen Moment and the real World, Becker could not figure out what it was. The food Jackal laid on the table—a mix of venison, lamb, and three types of fish—was as good as (if not better than) any Becker had ever tasted, the homebrew just as cold (if not colder), and the company just as lively (if not livelier). As the laughter and good cheer filled the room, Becker couldn't help but think that for someone Lost in Time, Tom Jackal had done pretty well for himself.

The entire family had been there the previous day when Tom returned from his fishing trip bearing a nearly frozen boy, and wanted to know all the juicy details. Since Becker wasn't sure what his fellow Fixer had told them about The Seems, if anything, he quickly crafted an off-white lie about how he'd been hiking with his tour group from the United States and wandered off the path to explore what he thought were some ancient Viking ruins. The kids were intrigued by this, of course, telling Becker all about the old shack in the woods where Eric the Red was supposed to have summered, which only forced the Fixer deeper into his own tall tale.

"Ever since I was a kid, I've been waiting for them to change Columbus Day to Bjarni Herjolfsson Day." Becker polished off his last piece of strawberry rhubarb pie. "Because he was the one who really discovered America."

Jackal and Rhianna looked at each other and laughed, then checked their watches, almost at the exact same time.

"All right, you two," the man of the house announced. "Time to hit the hay."

Amid a chorus of "Aw, Dad, do we have to?" Jackal led the troop upstairs, but not before they pleaded with Becker, "Promise you'll stay long enough for us to take you to Eric's house?"

"I'll do my best," answered Becker, even though he knew the chances were slim. Half a day had gone by since he'd fallen into this Moment, and Becker knew it was time to get back to the Mission. But as Rhianna started to clear the table, he again chose to bide his time.

"Here, let me help you with that." Becker gingerly picked up a few of the larger dishes and carried them to the sink. It was tricky with the bandages, but he managed to stack them in the crook of his arm. "Those are some awesome kids you have."

"They are." She smiled proudly. "And you're not so bad yourself."

As the warm water from the sink washed across the serving platters, Becker was reminded of the first time he Briefed for Lisa Simms, when he'd stammered and blushed his way through an entire Mission. It took a minute for him to get over how pretty Rhianna was too—yet she was so easygoing that Becker soon felt completely relaxed.

"So when is your tour group coming to pick you up?" she asked. "Your parents must be worried sick."

"Excuse me?" Becker forgot for a moment what she was referring to, but scrambled back to his feet. "Oh yeah, yeah—um, I spoke with my history teacher, Mr. Gomez, a few hours ago and we're gonna try to find a place to rendezvous in the morning."

"I see."

There was an awkward silence and Becker worried that the cat was out of the bag.

"You know, Becker, when you've been married for ten years, you become very adept at sensing when something's not right with the person you're married to. When they're upset about something . . . when they're hurt . . ." Rhianna handed Becker another clean plate. "And especially when they're afraid."

"I can imagine." Becker dried the plate and placed it in the dish rack without looking up.

"And for the first time in many, many years, *afraid* is how my husband seems." The sink was now empty, so Rhianna shut off the faucet and turned to Becker. "What do you think he's afraid of?"

Becker could feel her eyes burning into his neck, and knew he had no choice but to finally look into them.

"I don't know, ma'am," said the Fixer, though he had a pretty good idea. "Maybe because I need his help."

"With what?"

Becker wasn't sure how to answer that question. He knew

from the occasional arguments between his mom and dad how dangerous it was to get between a husband and wife, and besides, the details of his Mission were highly classified.

"Something very important."

"I suppose The World needs Fixing again, eh?" Now Becker *really* didn't know what to say, but thankfully she said it for him. "Of course I know what Tom used to do . . . there are no secrets between us."

"I'm sorry. I wasn't sure if—"

She smiled, but her voice was quivering. "Are you here to take my husband away from his family?"

Ooof. Becker couldn't deny that from the moment he met Jackal, he'd been hoping the legend would come to his aid and help him Fix the damage wrought by the Time Bomb. But the last thing he wanted to do was break this woman's heart.

"I . . ."

"What are you two talking about?"

Becker and Rhianna turned to see the man of whom they were speaking, standing at the bottom of the stairs, a storybook still in hand.

"Nothing," lied Rhianna, turning off the faucet. "We were just finishing up the dishes."

"Excellent." Jackal could sense the tension between his wife and the boy but decided to ignore it. "I was going to see if our guest felt like walking off a little of this meal?"

"I'd love to," responded Becker.

"Just make sure you dress warm." Rhianna hung the dish-towel on the fridge, then she smiled and kissed Becker on the cheek. "And don't stay up too late."

She gently touched her husband on the shoulder, then made her way upstairs. Tom watched her go, then quietly turned to Becker.

"Shall we hit the road?"

The night sky above Greenland was crystal clear, and Becker felt as if he had never seen so many stars in his life. The wind and snow had tapered off sometime during dessert, and as the two Fixers tramped through the fresh powder, the woods took on the look of a gingerbread world.

". . . and so my plan is basically to put the Split Second back together before it turns The World to dust." Becker was now wearing a borrowed peacoat, gloves, and boots (he was roughly the same size as Sander), and though his hands were warm, they still throbbed with pain. "I just need to get back on the trail and isolate which Moment it's bouncing around in."

"It's a decent strategy," Jackal assured his young peer. "Unfortunately, it'll never work."

"What do you mean?"

Tom shrugged, as if the answer was obvious.

"You'll never catch up to the Second if you chase it. You have to make it come to you."

"Oh." Despite his full year of active duty, Becker had the distinct impression that he was now out of his league.

"Your best bet is to put together a Containment Field—say, ten-feet square—and make sure the floor is made out of grass, not dirt, so the Essence of Time doesn't seep through. Then take a handful of Firsts and Thirds and scatter them inside. The Split Second will be drawn to it like a magnet."

"That's it?"

"Catching it is the easy part." Jackal chuckled, then bent over to pick up a stick. "The problem is how to put the two halves of the Second back together without getting fried in the process. I'm not sure it's even possible."

Becker could tell that #7 had caught the old Fixing bug so he figured now was the perfect time to ask. "Help me Fix this thing, Tom."

"Me?" Jackal laughed, but in the same mirthless manner that his wife had smiled in the kitchen. "I'm a cautionary tale, remember?"

"You're the best that ever lived!"

"What about Li Po? Or the Septuagenarian?"

"She's the Octogenarian now."

"Good for her!" This time Jackal's laughter felt a little more real. "Surely she or one of the others could help out more than a washed-up old Welshman."

"Maybe so." #37 stopped in his tracks. "I just never thought I'd hear a Fixer try to pass the buck to someone else. Especially Tom Jackal."

It was a low blow, and Becker knew it. But Jackal simply threw the stick into the night and continued walking.

"When Jelani was teaching you about the Day That Time Stood Still, did he ever mention *why* I had no Mission Inside the Mission?"

Becker thought back upon the lesson, and shook his head no.

"Not surprising. He may have been my best friend, but there are some things every man keeps to himself . . ."

The woods grew dark and deep and the thin deer trail they had been following vanished beneath the drifting snows. But Jackal seemed to know exactly where they were going.

"Fixing . . . is the best job in The World, but it can also be the loneliest. The pressure, the stakes, the 25/7 hours. Sometimes there's not room for anyone else in that world, and even if there was, would you want to bring them in?"

Becker could more than relate, having seen many of his friendships in Highland Park grow distant, and the one person he wanted to bring into his world—Jennifer Kaley—had been banned from it.

"By the time I fell into that pool of melting Moments . . . ," Jackal confided, "there was nothing left in my heart to wrap a Mission Inside a Mission around."

A gust of wind rippled through the pine needles, and a few icicles fell to the ground.

"But then I tumbled into this place . . ." He motioned to the rolling countryside of Myggebungen, the province where the Jackal family had staked their claim. "And for once, the Agents of L.U.C.K.[18] were on my side."

Even in the darkening forest, Becker could see Tom's face lighting up at the Memory.

"When Rhianna walked out of the forest, she was the most beautiful thing I'd ever seen. And before we even said a word to each other, I knew. I just knew . . ."

18. The agency responsible for dispensing Little Unplanned Changes of Kismet to The World.

The pathway Jackal was carving through the powder suddenly sloped, forcing them to hold onto branches and trees as they descended into a frost-covered glade.

"I guess I must have interrupted the Frozen Moment she was about to have . . . because unlike all the others I'd been to, this one never fell apart." Jackal jumped the last few feet of the slope, as if to prove to himself the ground was solid. "And after those first few years—when I waited for it to crumble and send me falling away from everything I loved—I finally accepted that this was my life. And that it was okay for me to be . . . happy."

"But Tom," said Becker, not wanting to be the one to say it. "None of this is real."

"Isn't it?" Jackal picked up some snow and let it filter through his fingers. "This snow is cold . . . the laughter of Sander and Katia rings in my ears . . . and when the sun rises and I see my wife beside me, it feels more real than anything I've ever known."

Becker couldn't argue with what Jackal was saying, especially with the feast still stuffing his belly, and how close he'd come to freezing to death.

"Nothing . . . ," whispered Jackal, and Becker at last heard the fear that Rhianna had sensed in her husband, ". . . not even the very destruction of the World—will make me leave that all behind."

The older man stopped before a tall, snow-covered mound and Becker could tell they'd finally reached his chosen destination.

"Where are we?"

Tom reached forward and when he brushed away the first layer of snow, Becker could not believe what he saw.

"A Door?"

Indeed, Jackal had uncovered one of the Doors that since the beginning of Time (and until the ratification of the Skeleton Key) had served as the gateways between The World and The Seems. And just like the one at an abandoned lighting factory in Highland Park, New Jersey, the Door was stamped with the logo of The Seems.

"Amazing, isn't it? Every Frozen Moment is like a snapshot of the entire World." Jackal pointed to the east. "If we hiked two hundred miles that way, we would come to the city of Nuuk. And if we boarded a plane and flew to the town where you lived, there would probably be another you there. In ten years of exploring this place, I've yet to find the limit . . ."

Becker's mind bent as far as it could to grasp how this was possible.

"This Door is right where the Manual said it would be, and I'd wager it somehow leads directly back to The Seems."

Fixer #7 looked down at #37, and made it clear that it was time for him to depart. But Becker wasn't quite ready to go.

"Can't you help me fix Time, then come back when the Mission is over?"

"I don't know what you know about Frozen Moments, but they can only be entered once." Jackal dropped his head, somewhere between resignation and shame. "The moment I walk through that door, I'll never be able to return."

"Then what am I gonna do?"

There was a long beat of silence and Becker saw on Jackal's face that part of him *did* indeed long for the pressure, the stakes, the 25/7. Somewhere in the distance, an owl's cry echoed through the trees.

"The only person I can think of who can help you Fix Time . . . ," Jackal's voice betrayed that even he wasn't sure his idea was a good one, ". . . is the person who invented it."

Becker shook his head, disappointed that this was the best the living legend could do. "But no one knows where she is."

"Somebody must know. A Case Worker . . . one of the Powers That Be. Everybody leaves a trail." Jackal smiled at the irony of his statement. "I did."

As Fixer Drane nodded and prepared to depart, Jackal reached into his coat pocket and pulled out a dusty Fixer's Badge. It depicted him wearing the jacket and the helmet he'd pulled from the chest of mementos, and when Tom slid it across the black swipe pad, there was a loud *click* on the other side . . .

"Say good-bye to Rhianna for me." Though Becker's heart was heavy, he couldn't deny that it had been an honor and a privilege to spend even one night with the Jackals. "And tell the kids I'm sorry I couldn't see Eric's shack."

"They'll be heartbroken, but I'll be sure to pass on the message."

Jackal handed Becker his old pair of Transport Goggles, for he would never need them again.

"Do you want me to send a message to anyone?" Becker slapped the Goggles over his eyes. "Fixer Blaque? Or Lisa Simms?"

"Tell them . . ." Jackal thought long and hard. "Tell them you never found me."

As Becker reached for the knob and pulled the Door open, he wanted to say, "Thank you for saving my life, Tom," and Jackal wanted to say, "I wish you luck, kid," but neither of them could get their mouths to speak the words.

The rest was lost in the roar.

Meanwhile

Alton Forest, Caledon, Ontario

"Do you guys think there's a plan for everything that happens?"

Jennifer Kaley stared up at the clouds from the newly finished addition to the headquarters of Les Resistance. "Or is it all just, like, random?"

"JK, must we figure out the meaning of life right now?" On the other side of the circular perch, Vikram Pemundi dozed in and out of consciousness, enjoying the elevated view of Alton Forest. "Can't we just chillax?"

"I'm serious."

"There'd better be a plan," answered Rachel Mandel, taking a long swig of lemonade from a bottle. "If there isn't, I'm gonna be seriously mad I never ate bacon."

Though Jennifer and Vikram were the original founders of the "the resistance" (against whom or what they were resisting was never fully articulated), their number had quickly grown to five. Rachel—an Orthodox Jewish girl who always wore sleeves past her elbows and skirts past her knees—was the third member, followed quickly by the Moreau twins, Rob and Claudia. All of them were basking in the glow of a construction job well done.

"Totally random," interjected Rob Moreau with disdain. "Anybody who believes there's rhyme or reason to the universe is living in a fantasy world."

"I agree with Moreau." Claudia took a bite of a big juicy peach. "Nothing would make me happier than to believe that things happen for a reason, but who's kidding who?"

The Moreaus had been dubbed "the Peppers" by some of the bullies because of their French-Canadian roots, but in fact they were just a little too ahead of their time to fit in. They both had Bluetooth before anybody knew what that meant, they both listened to Kruder & Dorfmeister, and they both wore argyle, in anticipation of its long-overdue comeback. Yet despite all that, they loved to do nothing more than watch bad TV and eat Cheez Doodles from the bag (like Rob was doing right now).

"All you have to do is watch the news any night to see that the world's totally messed up." Claudia chucked the half-chewed peach pit into the waiting woods.

"Life is what you make of it." Vikram smiled, his eyes still half-closed. "If you choose to see randomness, you will see randomness. If you choose to see plan, you see plan."

"Oh my G-d!" Rachel cried out, scaring everyone half to death. "There's no 'K' or 'OU' on this bottle!" She held up the lemonade to let her friends know that the juice she was drinking wasn't kosher, but they just laughed it off, because Rachel always was breaking the rules, worrying about it, then finding a brilliant rationalization for why it was okay. "Then again, I am stuck out in the woods and this is my only means of survival."

"You know what I was thinking?" Jennifer abruptly pulled her head out of the clouds. "What if there was like this other world that was responsible for making our world but instead of being lame, it was cool, and there were all these people working to make sure everything goes right for us?"

"Please," answered Moreau (Rob). "Have you been drinking the non-kosher juice too?"

"No," said Jennifer. "But I did have this really weird dream once . . ."

"It's all a dream, JK," promised Vik. "Our challenge is to wake up."

Jennifer was about to tell Vik and the others more about what happened in that dream, when—

"Ow!"

"What's wrong?" asked Rachel, seeing Jennifer slap her hand to the back of her neck.

"I don't know—my neck's been bothering me all day."

"Is it muscular or skeletal?" asked Vik, whose father was a doctor.

"First it was just chills, but now it's starting to hurt," Jennifer explained. "And this is gonna sound crazy. But I have this terrible feeling that something is about to go . . . I don't know . . . wrong?"

The members of Les Resistance cracked up at first, but seeing she was deadly serious, immediately scrambled into action. Vik checked the support beams of the fortress, the Moreaus the foundation, and Rachel scanned the woods for any sight of

139

the slavering grizzly she always worried was watching and waiting for just the right moment to eat them for lunch. But when everything was hunky dory, they breathed a sigh of relief.

"That was so not cool." Rachel exhaled, waiting for her heart to slow down. "You totally freaked me out."

"I'm sorry, I just . . ." Jennifer was struggling to explain the pit in her stomach that was telling her something really bad was about to go down. But then that same pit told her to go over to the telescope they'd installed and point it 35 degrees south by 42 degrees west and take a look at the—

Crack!

"Oh no," she whispered, eye pressed to the lens.

Crack! Crack! Crack!

Through the telescope, Jennifer saw the base of a huge tree begin to wobble and shake.

"What are you doing, JK?" asked Rob. "You're acting really loopy."

"We gotta get outta here . . ." Jennifer backed away, her own heart starting to pound. "Now!"

But before she could gather the troops, the cracking echoed through the forest again, so loud that this time her friends could tell where it was coming from too.

"That tree." Rachel pointed in the direction of the shadow that was looming larger and larger over their heads. "It's heading right for us!"

Indeed, the massive oak that stood sentry over Alton since time immemorial had inexplicably collapsed, and was now making its final, lurching journey down to the forest floor. Worse yet, it would undoubtedly smash the clubhouse of Les

Resistance to smithereens. Not to mention Les Resistance themselves.

"Hit the fire pole!"

Moreau (Claudia) was the first one down the emergency escape hatch, which—thankfully—her brother had insisted upon for just such a crisis, closely followed by Vik, Jennifer, Rachel, and Moreau (Rob). As the sound of falling timber built to a roar, they collectively ducked beneath the tilted pine and into a small underground storage space they had dug to hide a stack of magazines and canned goods.

"Hold on," cried Vik, and that's exactly what they all did, hugging each other tightly and hoping for the best. But instead of the devastating crash they expected, or the explosion of branches and leaves, all they heard at the moment of impact was a *"whoooosh"*—as if a giant bag of sand had suddenly been emptied out above.

Then silence.

"Everybody okay?" asked Jennifer, and the others nodded back, frightened but ecstatic to still be in one piece. "C'mon— let's go check it out."

As they tentatively lifted the bamboo trap door, the five friends expected to see a pile of trees laid across the woods like giant pick-up sticks and their beloved clubhouse in shambles. But when they staggered into the light, all they found was a plume of ashes, billowing through the air like thick, gray smoke . . .

The massive oak had literally turned to dust.

"Guys?" asked Jennifer Kaley, hand still holding her stomach, though the pit inside was gone. "What the heck just happened?"

"What the heck just happened?" Tony the Plumber pulled his head from the mass of thermal coils and fuses that were responsible for climate control. "My 7th Sense is ringing off the hook!"

As the Fixer grabbed his Blinker and toggled over to "Missions in Progress," Permin Neverlåethe, Administrator of Time, anxiously looked on. This terrible day was quickly getting worse, and he couldn't help feeling that it was entirely his fault.

"We got Essence of Time strikes in five Sectors . . ." Tony's face darkened as the data scrolled across his screen. "Last one looks like Canada."

"It must be runoff from the Split Second . . . ," whispered Permin, dropping his face into his hands. "Was it a heavily populated area?"

"Negative. Looks like it hit some forest or wildlife refuge or something."

"Thank the Plan."

"Don't thank the Plan," the Fixer retorted with his trademark swagger. "Thank the Agents of L.U.C.K."

Though Fixer #26 had not been called in for over six weeks, he'd still had the presence of mind to request that Agents of L.U.C.K. shower the Fabric of Reality with their precious salve. Thanks to these efforts, the remaining four strikes had fortuitously avoided population centers and instead hit the middle of the Indian and Pacific oceans, the Caspian Sea, and the Ellsworth Mountain region of Antarctica.

"Okay, Mr. Thermostat." Tony the Plumber returned his

attention to the frigid conditions in Time Management. "I need you to start cookin', or we're gonna have a little problem."

If the thermal coils heard him, they had nothing to say in response.

"Lemme put it another way. Neither of us wants me to go get my lug wrench and start diggin' around in your tummy, so why don't we compromise on a cool forty-eight?"

Apparently those terms were acceptable, for the coils took on an orange glow, and the temperature in the room began to rise.

"That's incredible," Permin marveled.

"All in a day's work." Tony tossed his work gloves into his Toolkit and made his way over to the Frozen Moment pool, where happily the thin layer of ice that had formed on the surface was already crinkling. As long as that pool stayed melted, the Jersey boy still had a fightin' chance. "I gotta tell ya though, Permie, somethin' don't smell right here."

The Administrator sniffed the air, before realizing that the Plumber was speaking metaphorically. "What is that supposed to mean?"

"Time was on a twenty-five-hour lockdown and still these guys managed to plant a Bomb smack dab between the gears?" Tony looked the Administrator straight in the eye. "I think we got an inside job."

"How dare you accuse my people on a day as tragic as this?" Permin shot back, insulted. "Keeping the World on schedule is their reason to be!"

"All I'm sayin' is, maybe one of them is surfin' the wrong wave, if you catch my drift?"

Permin stormed out of Time Management—but not before

muttering under his breath, "I'll go check the time cards . . . see who was on duty when the Bomb was planted."

"You do that." Tony pulled his pants up to their normal position, then called out to someone in the adjoining room. "Yo, Brief, I need to talk with you for a sec."

Every Fixer has a favorite Briefer, someone trustworthy to be the right-hand man (or woman) beyond all others, and Fixer #26 was no exception. Tony's preference was a med student from the Baldwin Hills section of south-central Los Angeles, who grew up on the same side of the tracks that he did and shared a similar love for greasy food, professional sports, and high-end automobiles.

"What up, T the P?" Briefer Harold "C-Note" Carmichael poked his head into Time Management. "I'm almost done oiling the gears."

"Drop that, C, and bust out your Transport Goggles."

"Why? Where in The World am I goin'?"

"You ain't goin' to The World." Tony knew that if the Essence of Time had leaked into The World once, it would likely happen again, and the only way to stop it was to cut it off at the pass. "You're goin' In-Between."

I-95 North, Pawtucket, Rhode Island

"You guys are being so good back there . . . ," announced Professor F. B. Drane, switching his Garrison Keillor CD over to disc two. "This could mean double scoops for everyone when we get to Sundae School."

Benjamin wanted to shout "yay," but he was still scooched against the window in the backseat, peeking intermittently at his "brother" to the right. For the last four hours, they had sat together in dead silence, Benjamin resisting the urge to dive into the front and tell his parents that there was an inflatable replica of Becker in the back. But the clear and present danger of the promised wedgie made him hold his tongue.

"Ice cream is all well and good, Dad," the Me-2 said with the same hint of sarcasm that the real Becker Drane would have used. "But if I have to listen to one more Lake Wobegon story, I'm gonna tear my own ears off."

Benjamin cracked up despite himself, then slapped his hand over his mouth, because he knew how much his father loved those old homespun tales.

"Laugh it up, half pint. If I had a nickel for every Rafi or Wiggles song I had to listen to to keep you two pacified, we'd be flying to the Cape on a private jet."

As if to rub it in, Professor Drane pumped up "A Day in the Life of Clarence Bunsen" in the rear speakers—just loud enough to torture his kids and still avoid waking his sleeping wife in the front.

"Yo, B?" the Me-2 whispered, seizing this golden opportunity to speak to Benjamin undercover. "I gotta talk to you."

Still a little freaked out, Benjamin inched a little closer.

"Listen, I know we got off to a rocky start." The Me-2 glanced up front, where the professor was again immersed in his tape. "But you shouldn't be scared of me. We've hung out lots of times."

"We have?"

"Remember when we went fishing with Grandpa and caught the rainbow trout? Or that time we won the three-legged race at Ag Field Day?"

"That was you?"

The Me-2 nodded, fondly remembering the victory and the shiny blue ribbon.

"We totally housed those guys."

Benjamin was starting to get the picture, but instead of feeling better about things, he was actually feeling worse. A lot worse.

"What about the time you and the Croziers told me I was a loser and wouldn't let me come sledding with you down at the park?"

"That was all Becker!" The Me-2 wasn't about to cop to something it didn't do—but passing the buck didn't seem to be cheering Benjamin up. "What's wrong, pal?"

"It's just . . . I don't even know who my real brother is anymore!"

The duplicate took another peek up front, then kicked Benjamin on the foot.

"Becker's your real brother, and I know for a fact he loves you very, very much."

"How do you know that?"

"Because we talk about it all the time. When he was away at Training, he always called to see how you were doing. And whenever he comes back from a Mission, you're the first person he wants to see." The Me-2 gave him another brotherly little shove. "Just because me and you hang sometimes doesn't mean that any of that has changed."

Benjamin might have nodded—but he wanted to make the Me-2 feel a little guiltier, so he kept his eyes on the floor mat.

"Is, um . . . my brother okay?"

The Me-2 turned toward the passing landscape, not wanting to betray the look in its mechanical eyes. The truth was that the Memory Bank account it shared with Becker had gone silent over two hours ago, right after he'd jumped into the Frozen Moment pool. At first, the Me-2 had written it off as a typical delay at the deposits window . . . but now it wasn't so sure.

"He's fine, B." The Me-2 turned back to the boy, thankful that it had been quite well programmed to cover for its Fixer. "The Mission's going great."

Meanwhile, The Seems

Far, far away from Interstate 95 or even the devastated village of Time Square, Briefer Shan Mei-Lin stumbled through the darkness and cursed the Case Worker who had steered her to this Plan-forsaken place.

"Helpful Hints, my butt!" Shan took a moment to reignite her Flash in the Pan, which was the only thing that allowed her to see her own hands, let alone where she was going. Unfortunately, she was running out of Flashes. "How 'bout throwing me a Bone or a Big Idea once in a while? And I could really use a Shove in the Right Direction about now!"

The only response to Shan's pleas for assistance from the Big Building was a deep, deafening silence. It was as if her words had been choked before they'd ever left her lips, and soon it was the Briefer herself who began to feel smothered by the blackness around her.

"*Hun dan!*" she swore. "*Hun dan!*"

When Shan found the footsteps leading off from the water-fall of Frozen Moments, she was convinced that Fixer Drane had somehow preceded her to this location, and she sprinted through the mud to ensure that she would be at his side when the Split Second was captured. But then she realized that the prints were made by someone wearing boots—not Fixer #37's Speed Demons™—and her pace slowed to a cautious jog. When they abruptly ended midstride, she was forced to stop altogether.

"Briefer Shan to Fixer Drane, come in, sir!" she called into her Receiver, but just as with her previous attempts, static was the only response. Even more disconcerting was the fact that there didn't seem to be any natural source of light in this place besides the churning waterfall, which had faded to a distant glow behind her.

The prudent thing would have been to return to the falls and wait for help to arrive, or at least try to find a way to climb back to the top. But Shan Mei-Lin had been moving forward for as long as she could remember . . . ever since she was a child, when she had scored so high on her placement tests she'd been taken from her hometown of Dunhuang and sent to live with the other "gifted students" in Beijing. Moving forward (not to mention upward) had led her to become the top-ranked student at every school she'd ever attended, and after she'd been recruited by Human Resources, she had done the same at the IFR. Moving forward was all she knew how to do.

So she raised her last Flash in the Pan, and headed into the black.

———

Hours later (or was it days?) Shan continued through the darkness, but gradually that word had come to lose its meaning. The Flash had flickered and gone out and when the Teflon-coated Pan slipped from the Briefer's fingers, she didn't bother to pick it up. Her Night Shades™ didn't help her see anything (because there was nothing to see) and even her coveted 7th Sense—the beacon that every Fixer and Briefer follows—was faltering as well. Not one hair stood, not one goose bump raised, not one twinge in her stomach told Shan the news that she was on the right track.

In *The Compendium of Malfunction & Repair* (aka the Manual), there is an appendix known as "Places You Don't Want To Go," and Shan had studied it all too well. In these pages, there is talk of the Jaws of Defeat, the Point of No Return, and of course, the village of Who Knows Where. But tucked amid the maps and warning signs is the small account of a place where Time does not exist. A prison, with no obvious entrance and no known way out, whose walls shape around the mind of the unfortunate soul who somehow finds their way inside. Briefer Shan felt a cold weakness descending over her body, and for the first time she was forced to face the real possibility that she had stumbled into Meanwhile.

"Central Command, come in!" Shan called out desperately. "Briefer down. Repeat, Briefer down! Requesting immediate backup, please respond, over!" Even the static that Shan had once hated would have been music to her ears, as opposed to the mind-numbing silence.

"Never be afraid to be afraid," Shan chanted to herself. "Never be afraid to be—" But she *was* afraid to be afraid, and never in her life had she been as afraid as she was right now. Not even the time she had wandered into the Magao caves as a child and couldn't remember which corridor would lead her back to the light. She'd begun to cry and run through other passageways, but they just led her deeper into the maze. Rescue only came through the ingenuity of her older brother, whose rhythmic knocks on the cave wall drew her from both panic and the damp corner in which she crouched. But today, Bohai would not be coming to rescue her. Nobody would.

"Help!" she screamed as loud as she could, because *someone* had put those footsteps in the sand. But for all Shan knew, they'd been put there years ago and that someone was just as lost in the infinite darkness as she. "Help!"

It was at this moment that she at last grasped the importance of the ancient axiom that she'd always mocked as a pointless exercise in self-trickery. For if she only had a Mission Inside the Mission right now, she would have something small to wrap her heart around—something to help her transcend the fear. But in the place of that small gem, all that was left was the fear itself.

Her heart began to pound, and her mouth felt like it was filling up with sand. Shan curled up in a ball and closed her eyes and did her best to block out the memory of the final entry in the Manual regarding this bleak and terrible place. But the words kept writing themselves across the back of her eyelids . . .

"Those who enter Meanwhile are never seen again."

The Keeper of the Records

Hall of Records, Department of History, The Seems

"Someone's coming! Someone's coming!"

Daniel J. Sullivan—or "Sully," as he was known to the few friends who still checked in on him from time to time—removed his stereophonic headphones and put down his paper and pen.

"I'm sorry, Linus. Did you say something?"

"Someone's coming!" A voice that sounded like fingernails on a chalkboard echoed through the room. *"Someone's coming!"*

"Don't be ridiculous. We haven't had a visitor since the Revisionist stopped by and that was eons ago."

Sully was speaking not to an assistant or a co-worker, but to the Gray-Headed Lovebird (*Agapornis canus Seemsius*) who was his only company in this desolate corner of The Seems. The brightly feathered parrot (only the head of a Grayhead is gray) was presently in a highly agitated state, shaking the bars of its cage like a rioting prisoner.

"All right, already!" The man with the frizzy hair and bleary eyes put his headphones back on and turned up the volume. "Don't get your feathers in a bunch."

Of all the positions in The Seems, few are less coveted than an assignment to the Hall of Records. This crumbling stone depot was officially defunded by the Powers That Be several years ago and claims but a single employee—a position manned over the years by Seemsberian ex-cons, a ne'er-do-well son-in-law of a Power That Be, and a disgruntled nature buff whose insubordination had angered one too many higher-ups. But of all the people who've held this lonely, dead-end post, it is safe to say that only one of them truly loved it.

"By the Plan, you're right!" Sully's headphones were connected to an enormous Gramophone, on which a vinyl disc six feet in diameter was slowly spinning around. Whatever he was listening to, it seemed to have something to do with what was about to happen. "If I know History—and I do know History—he'll be here in less than five minutes!"

The hall's lone staff member jumped to his feet and scrambled into action. A chalkboard was flipped over and the other side erased of all its equations. Handwritten pieces of paper were gathered off the floor and stuffed into desk drawers. Even the two remaining buttons of a collared white shirt were hastily secured, which only served to emphasize the disheveled nature of the pin-striped tie that hung loosely around Sully's neck.

"Time for the gnomes!" screeched Linus from inside his cage, *"Time for the gnomes!"*

"Quiet, you stupid pigeon!" Sully wheeled and flicked an

eraser in the general vicinity of the cage. "No one knows what I've been working on and I wanna keep it that way!"

"Time for the gnomes! Time for the gnomes!"

"Fine!" Sully made his way over to the small black-and-white TV that was plugged into the outlet above his work station. "But don't complain if it's a rerun!"

As Sully returned to his frantic cleanup, Linus focused his attention on the fuzzy monitor, where another episode of *The Jinx Gnomes* had just gotten underway. Based on the popular comic strip of the same name, this half-hour animated series depicted the adventures of the crack unit dispatched to The World whenever a person overcelebrated a bit of good fortune. It was now the top-rated show in The Seems, and counted among its many devoted followers a certain ornery bird.

"Rerun! Rerun!"

"Send a letter to the network!" Sully scanned the hall to make sure that all the evidence of his life's work was concealed, then snuck a peek at the monitor himself. "Is it 'I'm Just Glad There's No Traffic'?"

" 'Perfect Day for a Wedding.' 'Perfect Day for a Wedding.' "

But Linus's joy at watching the blushing bride get her comeuppance was rudely interrupted when the locked and dusty door that Sully had always assumed to be an old janitor's closet suddenly burst open. Blue light and wind spilled out, followed shortly by a thirteen-year-old boy, with a borrowed peacoat and fraying bandages all over his hands.

"Where am I?" shouted the strangely dressed kid, staggering to his feet. "Am I back in The Seems?"

"Of course you're in The Seems." Despite the fact that Sully was rarely in the presence of other humans or Seemsians, he hadn't forgotten his manners. "Welcome to the Hall of Records."

Becker Drane pulled the frost-covered Transport Goggles off his face and took in the sight of his new surroundings. It looked very much like the reading room of an old library, with stained-glass windows and shelves stretching from parquet floor all the way up to domed ceiling. What was contained in these stacks didn't appear to be books, however, but record albums—like the kind his father kept in the "Do Not Touch" corner of their basement—except a whole lot bigger. To make matters weirder, the only two inhabitants of this place seemed to be a frizzy-haired lunatic dressed in rags and a parrot watching TV.

"The Hall of Records?" Becker was still frazzled from the craziest trip through the In-Between he'd ever taken. "I didn't even know there *was* a Hall of Records."

"It's actually a division of a sub-department of the Department of History, if you want to get technical." Sully offered the boy a stool. "I'm pretty busy right now, but if you don't mind waiting, I'd be happy to give you the grand—"

BLINK! BLINK! BLINK! BLINK! BLINK!

Becker whipped off his heavy peacoat and pulled his flashing Blinker off his belt.

196 MISSED CALLS

Uh-oh. Someone had been trying to reach him for quite some time—a lot of someones—and judging by the "911" next to each communication, he wasn't sure he wanted to hear what they had to say. In fact, the whole thing was giving him a terrible Déjà Vu of the worst nightmare (beta) he'd ever had.

"Forget about *where* I am!" Becker's eyes darted about for a Time Piece or a clock, but found none. "*When* am I?"

"When are you? I'm not sure I under—"

But the Fixer was already scrambling over to the black-and-white boob tube and spinning the dial through the staticky broadcasting band known as UHF.

"*PARTY FOUL! PARTY FOUL!*" squawked Linus, furious that Becker had turned off his favorite program.

"Linus, if you don't shut your trap, I'm going to cover up your cage again." Sully grabbed an old bedsheet and held it up to the Lovebird. "And we all remember what happened last time . . ."

As Linus quickly settled down (while making a mental note to imitate the smoke alarm as soon as Sully fell asleep that night), Becker found his way to channel 64, better known as the Seemsian News Network. To his profound and lasting relief, the date and time stamp running across the SNN ticker revealed that although he'd spent what seemed like several days falling through the Frozen Moments, only six hours of real Time had passed since his Mission had begun.

". . . at present all attempts to contact Fixer Drane have failed," reported SNN's continuing coverage of the crisis. "But our sources inside the Big Building confirm that at least for the moment, The World is still on schedule."

"Thank the Plan." Fixer #37 on the Roster felt his heart start beating again. "Thank the Plan."

Becker turned down the volume and recounted the strange journey that brought him here. First, he'd opened a Door inside a Frozen Moment. Second, he'd tumbled into a tube that looked like the blue electricity that powered it had gone out decades ago. And third, he'd found himself in an artery that was so narrow that his only choice was to wriggle his way through like a rat in a pipe. In all his trips through this nether region, Becker had never been as happy to see the white pinhole of light that heralded The Seems.

"Only thing I don't understand is why I didn't end up in Customs?"

"It makes perfect sense," said Sully, unrolling a map of The Seems that featured the pre–Seemsiana Purchase layout, including defunct departments such as Justice, Mystery, and Ladies' Shoes. "The Hall of Records used to be the Department of Transportation, till they built that fancy new Terminal. Who knows how many old Doors wind their way back here?"

As the Fixer studied the scroll, the Keeper of the Records finally started to relax. When he'd confirmed the parrot's assertion that someone was coming, Sully fretted that this was a random inspection or worse yet, the long-dreaded day when HUD[19] would decide to turn this place into "industrial condominiums." But now that someone was here, he couldn't help but swell with pride.

"Personally, I'm glad they made the switch." He motioned to the stacks of giant LPs. "Here in the Hall of Records, everything

---

19. The Department of Housing & Useless Development.

that has ever happened in The World or The Seems is recorded in wax and made available to the general pub—"

"No offense, dude." Becker didn't want to be rude, but he didn't really have time for tea and cookies. "I'm sure this is an awesome department, but I need to make a phone call."

Becker tucked himself into an abandoned listening booth and dialed the number for Central Command.

"*Number 37!*" The Dispatcher made no attempt to hide the relief in his voice. "*Where in the name of the Plan have you been?*"

"Shan and I got separated in the Frozen Moments." Becker kept it to himself as to why that had happened. "Any word from her yet?"

"*Negative.*"

Becker stifled a pang of guilt and prayed that Shan was as good as Shan thought she was.

"She's a professional. She'll find a way out." Becker had to stay focused on the task at hand. "In the meantime, I need you to supervise the immediate construction of a Containment Field—ten-feet square, with a floor made of grass, not dirt. Scatter a handful of Firsts and Thirds inside, and the Split Second will be drawn to it like a magnet."

There was a brief pause on the other end of the line, and Becker briefly considered attributing his plan to Tom Jackal, but he couldn't deny the thrill of hearing the Dispatcher speechless.

"*I'll put #26 on it right away.*" The Dispatcher shouted for someone to get Tony the Plumber on the line. "*Where are you gonna be?*"

Becker swallowed hard because he knew this would be a bombshell.

"I'll be looking for the Time Being."

"You must be joking."

"Somebody has to know where she is. A person of that magnitude doesn't just vanish into Thin Air."

"We've already checked Thin Air—several times—and there wasn't even a trace."

Becker knew this to be true, because searching for the woman known as the Time Being in The Seems was kind of like looking for Amelia Earhart in The World. Back in the Day, she had been a leading voice on the design team that built The World from Scratch and was famed for her controversial choice to inject Time into the very Fabric of Reality. The popularity of that decision in The Seems led to her election as the original Second in Command, and she was always well liked even after she tendered her resignation. But she vanished without a trace over fifty years ago, and hadn't been seen since.

"Excuse me—," interrupted Sully, but the Fixer ignored him.

"Well maybe we can talk to one of the original members of the Powers That Be." Becker cupped his hand over his ear and spoke louder into the Receiver. "All I know is I have it on good authority that we can't complete this Mission unless she—"

"Excuse me!" Sully was now shouting.

"What?" Becker shouted back, seeing that the Keeper of the Records was now looming over his shoulder.

"I don't mean to be a bother, but can I interpret from your conversation that you're on a quest to find the Time Being?"

"Uh . . ." Becker didn't really know what else to say, so he just said, "That's right."

Sully smoothed back his hair and tightened up his tie to near respectability. As far as he was concerned, the Hall of Records had a lot to offer, but it had fallen so far off the Radar that he rarely, if ever, got a chance to make a difference in The World. Now that the opportunity presented itself, he was going to relish it.

"Well, why didn't you just say so?"

Gandan Monastery, Sühbaatar Province, Outer Mongolia

An entire World away, two figures garbed in traditional red gis sat in the lotus position on a rice paper mat. As a bell tolled, the statues of the great warriors who came before seemed to watch their every move.

"*Devasyaaaa . . . ,*" chanted the voices of their fellow monks. But the incomparable Li Po and his new Initiate did not join them.

Six months earlier, the lanky young Seemsian had come to Gandan to study under Fixer #1, and at Po's instruction he'd forsaken his name and taken a vow of silence. The Initiate had also shaved his head, blindfolded his eyes, and covered his ears, tongue, and fingertips with beeswax—all in an effort to avoid deception by the five primary senses. For it was mastery of the fabled 7th that he now pursued.

"Focus!" The Initiate admonished himself with his inner voice. "Reach for that feeling that something is wrong!"

Those born in The Seems have no 7th Sense, but on a fateful night in the Department of Sleep, the Briefer turned seeker had felt the subtlest of twinges. Now he used the raised neck hairs, goose bumps, and chills down his spine to track the path of the Split Second, and even from this great distance, he could see in his mind's eye that it had reached the launching point from which it would soon annihilate The World.

"Do you feel it, master?" asked the Initiate, though not with the help of his vocal cords. Affixed to his belt was a small pouch of tiles, each inscribed with Olde Seemsian characters that allowed one versed in their ways to say much without saying anything at all. But the way his hands shook as he arranged the ivory squares betrayed the fear that welled inside him. "The Essence of Time is loose."

"The Powers That Be will determine if and when we are needed," Li Po responded via his own set of squares. "I strongly suggest you return to your exercises until that moment arrives."

"But The World is in grave danger!"

"The World is always in grave danger, young one. For its very existence depends upon the thinnest thread in the Fabric of Reality, and the simplest Twist of Fate." Po had raised the act of silent communication to an art form, and his fingers now arranged the tiles with the speed of a World-class pianist. "Only by harnessing the power of our 7th Sense—and by releasing what we cannot control—can we ensure it will remain safe."

The words rang of truth, but the Initiate's ears were not ready to hear. In his heart was not the stillness of deep water, but rather the impatience of youth.

"I must go."

"You are not ready."

"Then I will fail, Master, but still I must go."

The Initiate bowed to honor the lessons he had already learned, then made his way to the antechamber where travelers left their shoes and possessions. Hanging from a hook on the wall was a Briefcase, filled to the brim with Tools both new and old. Most of these devices had been a gift from his beloved grandfather, and part of him longed to pick up his Receiver and dial "Crestview 1-2-2." But his 7th Sense told him that if The World was going to be saved this night, the only help he would get would come from within.

The Initiate removed the Tools and, one by one, began to strap them across his body.

Hall of Records, Department of History, The Seems

Though the SNN report had painted a rosy picture of the situation in Time, Becker knew the truth was a far different matter. The World had been hit by two more bursts of Essence and the Agents of L.U.C.K. would be able to steer them toward uninhabited Sectors for only so long. But what really got under the young Fixer's skin was the fact that Shan Mei-Lin had still not returned from the Frozen Moment pool and was feared to be PIA. This was entirely his fault—for he had abandoned his Briefer to be with Amy Lannin one last time—and he whispered a prayer that Shan could find her own Door, or some other escape route back home.

The only positive development was that his arrival in History might have been the lucky break he needed. According to the Keeper, the Records that filled this Hall contained not music but the symphony of life itself. Every decision that was made in The Seems and its consequent effect in The World was recorded in ten-year increments upon their shellac surfaces, and Daniel J. Sullivan claimed to know them all like the back of his hand.

He began his search for the Time Being by cueing up the bonus track of a dusty old album called *The Beginning of Time,* when the inventor had thrown the switch to activate her particular department. Once Sully picked up her audio trail, it was an apparently simple process to isolate her "life's path" on whatever LP she popped up on next.

"You can run, my dear . . ." The crazy-maned historian closed his eyes, leaned back on his favorite bean-bag chair, and turned up the volume. ". . . but you cannot hide."

As a Record called *The Fifties* continued to spin, Becker sifted through the giant .33s and .45s that were splayed out all over the floor. He couldn't for the life of him fathom how everything that ever happened could be contained on these discs, or how anyone could pick through a seemingly infinite Chain of Events to find the pathway of one person's life.

"Are you sure this is gonna work?" asked the skeptical Fixer.

"Trust me. I've done nothing but listen to the course of History for the last eight years. Everyone in The World or The Seems has their own unique frequency, and the Time Being is quite audible at 1,233,456,789.1703 Seemsahertz."

Becker felt a hole growing in his stomach. He had watched a lot of classic movies with his mom on AMC, and the gentleman in the headphones was bearing an alarming resemblance to some of the patients from *One Flew Over the Cuckoo's Nest.* But without any other promising leads, the Fixer had to put his Mission in Sully's hands.

"There she is in '59!" The historian pumped a fist and pulled off his trusty AKGs. "Get me *The Seventies*!"

Fixer Drane climbed to the top of a tall wooden ladder that

rolled around the room on brass casters and gave access to the custom-made shelves that had been built into the walls.

"You mean the big Records?"

"No," shouted the Keeper. "The 1970s!"

This batch of albums was located in the relatively new section of the library, where the jackets were less dusty and the Art Department had been given a little more free rein in terms of cover design. Becker pulled the Record out from its place between the 1960s and the 1980s, and was pretty much blown away by the combination of gritty realism and mellowed vibe that graced the cover.

"Am I crazy or has the Time Being been alive for like a million years?"

"Anyone who was around before the Beginning of Time never gets old, unless they go to a Time Zone or spend too much time in The World." Sully was trying to talk and listen at the same time. "Now can you come down here and cue it up for me? I think that's gonna be our ticket to ride!"

Becker slid down the ladder without touching any of the rungs, and walked over to where Sully was manning the turntables. Unlike most of the equipment in the room, these had no dust or cobwebs at all, and were obviously kept in tip-top condition. In fact, they kind of reminded Becker of some of the same ones that his friend Seth Rockman's brother Matt had in his bedroom.[20]

"How come we're skipping *The Sixties*?" asked Becker,

---

20. You can catch Matt Rockman spinning discs every Thursday night from one a.m. to four a.m. on WVHP, Highland Park High School's student-run radio station.

pulling the bulky disc out of its sleeve and placing it on the unoccupied spinner.

"From what I can tell, after she dropped out she pretty much hit the Road. Lived in Obscurity for a while, holed up in the Sticks, even spent a little time trying to find Herself." Sully turned up the treble via one of the countless dials. "But when it came time to settle down, she picked a place where no one would think to look . . ."

Becker hit Play on the console and the needle swung out on a lever, resting ever so gingerly above the spinning disc.

"She was flirting with moving there all through the forties and fifties." Sully was wearing two sets of phones so that *The Fifties* was in one ear and *The Seventies* in the other. "But something tells me she didn't pull the trigger until around '73!"

He lowered the needle and, placing hands on both of the discs, began to slide them back and forward through Time. It was almost as if he were trying to find where one song perfectly transitioned into the other, and Becker had to admit that despite his unkempt beard and broken glasses (or because of them), he looked like a fresh DJ scratching on the 1s and 2s.

"Bingo!" Sully shouted triumphantly.

"You got it?"

"Of course I got it!" The Keeper turned off the turntable and hopped down off his stool. "And I promise you she's still there!"

Before Becker could get a listen for himself, Sully was madly dashing toward the only other working piece of machinery in the Hall of Records—the old-fashioned Gramophone, which wasn't playing anything, only recording.

"This is what's happening right now . . ." He pointed to where the needle was cutting microscopic grooves into the face of the Record. "On first listen, it's been a pretty rocky decade, but you can never tell until you hear it a few times."

On the back of the Gramophone were RCA cables with the symbols of every department and sub-department in The Seems. There was also an "audio out" jack, and Sullivan affixed a one-eighths to one-fourth adapter and plugged in the cord.

"See if this rings a bell."

When Becker pressed the cushiony leather of the headphone against his ear, he was hoping to hear the answer to the whereabouts of the one and only Time Being. But all that assaulted his ears was a hideous clamor.

"Dude, it's totally garbled!"

"That's because you're not used to what life sounds like when it's happening all at once." Sully pushed up his glasses over the bridge of his nose. "Gimme two more seconds to isolate her track!"

Watching the Keeper of the Records madly adjust the knobs on the front of the machine did little to instill confidence in Fixer #37. Nor did the piles of white pages that were crudely stuffed into every drawer, box, and file cabinet in the hall. Sully continually brushed off inquiries about the papers by mumbling something about his "project," which only served to increase Becker's dread that he'd been sucked into a wild goose chase.

"Are you sure you found her?"

"*One more second!*" screeched Linus from inside his cage. Though he and Sully were often at odds, he would never bite the hand that fed him. "*One more second!*"

Becker was now *totally* convinced that he had stumbled into the loony bin—until suddenly the "music" in his ears came perfectly into sync. He could clearly hear the sound of horns honking, people shouting in many different languages, even a distant siren. And underneath it all, an exhilarating hum that vibrated through his body and made his adrenaline soar.

"I know where that is . . ." Becker also heard the sounds of quiet footsteps amid the hustle and bustle, and had the distinct sensation that he was listening through somebody else's ears. "I totally know where that is!"

"Half The Seems has been looking for this woman for fifty years," said Sully, proudly watching the realization dawn upon the Fixer's face. "And she's been right under their noses all this time!"

Becker allowed the headphones to fall around his neck, then quickly formulated a game plan. He would need a change of clothes—probably something black, so as not to stand out like a sore thumb. A replacement Toolkit would also be required, messenger-bag style. And lastly, he would have to score a fully loaded Metrocard. Because according to this Record, the Time Being was not hiding in any little out-of-the-way corner of The Seems . . .

She was living in New York City.

The Big Apple

Central Park, New York, New York

Becker Drane and Daniel J. Sullivan emerged from a Door that was marked with a leaf—perfectly imitating the seal of the NYC Parks Department—and stepped into the eight hundred and forty-three acres of rolling green known as Central Park. Sully immediately tried to shield his eyes from the bright sun, infused as it is with far more ultraviolet and infrared than that of The Seems. But even with his elbow above his forehead he couldn't stop the sights and sounds of New York City from rushing in.

A Rollerblader blasted by, joyfully using the Fixer and Keeper of the Records as pylons in her obstacle course. Tall stone and glass buildings loomed over the park on all four sides, while the sounds of ambulances, jackhammers, and two men haggling over the price of a shish kebab melded together in a pop single worthy of one of Sully's precious Records. In his adventures in The World and The Seems, Fixer #37 had been to many strange and out-of-the-way places, but none of them flooded all twelve of his senses[21] like this one.

"Welcome to the Big Apple, Sully."

Sully was still a little shell-shocked, so Becker helped him over to a park bench. Persuading the older man to come to The World hadn't been easy, for the Keeper was intent on getting back to his project, and besides, who would take care of Linus? But a quick call to Central Command had brought one of the Skeleton Crew to watch over History (along with the complete first season of *The Jinx Gnomes* for the obsessed parrot), and once Becker had declassified some of the details of his Mission, Sully finally agreed.

"You okay, dude?" asked Becker, seeing that his companion was trembling from head to toe. "Can I get you a water or a Diet Coke?"

"No, no. I'm fine."

When Sully opened his eyes again, Becker could see that his comrade was not suffering from shock and awe, but rather from genuine emotion.

"It's just . . ." Sully wiped a tear from the corner of his eye. "I forgot how beautiful it was."

"When was the last time you came to The World?"

"For Y2K. I've been meaning to come back ever since, but I've been so focused on my project that I never had time."

"Gotta stop and smell the roses, Sully."

Becker laced up his suede Pumas and cuffed his replacement

---

21. 1. Taste. 2. Touch. 3. Smell. 4. Hearing. 5. Sight. 6. Humor. 7. The 7th Sense. 8. Direction. 9. Style. 10. ESP. 11. I See Dead People. 12. Common.

Levi's just once. The Wardrobe Department had also hooked him up with a black Old Navy T-shirt and a nice pair of Vuarnets, but they had struggled to come up with something workable for the Keeper. Presently, he was stuffed into a white "I Love New York" T-shirt, red Adidas sweat pants, and clunky Doc Martens, which made him look like a cross between an outpatient from a mental hospital and a homeless man.

"Where did you say she lived again?" asked the Fixer.

"Let me double check." Sully turned up the volume on the old-fashioned Sony Walkman that was clipped onto his pants. Inside the device was a dub of the last three years, and he listened intently, covering the orange foam headphones with his hands. "I heard her mention 274 West 12th Street on at least three occasions."

"Then we're gonna have to take the subway downtown." Becker scanned the park for the closest passerby. "Hold on, let me ask somebody how we get there."

A man in a business suit and sunglasses was in shouting distance.

"Excuse me, sir?"

The man just flipped a quarter at Becker and kept right on walking. The next two people he approached simply put up their hands and said, "I already believe in Jesus," until finally, a mounted police officer was kind enough to tell him, "You need to take the 1 train to 14th Street, boss." He pointed to the station entrance that was visible over the stone wall surrounding Central Park. "It's right over there."

Fourteenth Street was only two blocks away from where they believed the Time Being had been hiding for the last thirty-odd years, and if they were lucky she'd be home. And if they were *really* lucky, she'd be able to tell them how to put a Split Second back together. But even though the stakes for the Mission couldn't be higher, Becker found himself embarrassed by the ragged sight of his traveling partner.

"And Sully?"

"Yeah?"

"I don't want people to think we're bridge and tunnelers[22], so try to be cool."

"Cool? I'm cool." Sully was deeply offended. "Cool's my middle name."

But as the Keeper followed Becker toward Columbus Circle, he could feel the eyes of even the most jaded New Yorkers upon him.

"Correction. My middle name is Jehosephat."

Meanwhile, The Seems

Briefer Shan Mei-Lin sat with her legs crossed in the cold and empty darkness. There was nary a sound nor a speck of light, nor even a hint of movement in the shadows (of which there were none, for shadows themselves can only be created by the presence of light). In fact, the only things that confirmed that she existed at all were the sound of her heartbeat—which she controlled via the Buddhist technique of anapanasati, or "mindfulness of breathing"—and the feel of the hard ground beneath her.

---

22. A derogatory term hurled by Manhattanites at citygoers who hail from the outlying boroughs (and particularly New Jersey).

When she had first entered Meanwhile, panic had threatened to tear Shan apart, but the tutelage of IFR instructor Jelani Blaque had served her well. He implored his Candidates to view even the most mind-numbing terrors as Tools by which the innermost portions of one's own self could be mapped and explored. Yet when she looked inside to see what she really was terrified by, it was not the fact that she was going to die in this black prison, but the fact that nobody would really care that she was gone.

"How is this possible?" the girl asked herself, resisting the impulse to wrap her arms around her knees. "I've always tried the best I could."

This was undeniable. Her life had been one long succession of triumphs, all of which were memorialized on plaques and papers in two separate worlds for all to see. And yet, the distance she felt from those around her was also undeniable.

"You've become the best at the wrong game."

Shan's eyes opened with a start. She had definitely heard a voice, but she couldn't tell if it had echoed from the darkness or from the corridors of her own head.

"Say that again?"

"I said you're playing the wrong game."

Shan knew that hearing voices was one of the telltale signs of dementia, but listening to something imaginary was better than nothing at all, so she decided to play along.

"Then what would be the right game?"

The voice went silent and Shan feared that she had asked too direct a question, but after a moment's pause, it piped up again.

"A game where you're playing for something other than your own high score."

As always, the Briefer resented the implication that she had failed or even struggled with something, but she let the hot flash of anger pass before responding.

"I didn't make the rules."

"But you continue to play by them, at the expense of all else."

Shan tried to fire back, but she couldn't argue that in her endless drive to succeed and achieve, those around her—her fellow students, the Candidates at the IFR, even Fixers Chiappa and Drane—had become competitors (if not enemies) or fools that stood in her way. In fact, she could not think of a single person in the World or Seems whom she could honestly call her friend.

"And when was the last time you talked to your brother? Or to your mother and father?"

"I . . . I . . ."

"Or even to your precious Ye Ye?"

Whoever the voice was, Shan was starting not to like him. The truth was that the Briefer had not spoken to her family in years. Not since they made the long trip to Beijing to celebrate her graduation from secondary school. Pride had been written all over her parents' faces, but instead of enjoying it, the young student had felt surrounded by strangers, whose humble clothes and manner had embarrassed her.

"What do you know of me or my family?" Even she could hear the defensiveness in her voice. "They were the ones who sent me down this path in the first place!"

This was also true. Perhaps the most indelible mark on Shan's memory was the day two government educators came to take her to a school on the other side of the country. She had kicked and cried that day, begging her parents not to send her away from everything she cared about, but they had let it happen anyway.

"Only so you wouldn't have to live the hard lives they did. Only out of love."

As much as Shan felt the hurt and anger coursing through her, the voice had spoken honestly.

"Sorry, little flower. I'm only trying to help."

"How?" Shan forced the tears back into her throat. "By making me feel bad?"

"By showing you the world you've created for yourself."

The Briefer had to admit, it was not a pretty world she lived in. In fact, it strangely mirrored the one she resided in now: cold, dark, and lonely. And yet if the voice was right, and that world had been one of her own creation, then it stood to reason it was possible for her to make a new one.

"Now you're starting to see the light."

"Yeah, but what good will it do me if I'm stuck here in Meanwhile?"

"No," said the voice, and Shan almost felt like someone had whacked her on the back of the head. "You're *really* starting to see the light."

It took her a moment to see that the voice wasn't talking about a metaphorical light but a real light that was emanating from somewhere ahead in the distance. It wasn't much—just a change in the shade of the blackness, really—but it was the first inkling that there might be a way out of this abyss.

"Well," said the voice, and its eyes would be twinkling if it had any, "what are you waiting for?"

Having no answer to that question, Shan got up off the

ground and slung her Briefcase over her shoulder. She was tempted to thank the voice or ask for its name, but she still wasn't positive if there was a voice at all. So she just started tramping off toward the light.

"You're welcome!"

Shan stopped in her tracks, afraid she had offended the speaker (or herself), but a good-natured laugh greeted her instead.

"Travel safe, little flower. And don't forget—it is you who make the rules of the game . . ."

1 Train, New York, New York

"Next stop, 28ᵗʰ Street!" came the barely audible crackle from the speaker above. *"Please stand clear of the closing doors!"*

Sully and Becker stood inside a packed subway car and held onto the metal straps for dear life. A slideshow of graffiti, pipes, and mosaics zipped by the windows, matched only by the theater on the inside—commuters of every shape, size, and color, all looking a little worse for the wear after a long day on the job.

"It's amazing, isn't it?" marveled Sully. "To be in the presence of the Plan in action instead of listening from afar?"

"How did you end up in History, anyway?" asked Becker, ignoring the woman in a business suit who jostled him from behind. "That's a pretty random job."

"Actually, I used to work in the Big Building." Sully switched his grip to one of the passenger poles. "But that was another life ago."

"The Big Building?" Becker was struck by a moment of recognition. "Waitamminnit—you're not *Danny* Sullivan, are you?"

A wistful smile crept across the Keeper's face.

"That would be me."

Everybody in The Seems knew the story of Danny Sullivan. He had been one of the top Case Workers in the Big Building, and rumored to be in line for a spot among the Powers That Be. That Danny Sullivan had effortlessly managed entire Sectors and was famous for pulling sweet moves, sometimes years in the making, that led his Cases toward a greater sense of happiness. But his fall was nearly as meteoric as his rise.

"They found me staring at the wall in my office, catatonic," Sully confessed over the tinny hip-hop piping out of some kid's iPod. "The transfer to History was more of just a sympathy vote . . . so I could keep my benefits and not embarrass anyone. But it turned out to be the best thing that ever happened to me."

The door leading to the adjoining car slid open, and with it came the squeals of the metal juggernaut as it barreled down the tracks. They turned to see a man with no legs and a simple cardboard sign that read "Veteran—need $ for food" wheel himself into the car. Most of the crowd pretended he was invisible and cleared the center aisle, though a few people dropped coins into his paper cup. Becker searched his own pockets thoroughly, and finding only the supply of Slim Jims he'd requested from Central Command, sheepishly handed one over. The man in the wheelchair issued a "thank you, brother," then moved on to the next car.

"It's hard to believe in a Plan that allows for that, isn't it?" asked Sully.

"Tell me about it." Becker was not only thinking about the vet, but about the people on the train platform in Time Square, about Amy Lannin and Tom Jackal, and about all of the painful moments that were still so fresh in his mind.

"That's why I got burned out, man," Sully explained. "Every day the decisions I made affected thousands, if not tens of thousands, of lives, and when it worked out, it was the ultimate rush. But when it didn't . . ."

Sully's eyes fell to the floor and Becker didn't want to ask what terrible Move or Chain of Events had sent the ex–Case Worker over the edge. When the train arrived at the 18th Street station, the crowd thinned out a tad, and he and Sully were able to find adjoining seats.

"The thing I could never come to terms with was why so many hard knocks, bad breaks, and natural disasters were built into the Plan." Sully waited for the train to head into the tunnel before he continued. "But once I got to History, I finally saw the big picture and started to understand."

"You mean there's like a really Big Picture on the wall in the Hall of Records?" asked Becker, wondering how he'd missed such a thing.

"No, no, no, no. I'm talking about seeing everything that happens in its proper perspective . . ."

Ring! Ring! Ring!

Suddenly, the Receiver on Becker's belt—which he had hidden beneath his black tee—started ringing off the hook.

"Hold that thought." As Becker lifted his orange headset to his ear, everyone on the train wondered: a) Where did that kid get such a funky, retro cell phone? And b) How was he getting service in the subway tunnel?

"Dude, I can't really talk right now," whispered Becker into the phone, trying not to be rude. "I'm on the train."

"I just wanted to let you know the Containment Field is locked and loaded," Tony the Plumber's Staten Island accent sounded right at home on this car. *"All we're waitin' on now is for that Split Second to come to papa."*

"Nice work, #26," Becker complimented the only other Fixer from the Tri-State area. "Any idea when it's gonna get there?"

"Better be soon. We got runoff Essence spoutin' into The World like a leaky pipe."

"I thought I felt something." Becker's stomach had been bothering him ever since arriving in the Hall of Records, but he'd hoped it was just the combination of the Jackal family dinner and being Lost in Time. "Have we considered sending someone up to the In-Between to divert future runoff?"

"C-Note's on his way."

"Cool. Gimme updates on the half-hour."

"Aye, aye, #37. And have a burger at the Corner Bistro for me, a'ight?"

"You got it, T."

The Fixer hung up the phone feeling almost optimistic.

"Good news?" asked Sully.

"Hope so," Becker tried to reassure himself as much as his traveling companion. "Just keep your ear on the Time Being, all right?"

"Next stop, 14th Street! Please watch your step as you exit the train!"

The closer she got to the light, the more Briefer Shan felt the oppressive weight of Meanwhile lifting from her shoulders. What had once been just the hint of a break in the darkness had become a healthy glow after a few minutes of walking, and now that she was jogging (if not sprinting) toward it, that glow had grown into what appeared to be a rectangle of bright yellow light.

"It must be the doorway out!" Shan shouted to herself aloud and doubled her pace. "I'm gonna make it! I'm really gonna make it!"

But it was more than just the prospect of escaping from this dreaded location that brought a giddy smile to her face. Whereas once she would have gloated over being one of the few to break out of Meanwhile, her thoughts were instead focused on her brother Bohai and the rest of her family, and the possibility that she would one day see them again.

But Shan also knew this reunion could never happen if the Time Bomb planted by The Tide had already destroyed The World. Her 7th Sense had suddenly reactivated when she'd seen the unexpected light, and judging from the chills running down her spine, she had to assume that there was still something terribly wrong in The Seems. Her only hope was that there was enough time to—

"Hold on a second." Shan's feet skidded to a halt. "That's not a doorway . . ."

Indeed, now that her mad dash had brought her close enough to the source of the glow, the Briefer could see she'd been mistaken. What she'd assumed to be a portal to The World out-side Meanwhile was actually a large glass box—perhaps ten-feet square—that held the intense yellow light within its transparent walls. She could also detect a faint, high-pitched sound emanat-ing from within. Shan again pulled out her Night Shades, this time because her eyes were having trouble adjusting to the bright light, and approached the mysterious structure.

The glass was thick, like ice on a pond in the middle of winter, and the floor of the interior was lined with red clay and dirt. Scattered all over the ground were a collection of perfectly spherical rocks, as silver and reflective as the shell of the Split Second that she carried in her Briefcase. She knew the small ones to be Thirds and the ones that were as big as boulders were Firsts—two of the three building blocks of Time—but she had no idea what they were doing in here or what inside the box was causing this fierce illumination.

"What are you?" she asked aloud, hoping the voice that guided her from the darkness would give the answer. But hear-ing none, she leaned forward and pressed her ear against the glass. The hum inside was not steady but rhythmic, and she could feel by the vibrations on her cheek that it was actually being caused by something hitting the walls. Something mov-ing so fast it couldn't even be seen . . .

"It's a Containment Field for a Split Second." A voice *did* give the answer, but this time it was a man's voice, hoarsely ringing out from the other side of the glass box. "The damn fools are gonna destroy The World!"

Though the man was clearly furious, his words sounded muffled, as if spoken through gritted teeth or a wired jaw. But it wasn't the quality of this new voice or even its totally unexpected appearance that made Shan's heart feel like it was about to burst through her chest. It was the fact that she recognized its owner.

Slowly she made her way around the enclosure, determined to hold her ground should this be yet another of Meanwhile's psychic assaults. But the person she found on the other side— his mouth gagged, his hands and feet tied to an old wooden chair—was undeniably real.

"Mr. Chiappa?"

Greenwich Village, New York, New York

The brownstone at 274 West 12th Street was on the hard-to-find block between West 4th Street and Greenwich Avenue (not to be confused with Greenwich Street). Like all the buildings on the street, 274 had a stoop. Unlike its neighbors, it also boasted two granite lions that stared out onto the street, as if standing guard.

"What do we do now?" asked Sully.

"I guess we see if she's home."

The two visitors climbed the concrete steps and leaned in to read the list of names posted on the intercom.

"Al Jelpert, #1" was boldly written in pen at the bottom, followed closely by "Funkytown Productions," which had been labeled #2 by a Brother P-Touch. Apartments #3 and #4 were just blank scrawls of metal, but it was the small handwritten label for the top floor that sent a jolt of electricity straight through Becker's body.

"There she is."

He pointed to the well-formed cursive letters that were capped off by an elegant picture of a flower. There was no first or last name, only a simple declaration that led straight to buzzer #5:

For the Time Being . . .

Both of them just stood there, not quite sure what to do next.

"Aren't you going to push it?" Sully finally exclaimed, unable to take the pressure any longer.

"You push it," replied Becker.

"You're the Fixer!"

"You're the Keeper of the Records!"

This type of bickering was certainly uncalled for, especially with the fate of The World at stake, so Becker finally pressed the black button and sent an electric signal up through the building walls. Tentatively, they waited for an answer—not sure what the Time Being's voice might sound like or if she would let them in—but only silence came back over the line. A second press of the button set off the same buzzer, but the result was the same.

"She's not answering," Sully worried aloud.

"Or maybe she's just not home," Becker speculated. "C'mon, let's find a good spot to stake out the building."

Across the street was the famed Corner Bistro—the same hole-in-the-wall burger joint that Tony the Plumber had recommended—but seeing a line stretching out the door, they opted for the small Italian coffee shop that had just opened up next door. As Becker and Sully ordered lattes and sat among the other bohemians who called the West Village their home, the Fixer told himself to be patient, that all of this was going according to Plan. But given the present circumstances, it didn't bring him much comfort.

"Back on the train," Becker stirred in the sugar with a wooden stick, "you were talking about seeing the big picture."

Sully perked up at the mention of his favorite topic. "Oh, yes. Of course."

"Care to expand on that?"

"Like I said before . . . once I began to dig into the Records, I started to realize that all those things I thought were so terrible—as small as someone breaking her arm to as big as war or hunger—take on a different light when looked at through the prism of History."

"What kind of light?"

"Most of us look at things in a cause-and-effect kind of way. 'I hit the lottery, therefore life is good.' 'My child was hit by a car, therefore life is bad.' But what we don't see are the Chains of Events that are connected to those things."

Sully took another sip of coffee and continued.

"A doesn't lead to B, Drane. A leads to B, which leads to C, which leads to D, E, F, G. And you can't tell if A was a good thing or a bad thing until you see how it ripples across the rest of the alphabet (not to mention all the letters that came before A!). Therefore, it can be said that the very idea of cause is an illusion . . ."

"I don't believe that," said Becker, and even though all the things he relied upon felt shaken by this day, he truly didn't.

"Neither do I." Sully smiled, happy that the boy had beaten him to the punch. "In fact, after studying the History of the World since back in the Day, I have come to believe that there was only one thing behind the Plan on the day it was implemented, and there is only one thing behind the Plan as we speak."

"Which is?"

Sully leaned back in his chair and put his hands behind his head.

"You'll have to read my book."

Becker flashed back to the stacks of paper sticking out of every possible nook and cranny of the Hall of Records (along with a host of equations, calculations, and graphs that had been half erased from multiple chalk and grease boards). Back then, he'd been pretty sure Sully had lost his marbles, and though the Fixer still wasn't convinced he hadn't, he wanted to hear more. But before Becker could pry any further, he spotted something across the street.

"Dude, is that . . . ?"

The woman who was heading up the stairs of building 274 had silver hair—the kind that only comes after years of being blond—and wore a simple white blouse, ankle-length skirt, and leather sandals. Her wrists were covered with bracelets and she was carrying a bakery box, but the only thing Becker and Sully were looking at was her face.

"I think it is, Drane," Sully whispered, incredulous. "I think it is."

Both of them recognized that face from paintings in The Seems—most notably the masterpiece known as "The 13th Chair," which depicted the founding members of the Powers That Be gathered around their conference room table. Sitting next to the symbolically empty seat at the head was the original

Second in Command—the same woman who was now fumbling with a set of keys and opening the outer door to the crooked brownstone.

"Excuse me!" Becker rose to his feet and called out across the street. "Can we speak with you for a second?"

As a thirteen-year-old Fixer and a mangy-haired Keeper of the Records tentatively approached the person they believed to be the Time Being, they did not notice a figure stepping out of the Corner Bistro with a paper bag in his hands. He was tall, thin, and bearded, his faded jeans and suede jacket fitting in perfectly with the downtown hipsters. In fact, the only thing about him that stood out from the crowd was the strange pendant that dangled from his neck—forged of black pewter and shaped into the image of a cresting wave.

The stranger sat down on the curb and started to eat his cheeseburger, all the while paying close attention to the conversation across the street. After a few more words were exchanged, the older woman opened the door and the trio disappeared inside.

"*Trés bien*, Draniac," said Thibadeau Freck, licking his fingers and putting on a pair of Serengeti shades. "*Trés bien.*"

For the Time Being

Tony the Plumber pulled off his "Iovino's Plumbing & AC Repair" hardhat and wiped the sweat off his furrowed brow. High above the mountains the sun blazed down and reflected off the Babbling Brook, a tributary of the Stream of Consciousness that flowed directly through this Time Zone.

"Where the heck is this thing already?" Tony spat on the ground and took a swig of much needed Diet Inspiration from his thermos. "I thought you guys said it was gonna be here like snap, crackle, and pop!"

Tony was speaking to the gaggle of Time Flies who had helped him construct the Containment Field on the banks of the brook. The ten-foot-square box of glass was finally complete, with a semipermeable membrane on the roof to allow the Split Second in (but not out), and Firsts and Thirds scattered on a floor of freshly mown grass. It had taken a lot of work, however, and as the crew lowered their shovels and glass cutters, they were caked with perspiration and dirt.

"Patience, brudda," said the dreadlocked foreman of the crew in his lilting accent. "The watched pot never boil."

"Yeah, but The World's gonna roast like my mom's braciola if this Split Second don't come marchin' through the door!"

"Man makes his plan," responded the foreman with a toothy grin. "And the Plan laughs . . ."

A chorus of "iries" went up among the work crew, and someone turned up the thick reggae coming over their portable radio. Like all the construction workers, affectionately known as "Time Flies," this bunch had been raised on the Islands in the Stream, where the perfect sunsets, tasty waves, and offshore breezes contributed to a decidedly mellow mind-set. They were also practically immune to the Essence of Time (probably because Time Flies were always having fun) and thus were solely responsible for mining First, Seconds, and Thirds from the three indigenous Time Zones in The Seems.

"Are you sure this astroturf ain't screwin' things up?" Tony pointed to the floor of the Containment Field, which had been made from the vanilla grass that grew on the edge of the Brook. "Maybe we shoulda used dirt instead."

"Trus' me, Tony Plumba mon. We do dis every day." The foreman pulled a First from one of the wheelbarrows. "Whenever we got one dat be cracked or damaged, we wrap dem in da grass so we don' get no runoff. In da mud or dirt da Essence jus' seep tru."

Tony tried to take their word for it, but the farther the sun set behind the mountains, the more his stomach drifted in the opposite direction. Part of that was probably due to the meatball parm he'd inhaled before starting the Containment Field, but the other part was no doubt related to something wrong in The Seems. Something very, very—

Honk! Honk! Honk!

Tony and the Flies turned to see a white golf cart bouncing up the dirt road that led to their work site. It was Permin Neverlåethe, who looked nearly as pale as his vehicle.

"What's the word, Permee?" asked Tony, as the vehicle pulled to a halt.

"I checked the log sheets, just as I promised," replied the Administrator, his voice shaking. "And it seems there was one Minuteman who didn't show up for work today."

"Who's that?"

"Ahem . . . his name is Ben Lum."

"Big Ben?" A murmur shot through the Time Flies . . . but not a happy one. "Dat boy crazy!"

"Not ta mention eight feet tall," blurted out another.

Tony the Plumber dropped one hand to his Receiver and raised the other to rub the back of his sunburned neck. Fixer #22 knew the feeling of a Mission coming together . . . but this one felt more like a Mission falling apart.

"Yo, Brief! How we doin' in there?"

The In-Between

"Chillin' like a villain," shouted Harold "C-Note" Carmichael over the roar of the In-Between. But if he had to be honest, "chillin'" didn't quite apply to how the Briefer felt right now. "Barely hanging on" was probably more like it.

C-Note was currently standing atop one of the countless Tubes that transported Goods & Services between The World and The Seems. Goggles shielded his eyes from the frost and glare, while his feet were lined with both Rubber Soles™ (to keep him from being singed by the electrostatic energy) and Concrete Galoshes™ (to keep him from drifting off into the infinite blue).

"My Blinker says that Essence just smoked an island off the Moldavian coast." Tony the Plumber's voice squawked over the Briefer's Receiver. *"You got a handle on where it's comin' from?"*

"Yeah, T. I'm lookin' right at it!"

The Briefer had been deployed to the In-Between to track down the pathway by which runoff from the Split Second was spilling into the World. Using his 7th Sense like a homing beacon, he'd field-tested thirty-six of the Tubes before hitting paydirt on the one set aside for Animal Affairs.[23]

"I just got off the horn with Administrator Hoofe and she says it's business as usual up there. It's gotta be slipping in from another source!" C-Note watched a bundle of zebra stripes pass below his feet. "You want me to keep lookin'?"

"Negatory. Get that Q-Turn™ on ASAP!"

C-Note reached into his Briefcase and pulled out the heavy, Q-shaped Tool. Anything that entered the mouth would automatically be looped around 390 degrees and sent directly out "the squiggly," but it was normally used for redirecting Creative Juices. Tony's hunch was that if his Briefer installed the

---

23. The Department in The Seems responsible for Leopard Spots, Lion's Roars, maps for Carrier Pigeons, updates on the secret plan among squirrels to overthrow humankind and force all other life forms into indentured servitude in the nut mines, etc.

Q-turn in the middle of the Tube, any future bursts of Essence could be diverted before ever hitting The World.

"I don't know, T. Essence might turn this Q into an R!"

It wasn't that C-Note was afraid to get his hands dirty. In addition to his job as a Briefer, he worked two other part-time gigs to put himself through med school: pizza delivery man and car detailer at Slick Willie's, the hottest polish house in LA. But tricking out the rims on a Bugatti Roadster was a whole different ballgame than finessing the Essence of Time.

"Got any suggestions?"

"Yeah, I got a good one."

C-Note could almost hear the devilish grin on Tony's face.

"Use your imagination!"

Meanwhile, The Seems

Shan Mei-Lin rushed to Mr. Chiappa's aid and quickly began to untie the straps that bound his arms and legs to the chair. The restraints had left deep welts in the English teacher's wrists, and his face and body looked like he'd been severely beaten.

"Who did this to you, sir?"

"Who do you think?" coughed Fixer #12, spitting the gag from his mouth. "The same *scioccos* who planted the Bomb in the first place."

Even though Mr. Chiappa was as bruised as he was angry, Shan was amazed to see that he showed no visible signs of aging. Everyone else in the radius of the initial blast had been turned to dust.

"How is this possible, sir? We all thought you were dead."

"So did I." Lucien Chiappa rubbed his sore arms and eked out a smile. "When the Split Second exploded through the Frozen Moments, instead of being aged, I was somehow taken along for the ride."

Shan offered her Fixer a bottle of Inspiration from her Briefcase, and the Corsican polished off the whole thing in one thirsty gulp.

"It yanked me through dozens of Moments—maybe even hundreds—I don't know, it was all a blur of color and sound until I splashed down at the bottom of some kind of waterfall . . ."

"That's how I got here too." The Briefer quickly recounted the tale of what happened after she and Fixer Drane had ventured into the Frozen Moment pool. Shan surmised it was Chiappa's footsteps she had followed into the heart of Meanwhile, but how he ended up bound and gagged was a wholly different tale.

"Now we know why The Tide has been so impossible to locate," said Fixer #12, sitting back down on the chair. "They're using places like Meanwhile for their HQs."

In addition to the Containment Field, equipment, weapons, and Canned Heat were scattered all over the place. There were also blueprints from the Department of Time tacked up to a corkboard, right beside employee schedules, minutes from a meeting of Time Managers, and even the design for the original Time Bomb constructed by Mr. Chiappa and Permin Neverlåethe. But what Shan couldn't see amid all the clutter was any kind of door in or out.

"How did they find this place?" she asked.

"Looks like John Booby's at it again." Chiappa pointed to a schematic of what was clearly a Skeleton Key—except with a few extra notches added to the end. "Who knows where our friends can get into now . . ."

Shan knew Chiappa was referring to the Tide cell who had carved a home for itself in this shadowy hole. "How many of them are there, sir?"

"I've seen five so far, and I think there's a sixth running operations from a remote location. And let me tell you, we don't want to be here when they get back." Chiappa approached the glass of the Containment Field. "But first, we've got to figure out what to do with this Split Second."

"Split Second?" asked Shan, eyes reflecting the light that pulsed from within. "I don't see a Split Second in there."

"That's because it's moving too fast."

Chiappa reached into his pocket and pulled out a broken pair of what looked like wire-rimmed bifocals.

"They took my Toolkit." He winked and handed the bent frames over to the Briefer. "But they didn't know these were my Hour Glasses™."

During beta testing for The World, Hour Glasses had been used by Reality Checkers to help calibrate the rate at which Time should travel. They allowed the wearer to adjust the speed of everything they saw, but once the decision was made that "things should move at their own pace," the Tool became obsolete. Now they only endured as charming trinkets and reminders of the Days of Yore.[24]

---

24. Referring to Yore Alvayez Ontim, the gregarious Administrator of Time, whose reign immediately followed that of the Time Being. Though few advances were recorded during this era, it was known to be a period where no one was in a hurry and Good Times were had by all.

Shan taped the broken pieces together, placed them on her nose as instructed by Fixer #12, then set the speed to "Crawl." As soon as the lenses reconfigured, it became abundantly clear what was causing the pulsing yellow light that had drawn the Briefer from the darkness like a moth to the flame.

"Wuh de mah."

Bouncing off the walls of the Containment Field was what looked like half of an egg, except this egg was metallic and the size of a volleyball. Where the yolk should be was some kind of liquid goo that propelled the strange object in a random pattern off the walls, ceiling, and floor. Every time it hit the ground, it would leave a droplet or two behind.

"I think the Essence of Time is slowly beginning to escape the field," said Chiappa, watching the goo seep into the mud. "Have there been reports of Sectors in the World beginning to age?"

"I don't know, sir. I've been out of commission since I lost contact with Fixer Drane."

"Permin and I were convinced that dirt would be enough to keep a Split Second contained, but we were wrong." Chiappa's rage had become a slowly boiling stew. "And now The Tide is too."

"But look, sir." Shan whipped out the other half of the "egg," which she had carried ever so vigilantly after she and Becker had found the wreckage of the Bomb. "Maybe we can put it back together?"

Chiappa smiled, admiring his Briefer's tenacity. "It's a nice thought. But not even a Time Fly could withstand that much raw Essence."

"We have to try, sir! The fate of The World is at stake."

Fixer Chiappa looked at Shan again, and for the first time he saw a passion for something other than herself shining on her face.

"All right, Shan Mei-Lin. If you're game for this, then so am I."

But before they could hatch a plan, a circle of blue light—just big enough for a body to slip through—began to draw itself on the ground: the telltale sign of a Skeleton Key in action . . .

"It's them!" Chiappa turned white with fear, then scooped the ropes and gag off the floor. "Quick—tie me back up!"

Heart thudding, Shan bound the man from the isle of Corsica back to the chair, then slipped into the shadows behind the corkboard. Just in time too, for as soon as the blue circle was complete, it popped open like a porthole door, and five figures crawled out. They wore black bodysuits with their faces obscured by masks and began to gather their supplies with a great sense of purpose. But if the Briefer held out hope that they would be leaving just as quickly as they came, it was dashed when the burliest member of the group grabbed Mr. Chiappa by the throat and lifted him off the floor, chair and all.

"Time to take a ride, old man."

274 West 12th Street, New York, NY

Apartment #5 of 274 West 12th was a five-story walk-up, but despite the seemingly endless parade of stairs, it was well worth the trip. This quirky penthouse had wood floors and white plaster walls that stretched across the entire top floor of the building.

Fresh flowers were placed intermittently in shelves and alcoves, the light was pale and perfect, and due to its height above most of the other buildings nearby, street noise was replaced by the chirping of birds.

"You boys make yourself at home," called out the silver-haired woman from the kitchen. "I'll be right with you."

Becker and Sully sank into the velvet cushions of the living room couch. On the exposed brick wall across from them sat an original Topher Dawson photograph that depicted the Manhattan skyline at dusk, silhouettes of archaic wooden water towers looming on top of buildings.

"Is that the Department of Weather?" asked Sully, no doubt recognizing the signature design of the tank that held all The World's rain.

"They've been using those things in the city for a hundred years," Becker explained. "Lots of Big Ideas in The Seems find their way into The World."

"Is that why Machu Picchu looks like the Big Building?"

"Actually, the Big Building was more influential on the Tower of Babel," again the voice carried back from the kitchen, along with the clanking of dishes. "Although there are some elements from the executive conference room that did leak their way into Inca culture."

Becker nervously glanced at his traveling companion, then down at his Time Piece. He wasn't here to make a social call, and part of him was still concerned that this wasn't the Time Being at all. Maybe the woman who looked so much like the former Second in Command was just an out-of-work actress or eccentric bag lady—both of which were in greater supply in Manhattan than transplants from The Seems.

"The Plan got us this far . . ." Sully noticed that Becker's leg was jittering like someone afflicted with RLS.[25] ". . . the Plan will provide."

The Fixer was in the process of rolling his eyes—because there was a fine line between believing in the Plan and sitting on your couch all day doing nothing—when the person they'd been looking for finally reappeared.

"Sorry that took so long, but you simply *must* try these cup-cakes."

Sophie Temporale, aka "the Time Being," laid down a plate with an assortment of vanilla-, chocolate-, and pink-frosted cup-cakes that looked out of this World and then fell into a wicker recliner. Even though Becker estimated her age at seventysome-thing (and knew that she was at least a million years older) she had a brightness in her eyes and a lightness in her step that reminded him more of the students in his father's classes than his grandma Ethel.

As Becker helped himself to a chocolate on chocolate, his anxiety was eased by the sight of a brass gear painted on the face of the serving dish. When they had first approached the woman on the stoop, she had responded to the somewhat awkward query, "Um, excuse me, ma'am, but do you happen to be the Time Being by any chance?" with a bizarrely casual, "Of course I am," then apologized for being late to their meeting. The Fixer obviously hadn't scheduled any such meeting, but she promised to fill them in on all the details upstairs.

"It's quite a good cupcake, Madame Temporale," admitted

-----

25. Restless leg syndrome, aka "the Shaky Jakes."

Sully, who had eaten the bottom first and saved the frosting for last. "And even more of an honor to meet you."

"Oh, please call me Sophie, and yes, I'm totally addicted to them." She polished off the one with the red-hot candies on the top, then turned to Becker. "What about you, young man?"

"Excuse me?"

"How do you like your cupcake?"

Despite his years of Training (and respect for his elders), Becker couldn't take it anymore.

"Enough about the cupcakes!"

There was a long, painful silence and Sully just shrugged as if to say, "I don't know this kid. He's just some runaway who's been following me around all day!" But the Time Being herself was completely unfazed, and smiled at the Fixer sympathetically.

"Sorry, ma'am. I didn't mean to be rude, but I just don't have the time for small talk right now."

"Of course you don't." The Time Being poured some hot tea into a cup and gingerly took a sip. "You need me to come back to The Seems with you and repair that Split Second."

A flood of relief poured over the Fixer.

"Thank the Plan I found you," said Becker, already looking for a spot in the wall to insert his Skeleton Key and open a pathway back to where Tony the Plumber had hopefully collected the missing half of the Split Second. "With any L.U.C.K., we can put this Mission to bed and be at Flip's in time for the Procrastinators'[26] second set."

---

26. A classic-rock cover band made up of guys from the Department of Time who occasionally play The Flip Side, Slumber Party, and high-end weddings and bar mitzvahs.

The Time Being nodded, got up from the table, and opened a window to let in a warm breeze. As the sounds of the city gently rushed in, she closed her eyes, as if listening to the same soundtrack of life that Sully had fallen in love with.

"I haven't been to The Seems in over fifty years. And having lived in this apartment for the last thirty, my feelings about The World are even stronger now than when I was first helping to bring it to fruition."

"I understand what you mean," said Sully, covertly swiping a second cupcake. "Just being here the last hour or so has totally reinspired my work in History."

The Time Being did not respond or even open her eyes, which started to worry the young Fixer.

"Anything you need, ma'am—I mean, Sophie—Tools, a place to stay, whatever, it's yours. And believe me, if you're concerned about your anonymity or the paparazzi, no one even has to know you were there . . ."

But his appeals, however earnest, seemed to fall on deaf ears. And Becker was not exactly thrilled by the look on her face.

"I love The World as much as anyone ever has, young man. After all, I was one of the people who helped make it in the first place. But as far as the Split Second is concerned?"

The Time Being finally opened her eyes, and when she looked the Fixer right in his, he knew what she was going to say long before she said it.

"I'm afraid I can't help you."

Tavanbogd Massif, Altai Mountain Range, Mongolia

Half a World away, a solitary climber dropped his pick-ax and collapsed upon an icy crag. Snow whipped mercilessly across the face of the mountain, and though he was draped from head to toe in the soft white fur of the Siberian Ibex, at this altitude it did little to protect him from the thin air or cold.

Why the only Door in the whole of Mongolia was placed in such an inaccessible location was a mystery, but it was not the Initiate's place to question the Powers That Be. Nor did he bemoan the absence of a Skeleton Key, for that invention had been reserved for Fixers alone. His lone concern was the terrible ache that racked his every muscle—symptoms of a 7th Sense grown stronger than his ability to control it—and the awful premonition it generated in his mind. The vision of a thirteen-year-old boy, his friend and colleague, reduced to a pile of dust.

This could not be allowed to happen—the Initiate would not let it—but the fury of the blizzard threatened to break his very spirit. It was only the favorite mantra of his master—the incomparable Li Po—that finally brought him back to his feet.

"No matter how the wind howls . . . the mountain will not bow!"

With a final swing of his ax, the Initiate dug deep into the ice and pulled himself up toward the summit.

Tidal Wave

274 West 12th Street, New York, New York

On the top of 274 West 12th was a rooftop deck accessible only to the lucky resident of Apartment #5. Sophie had taken full advantage of this perk and proceeded to furnish the roof as if it were a greenhouse. Ferns, sunflowers, and delphinium sprung up like the skyscrapers in every direction, and Becker was sure he'd noticed some Seemsadendrums crawling up the legs of the cedar patio furniture. But the greenness of her thumb was the last thing on the Fixer's mind . . .

"Five more strikes of the Essence just hit The World," pleaded Becker, slamming his Blinker on the table amid a collection of old and empty flower pots. "And it's a miracle that no one got killed!"

"I'm sorry to hear that." The Time Being wore gardening gloves and was in the process of pruning a bush. "It's always disconcerting when innocent people are put in harm's way."

"Disconcerting?" The breaking news on Becker's screen angered him even more. "A three-year-old in Patagonia almost got smoked!"

"Time is relative. A fly lives an entire lifetime in one day."

Following Sophie's refusal to assist on the Mission, Becker had tried every trick in the book to convince her otherwise. He'd reasoned with her, appealed to her love for The World, shouted at the top of his lungs, cried, and even threatened to reveal her present location to a crew of documentary filmmakers in The Seems who had been fruitlessly hunting her for years. But with each stratagem he employed, the Time Being only grinned and replied, "Do what you must." Finally, she had invited her guests to join her on the roof, because it was time for her to tend to her garden.

"I must admit, Madame Time Being—I mean, Sophie—" Daniel J. Sullivan suddenly popped from behind a thick patch of ivy. "Your taste in horticulture is outstanding!"

"Thank you, Daniel." She surveyed his unique attire. "I should say the same about your choice of wardrobe."

"Sully!" shouted Becker, furious. "Work with me here."

The Keeper looked down at his shoes, ashamed of what a space cadet he'd become. "I am somewhat perplexed by your decision to absolve yourself of all responsibility in this matter, though. With all due respect, of course."

"You said it yourself, Daniel—the Plan will provide."

"But this wasn't part of the Plan!" Becker had tried this tack several times already, to no avail. "The Time Bomb was planted by The Tide."

"The Tide *is* part of the Plan, Becker. That's what I'm trying to tell you." Not at all impatient or perturbed, the Time Being took off her gardening gloves. "Daniel, can you do me a favor?"

"Of course."

"On my night table downstairs is a pile of books. One in particular is called *The Grand Scheme of Things*. Can you bring it up here?"

"*The Grand Scheme of Things*?" Sully immediately yelped. "You have a copy of *The Grand Scheme of Things*?"

"It's the original." Sophie wiped the sweat from her forehead and took a sip from her tea. "The rest are just mimeographs."

Sully almost tripped over himself in a rush to get to the door, and Becker could hear him pounding down the spiral stairs. The Fixer was so filled with frustration and disappointment that he was afraid he would burst into tears again. All of his eggs had been placed in this one flimsy basket, and not only had they cracked, but the basket itself was going up in flames.

"Sit down, Becker." Sophie's calmness in the face of what was going on infuriated the thirteen-year-old, and he refused to take her suggestion. "There's a lot you don't understand."

She motioned for him to sit once more, and since there was nothing to be gained by being obstinate (not yet, at least), the Fixer finally plopped down in a wrought-iron chair. But he couldn't even bring himself to look at the woman who meandered through her garden as if this were an ordinary afternoon.

"Before The World was even a thought, there were just those of us who lived in The Seems. And don't get me wrong, it wasn't a bad life." As she spoke, Sophie picked a few mulberries from one of her trees. "In fact, it was pretty much paradise. Happiness could be harvested, Love was in the air, and Time could easily be avoided."

She popped a few of the berries into her mouth for emphasis.

"But when everything is provided for you—and you know it will last forever—even paradise grows stale."

Becker wasn't asking for paradise. He was happy enough just to keep The World the way it was. But listening was the only strategy he hadn't tried so far.

"It was that complacency, that . . . boredom . . . that drove us to seek out something we could believe in beyond our own pleasures and gratification." Sophie smiled at the memory of those heady days. "When the idea for The World was hatched, we felt alive again. And when we tried to devise a Plan by which that World would operate, all we cared about was how to make things There better than they were Here."[27]

The Time Being waved her hand in the direction of the seething metropolis below.

"This place was never meant to be perfect—and we did everything we could to ensure it stayed that way. Created Rules and restrictions in every department, built randomness into Nature, Weather, the very Fabric of Reality. Not because we wanted the inhabitants of The World to suffer, but because we wanted them to savor the experience of life in a way that we in The Seems never had."

Becker couldn't help but think that he could definitely

---

27. In Olde Seemsian terminology, "Here" refers to The Seems while "There" refers to The World. See also Appendix B, in *The Glitch in Sleep*.

savor the experience of life without sleet, the flu, and a possible World War III, but again he bit his tongue. Sophie seemed to know what he was thinking anyway.

"Were there certain things that went into the Plan that I didn't a hundred percent agree with? Of course." The Time Being turned to look at Becker with the wisdom of who knows how many years etched into the lines of her face. "But on the day of the ribbon-cutting ceremony for The World, we the Designers swore an oath that we would never interfere with its unfolding. And no matter how many times someone walked through my door and told me this or that just *had* to be changed or everything would be ruined, I've never broken it."

The wheels in Becker's mind were spinning. If this had been a philosophical argument, he would have felt more comfortable—after all, he had gotten an F (Fixer) in Planology 201 at the IFR and even scored a tie with Lucas Pamelius at the tryouts for the Lafayette School debate team. But it was hard to refute a personal vow.

"If everything's part of the Plan"—his only choice was to pull a back door trap—"then breaking your vow just this one time to help me on this Mission would also be part of the Plan, wouldn't it?"

"You're funny." The Time Being smiled with real affection. "Jayson[28] used to try that same argument on me."

"Did it work?"

"Nope. He could never get his head around the idea that bad things happen to good people—he called it a design flaw—but

---

28. Jayson Handry, Founder of the Fixers.

then again, Jayson wanted to Fix everything, even if it wasn't broken."

"That's because Jayson knew that The World isn't a laboratory experiment!" Becker pointed to the streets below. "It's a place with real people who have real hopes and dreams and lives, all of which are about to end!"

"That's the beauty of Time, is it not? The less you have of it, the more you begin to appreciate The World around you." Sophie held up her hands, both looking at and showing off the veins and wrinkles. "For the first time, I'm staring at the possibility of my own death, and never before has life tasted so sweet."

The Time Being smiled, put her gloves back on, and started pulling the dead leaves off some of her larger sunflowers.

"Please, Sophie. I'm not asking you to Fix the Split Second." Becker's voice again quivered with emotion. "I'm just asking you to tell me how to do it."

But if there had been a moment when the Time Being had been considering Becker's pleas, it had clearly passed, for she simply gripped the dying head of another sunflower and said, "Can you please hand me that spritzer? Mother Nature would never forgive me if she knew I was treating her children this way . . ."

Kids who grow up in the Drane household are trained from an early age that a certain list of curse words are unacceptable for use in public (if at all), and Becker was tempted to unleash all of them in an effort to describe what the owner of said spritzer could do with it. But before his rage could spill over . . .

"Chill out, Draniac," a voice rang out from somewhere behind them. "You're wasting your breath."

Becker and the Time Being turned to see Daniel J. Sullivan standing in the crooked entrance to the roof deck, holding a glass case with an old book inside. But the voice that had come from Sully's direction was not that of the Keeper of the Records.

"What's wrong, Daniel?" asked Sophie, shielding her eyes from the slowly setting sun. But Sully only jerked forward—like he'd been pushed in the back—nearly dropping the precious case as he stumbled across the wooden deck.

"Sorry, Becker. They caught me by surprise."

Stepping through the doorway behind him was a tall, bearded young man, wearing the same shades and tattered suede jacket that Becker Drane had admired for its casual cool on the day the two had first met.

"Thibadeau," whispered the Fixer, and his heart began to pound. Not out of the anger he'd felt ever since his old friend had joined The Tide. And not out of frustration that his Mission to Fix the Time Bomb had officially jumped the rails. In the simplest of terms, what was happening to his body was a normal physical reaction to the human emotion known as fear . . .

Because Thibadeau Freck was not alone.

Meanwhile, The Seems

When Shan Mei-Lin watched The Tide drag Mr. Chiappa and most of their equipment back through the portal they'd opened into Meanwhile, she'd felt a strange combination of powerlessness and relief. Powerlessness at the fact she'd been unable to help her Fixer, and relief that she'd gone unnoticed hiding on the outer reaches of their secret HQ. But then the Briefer realized that, once again, she was doomed to solitary confinement in this awful, lonely place.

Fortunately, the Mission at hand did not allow her the luxury of panic.

"Remember, Shan," she whispered aloud to make sure it was she who was speaking. "The World is counting on you!"

The Briefer approached the ten-foot-square box of Time-resistant glass that was Meanwhile's only source of light. Mr. Chiappa's Hour Glasses revealed that the Split Second was still reflecting between the walls of the Containment Field, leaving more and more droplets of yellow goo behind every time it bounced off the floor. But there was something else she saw inside that concerned her even more.

Not only had the Field become soggy and soaked with the Essence of Time, but the dirt itself seemed to be tinged with a luminescent blue. Upon closer inspection, Shan could see that it wasn't fertilizer or anything else on the ground, but small pinholes of light shining up from beneath it. And because she had spent the last several years of her life traveling back and forth through a place that possessed the exact same shading and hue, the color of the glow was familiar . . .

"The In-Between." Shan's heart sank. "Plan help me."

Somehow, the Essence of Time had dissolved a hole through Meanwhile and into the In-Between, and the Briefer could only surmise how much had already found its way to The World. What she did know beyond a shadow of a doubt was that it had to be stopped, and there was no one else here who could do the job.

Shan reached into her Briefcase for the empty half of the

Split Second, as if somehow it would tell her how to reunite it with its twin, but all the shell did was sit silently in the palm of her hand. If she entered the Containment Field, her Sleeve could protect her from the Essence for a few minutes, but prolonged exposure would turn her into a pile of dust—much like those poor souls swept off the platform in Time Square.

The Briefer wanted to save The World, she really did—but at the age of only nineteen there was still so much in life she wanted to experience. She had never seen America. Never walked the Great Wall of her own country. And never fallen in love. But none of those things would happen if she made the ultimate sacrifice that every Briefer (and Fixer) wondered if he or she were capable of making.

"You can do this, Shan. Death is just a part of life."

If those words were designed to spur her into action, they failed to accomplish their goal. Her feet felt leaden and she couldn't stop thinking about the unanswered letters her family sent to her over the years. Surely there was another way or more time . . .

"Oh no. No, no, no, no, no."

In the middle of the Containment Field, one of the pinholes of blue light had enlarged to become a slightly bigger dot. Worse yet, more like it were popping up all across the dirt. Soon puddles would form, creating openings through which the bouncing sphere would inevitably escape. So whether it was going to happen now or in a half hour from now, the choice was unavoidable: Fix the Split Second, or stand idly by and watch it destroy The World.

"May the spirits of the ancients protect me."

Shan rolled up her Sleeve and began to climb inside.

"Had enough, Draniac?" Thibadeau Freck stood above the bruised and bloodied Fixer, fists curled. "Don't make me embarrass you in front of everyone."

Becker took a deep and painful breath, lifted himself off the ground, and spit a broken tooth directly at his former friend. "It's you who's gonna get embarrassed."

A chorus of "doh's" and laughter shot up among the crowd gathered around the two combatants. Just moments earlier, six members of The Tide had washed up on this roof deck, and Becker's first instinct had been to pull out his Sticks & Stones™ and plant himself between the insurgents and the Time Being. Thibadeau had waved off his henchman, though, and challenged Becker to take him on *mano a mano*.

"Please, gentlemen," the Time Being calmly intervened. "I'm sure we can find a better way to resolve our differences."

The owner of this roof deck was sitting on a bench, guarded by two Tide members—a Flavor Miner and an unemployed Wordsmith whom Becker recognized as the same who tried to rough him up that night at The Slumber Party, when he discovered Thibadeau had joined The Tide.

"I got a better way!" cackled the burly Miner. He peeled back the top of his bodysuit to reveal arms rippling with muscles, along with the flavor-stained smock of his profession. "Let's toss him over the side with Thing One and Thing Two!"

Thing One and Thing Two was a reference to a pair of

bound and gagged employees of The Seems: the Keeper of the Records—who was sporting a freshly blackened eye—and much to Fixer #37's amazement, the unconscious Lucien Chiappa. But Becker didn't have time to wonder how and why his colleague was still alive—he was too concerned with keeping himself in the same state.

"Half of the Duty Roster is on its way to New York right now." Becker wiped the sweat and a piece of his lip from the corner of his mouth. "So I suggest you guys blow this taco stand before I break out my A game."

"You are a very bad liar, Draniac." Thibadeau popped Becker right in the noggin, causing him to see stars yet again. "No one is coming to New York to save you, because all of your transmissions have been jammed. And don't forget that I kicked your derriere so many times in Fight or Flight it was beginning to hurt my foot."

There was a grain of truth to what Thibadeau was saying. "Fight or Flight" was required coursework at the IFR, and the two had sparred countless times under the auspices of Fixer Blaque. But in all their matches in the rubber-walled arena, Becker had never been able to overcome Thib.

"Talk is cheap," the Fixer threatened. "I've learned a lot since those days."

"As have I."

Thibadeau swung with a kick, but this time his former classmate tumbled, tucked, rolled, and launched himself at the Frenchman, catching him square in the jaw with an elbow and staggering him back toward the ledge of the roof. This sent The Tide into a second round of guffaws.

"Need some help, boss?" asked the Flavor Miner, cracking his scarred knuckles.

"No, *merci*." Thib spat his own glob of blood from his lip, then raised his fists in front of his face. "It's time for the *coup de grâce*."

Like a cat, Thibadeau feinted his way behind the Fixer, then applied a pythonlike choke hold. For a second, quiet reigned over the rooftop, interrupted only by the combatants' labored breathing and the occasional honk of a taxicab below. Becker felt Thib's hot breath against his ear, and he was certain it was to deliver one last taunt. But instead . . .

"Stop fighting, Draniac," Thibadeau whispered. "I'm trying to protect you."

"Thanks . . . for . . . nothing . . ."

"Believe me, my people will kill you if you get in their way. Your only chance to stay alive is say uncle, and say it now."

Becker stopped struggling and wrenched his neck around to look directly into his old friend's face. Behind the beard, behind the necklace of the cresting wave, behind even the betrayal of planting the Time Bomb, the Fixer saw genuine concern. And he knew that in some sick and twisted way, Thib really was trying to protect him.

"Uncle."

Lucien Chiappa's eyes slowly opened and surveyed the bizarre scene that unfolded before him. He knew he'd been administered some kind of sedative before his trip out of Meanwhile—the fruity taste on his lips told him it was probably Knockout

Punch—but the last place in the world he expected to be when he regained consciousness was on a rooftop in Manhattan.

"Please be patient, mademoiselle," said a bearded young Frenchman who looked like he'd just been in a fist fight. "We'll be ready in a matter of moments."

"No hurry." An elegant-looking woman with long gray hair crossed her legs and sat back against the slats of a bench. "I have all the Time in The World."

Chiappa recognized the Frenchman as Thibadeau Freck, but the sight of the older woman was a stunner. As an expert on Time, Chiappa had voraciously studied the life and work of Sophie Temporale, and though he'd always dreamed of meeting her (he even spent a year casually searching for her whereabouts), he was unprepared for the emotions that swelled within him at the very sight of the Time Being.

"What are they doing?" Sophie was watching a wiry kid in glasses and a raven-haired young woman run cords to and from a square metallic plate on the ground.

"We're setting up a Calling Card," answered Thibadeau. "There's someone who wishes to have a word with you."

"Why doesn't this someone just come see me in person?"

"He is a very private man—so much so that his identity is hidden even from us. And I might also add that you are not exactly the easiest person to find."

The Time Being glanced to her left, where Becker Drane and a guy who looked like he'd stuck his finger in an electric socket were bound and gagged. "I had no idea I was so popular."

"I'm sure Fixer Drane informed you of what happened in the Department of Time today?"

"He did."

"Despite what he may have told you, our intention was never to harm The World—or anyone else, for that matter—we simply needed a way to draw you out of hiding."

Once again Mr. Chiappa's blood simmered that The Tide would play dice with The World just to achieve its political ends, but it served no purpose to reveal that he'd regained consciousness. So he remained motionless as Freck continued.

"We were worried when you did not appear after the initial blast, but thanks to my old friend's ingenuity, our plan came together nonetheless."

Chiappa watched in silence as the Time Being shook her head, then sadly looked off toward the setting sun. "There have always been differences in The Seems about how best to manage The World. But it shouldn't have come to this."

Thibadeau was slow to answer, but the Wordsmith was more than ready to sell the party line. "The Powers That Be have refused to listen to reason and are unwilling to accept any adjustments to the Plan. Someone had to take matters into their own hands."

"Arg . . . napn . . . eklc . . ." Fixer Drane was trying to speak, and after furiously shaking his head back and forth enough times he was finally able to wriggle free of the gag. "All just to find her? Was it also your plan to age The World into dust?"

Smiles and chuckles shot between the Tide members.

"Don't worry, Draniac," assured Thibadeau. "The Split Second is safely contained."

"Then how do you explain why the Essence of Time hit Alaska not twenty minutes ago? Or the Isle of Madagascar?"

This seemed to catch Thibadeau utterly by surprise, and not in a good way.

"You lie."

"Then why are you shivering?" Becker knew that, just like himself, Thibadeau's 7th Sense was firing on all cylinders. They were both trained in the art, and both would be feeling the impending doom of the Split Second in a major way. "Or why don't you take a look at my Blinker and see for yourself."

Thibadeau reached down and pulled the communications device off Becker's belt. Even though he hadn't used one in over a year, it only took him a minute to toggle to Missions in Progress and confirm what the Fixer had said.

"Nice job saving The World, bro." Becker's smile was even more caustic with a missing incisor. "With friends like you, who needs en—"

"Button it up!" shouted the Flavor Miner, who then smacked Becker across the face with the back of an open hand. Thibadeau nodded toward the edge of the roof, and his henchman roughly dragged the boy away, chair and all.

It took all of Mr. Chiappa's composure not to come to the aid of his fellow Fixer, but he had a plan of his own, and it was already in motion. Besides, Thibadeau Freck seemed shaken by the news he'd just received.

"Don't be unnerved, *mon cher*." The black-haired girl who had thus far let her beauty do the talking rose and joined the Frenchman. "Even if there's been some collateral damage, no revolution has ever succeeded without a cost."

"This is too expensive, Lena."

"If it makes you feel better," the girl stroked the back of

Thibadeau's hair, "let's send Ben back to check on the Containment Field."

The one Tide member who had remained in the increasing shadows stepped into the light. Like the others, he wore a black bodysuit and wave pendant, but he had yet to remove his mask. He was different in one other respect as well . . . Big Ben was literally eight feet tall.

"It's no problem, sir." The softness of the giant's voice belied his gargantuan size. "Besides, I always prefer to be close to the Essence."

Again, Lena ran her hand through Thibadeau's wavy brown hair. "Satisfied?"

"When I know the Split Second is safe." Thibadeau turned back to his humungous comrade. *"Allez!"*

Big Ben saluted, then pulled a modified Skeleton Key from a cord around his neck. He inserted it into a section of roof, and a blue circle drew itself across the bricks and mortar. Seconds later, the masked monstrosity was gone.

Beeep! Beeep!

"We got a signal, boss."

Everyone turned to see the wiry kid with glasses leaning over the Calling Card. From his hoop earring and seafaring tattoos, Chiappa thought he might be a Drifter. "Just give me a second to fix the vertical hold."

The kid made a slight adjustment to a dial, and with a surge of electricity the image of a figure they now knew to be a man materialized onto the roof. It was almost as if he was actually standing there among them, except for the fact that the face and body were masked by a digital fuzz. He turned directly toward the Time Being and made a slight but courteous bow.

"Allow me to introduce myself, Ms. Temporale . . ." The speaker's voice was as garbled and broken up as the image. "My name is Triton."

All Gave Some

From his spot by the edge of the roof deck, Becker Drane craned his head to hear the words of the leader of The Tide, but the distance and the street noise made it nearly impossible. It didn't help that the Flavor Miner who'd been assigned to guard him kept whispering sweet nothings in his ear.

"It must really burn you up, eh, Fixer boy?" The Miner stank of sweat and stale seasoning. "That everything you've done today was all part of *our* plan."

"Just don't let me get to my Toolkit, Butter Pecan." Becker motioned to his replacement Toolmaster 3001™, which had been discarded by some bags of birdseed. "I got a can of butt-whuppin' in there with your name written all over it."

"Big words for a little man."

"Little words for a big man."

Becker knew that though the Miner was impressive in size, he was nowhere near as well trained as Thibadeau Freck, and if the Fixer could goad him into action, there might be a chance to escape.

"Hey, I got an idea. Why don't you take these ropes off and we'll settle this out back like real men."

Just as he hoped, the Neanderthal smirked and started untying Becker's hands.

"I got a better idea," the leader of the cell stepped in between the two. "Go take a breather and watch the old man."

A long moment of eye contact between Thibadeau and the Flavor Miner stretched like a taut rope, but eventually the larger man backed down.

"I see you haven't lost your touch," the Frenchman chided Becker, alone with him for the first time since The Tide's arrival. "Fixer Blaque always said you had to get into the head of your enemy to fully understand him."

"At least one of us was paying attention." Becker was bummed, for though the ropes were loosened, he still couldn't pull his hands free.

"Maybe I was paying attention too much."

Thibadeau gave his prisoner a playful elbow and plopped down beside him. For a second, Becker was reminded of when the two Candidates were almost like brothers, and conversations like this revolved around getting their Badges or how to meet girls. But that memory was fleeting, and the truth was more like what Thibadeau had predicted when they'd parted ways at The Slumber Party. "Next time we see each other . . . it won't be the same," he had said. And it wasn't.

"I just want you to know . . . Big Ben is the best Minuteman in Time. The Split Second is in good hands."

"Whatever helps you sleep at night." Becker turned away

and stared at the building across the street, where some random New Yorker was unpacking groceries, unaware.

"Believe me, Draniac. I had no idea it would come to this." Thib seemed genuinely tormented by what had happened. "I was given assurances that no one would be hurt. In The World *or* The Seems."

"Then you're living in a fantasy World."

"No, I'm living in the real World—where things are a little more complicated than black and white."

Thibadeau shook his head, almost like there was something he wished he could tell Becker, but wasn't able to.

"I don't understand you." Becker's voice softened, though the muscles in his stomach were twisted in knots. "How can you try to be friends with me after everything that happened?"

"Because I *am* your friend."

"Do me a favor . . ." The Fixer shook his head in disbelief. "Put the gag back in."

Thibadeau angrily obliged, then headed back to where Triton was deep in conversation with the Time Being. But he stopped halfway.

"By the way . . . was it good to see Amy again?"

Becker felt his face flush with both embarrassment and rage. How could he know about that Frozen Moment, unless . . .

But Thibadeau had already turned away.

Alton Forest, Caledon, Ontario

The five charter members of Les Resistance tromped back down the trail to the bike rack that lay at the mouth of Alton

227

Forest. The day had been eventful not only because of the pre-planned goal of completing principal construction on the fort, but due to what had already come to be known as "the bizarre incident of the falling tree."

"I strongly believe the trunk was infested with termites and ready to go at any moment," announced Vikram, untethering his bicycle from its lock. "It's the only logical conclusion."

"I think it's magic," declared Rachel, attaching a series of clips and pins to her sleeves and skirt to avoid them being tangled up in the chain of the bike. "Things happen every day that can't be explained by modern science."

Whatever had happened, Jennifer knew the members of Les Resistance were likely to argue about it all night. That was part of resisting, she supposed, and it never got in the way of their fun. All around them, the crickets had begun to chirp and the magic hour of twilight bathed the forest in purple and blue.

"You guys hit the road . . ." JK pretended to be unlocking her bike as well. "I'm goin' the other way, 'cause I'm having dinner at my uncle's tonight."

Everybody put their hands in the center of a circle and on the count of three, they shouted the same cheer that adjourned any meeting of the secret order they'd grown to know and love.

"Les Resistance is never futile!"

After a few high-fives and hugs, Jennifer watched as the gaggle of misfits peddled into the night.

"Hey, Moreau. Do you think it's part of the plan if I kick you off your bike?" she heard the always-cutting Rob laugh and shout at his sister.

"Only if it's part of the plan if I kick you in the shin!"

Claudia chided back, and Jennifer cracked up. But as soon they had faded into the dusk, she left her lock squarely around her Schwinn and dialed her dad's cell phone. It rang twice before he answered.

"Jenny?"

"That's my name, don't wear it out."

"Is construction done for the day?"

"Yep. We managed to install the second-floor deck *and* the master bedroom!"

"Does this mean you're getting your own show on HGTV?"

"Very funny." Jennifer could hear voices in the background and knew that meant her father's party was still going on. "Listen, um, Vikram's mom invited us all over dinner and I was, uh, wondering—"

"I don't know, sweetheart. You've been out since early this morning."

"Pleeease, Dad. Everybody's going."

"On one condition."

"What?"

"Bring me back some of that flan she always makes."

"You mean naan!"

"Some of that too."

She could tell her father was in a good mood and his important day of fresh-squeezed orange juice and big deals must have gone well.

"And be careful. There's a lot of crazies out there."

"I will. Love you, Dad."

"Love you too."

Jennifer hung up the phone, then snuck back into the woods before any of the rangers who were closing up the park could notice. She was happy to be alone and unencumbered because that feeling she'd gotten right before the tree fell was still in the base of her stomach. She had definitely felt this sensation before, like when she was alone in her room late at night or before a thunderstorm. But this time it was speaking to her directly, and she couldn't stop thinking about what it said.

Something was on its way to Alton Forest—something big—and she wasn't going to miss it for the world.

274 West 12ᵗʰ Street, New York, New York

Daniel J. Sullivan, aka the "Keeper of the Records," had been largely forgotten among the proceedings on the rooftop garden of the Time Being. Like Becker Drane, he had been bound and gagged, but in all the fiddle faddle, no one had really stopped to give him the time of day. Sully had listened intently nonetheless, for this had always been his strong suit and because his intellectual curiosity was piqued—especially once the Calling Card lit up and the figure of Triton appeared.

"You don't have to answer me now," implored the head of the Seemsian underground. "I'm just asking you to consider the offer."

Triton and the Time Being had been communicating for over ten minutes and Sully had processed every word of their exchange. "The offer," as it were, was Triton's assertion that a veritable who's who of important figures in The Seems had already signed on to be part of the committee that would help The Tide fashion a new World. The only caveat was that they wouldn't fully commit unless the highly respected Sophie Temporale threw her hat into the ring as well.

"With you on board, our cause would gain real credibility amongst the Seemsian populace." The charismatic speaker was far less sinister in person than Sully had imagined. "And it would also be a chance to implement your proposals from the original World Project that were so thoughtlessly rejected at the time."

Sully's eyes fell to the ground, where a book known as *The Grand Scheme of Things* lay in the shattered glass case at his feet. Inside its plain white cover was the original design document for The World. The Keeper had been seeking a copy for most of his adult life, because he believed his theory of what was behind the Plan could be proved by what was on those pages. But if Sophie agreed to Triton's proposal, the question—and his long-suffering project—would suddenly be moot.

"Any changes to Time would be subject to your approval, of course." Triton's garbled image flickered for a moment before regaining its original strength. "But I was really hoping you would help us follow up on a recent discovery I've made about the Most Amazing Thing of All."

The Most Amazing Thing of All was what many believed to be the answer to an ancient riddle—"If The Seems is building The World, then who's building The Seems?"—and Sully wasn't the only one whose ears perked up.

"And I would still be able to keep my apartment in the city?"

"Of course."

"What about the old World?" asked the Time Being, betraying her interest in the process. "Are you planning to institute the changes gradually, or does it have to be scrapped all at once?"

Everyone close enough to hear watched—riveted—as Triton considered this point.

"Open for discussion."

He abruptly looked to his left, as if someone was coming, not here but from wherever he was broadcasting. When he turned back to the Time Being, his voice had dropped to a whisper.

"If you are interested in this offer, take the last train out to the End of the Line tomorrow evening, where I will be waiting to show you what I found. If not, I thank you for this opportunity, and wish you the best of luck in your future endeavors."

As his image began to dissolve into nothingness, Triton offered another elegant bow.

"Until we meet again."

On that note, the Calling Card went dark and the wiry Drifter unplugged the rabbit-ear antenna from the back.

"That's a wrap, boss."

"*Bon.*" Thibadeau snapped his fingers. "Then we too must hit the road."

Like a well-oiled machine, the remaining members of the cell collected their equipment, and Sully actually allowed himself to think he might survive this fiasco. This, he feared, was a terrible mistake, for something told him that the very thought in his head was already sending a signal to a certain firehouse in the fictional town of "Jinxville," where alarms were sounding and a team of pointy-hatted, curly-toed-boot-wearing Gnomes were gathering around their high-tech conference table to gleefully orchestrate an unpleasant Chain of Ev—

"Aren't we forgetting something?" The Wordsmith stopped at the entrance to the staircase and pointed to everyone on the roof who was not a Time Being or a member of The Tide. "These guys know who we are."

"Smithy's right." A malicious grin slowly spread across the Flavor Miner's face, and he focused on Becker Drane. "It's time to do a little roof cleaning."

"What's the point?" Thibadeau shrugged. "Our identities have already been compromised."

"Yours, maybe." The Drifter put the Calling Card back in its case. "But the rest of us weren't stupid enough to blow our covers."

"You don't think Central Command checked the Time cards?" Thibadeau shot back. "Or scoured that security cam footage for every last detail?" The look on the faces of his men said they hadn't considered these unpleasant possibilities. "Right now, a Fixer or a Briefer is rifling through your offices and dresser drawers, your friends and family members are being interrogated, and your careers in The Seems are as good as over."

"Unless we win," interjected Lena from beneath the cover of a small banyan tree.

"*Oui*, unless we win." Thibadeau turned to the woman whom Sully assumed was his girlfriend. "But I am not a murderer."

"Which is why this is not your decision to make." Lena emerged from the shadows and reached for the Frenchman, but he took a reflexive step backward.

"Madame Temporale," Thib was imploring the Time Being with his eyes as much as his voice. "Surely you cannot let this happen in your own home?"

Sophie's face remained impassive, however.

"I'm curious to see how an organization that seeks to make a new World handles such a situation," she said, taking a seat and crossing her legs. "Decisions like this will be an everyday occurrence should you become the Powers That Be."

Sully kind of wished she hadn't said that, because Lena's expression grew even colder, and she turned to the Flavor Miner. "Do it."

"My pleasure."

Faced with the prospect of his untimely end, the Keeper of the Records took some comfort in the fact that he would probably be the last of the three captives to be thrown from the roof. That would give him perhaps thirty seconds to dive to the ground, smash what was left of the glass case with his forehead, then use his chin to open *The Grand Scheme of Things* and find out if the foreword said what it was rumored to say. But as the Flavor Miner patiently donned a pair of black gloves, Sully was distracted by something over by the staircase.

It was the silhouette of a man, crouching on the steps that led to Sophie's apartment. The fallen darkness kept most of his face shrouded, but Sully could just make out an index finger being raised to a pair of bearded lips. Whoever he was, it felt to the Keeper like he was being invited into a really good game of hide-and-seek, as long as he kept his mouth shut.

"Then you leave me no choice." Thibadeau Freck stepped in between the Miner and the thirteen-year-old Fixer. "I can't let you do this."

"Suit yourself." The Miner motioned for the others to join him. "I always figured you for gutless."

The Wordsmith grabbed one of Sophie's shovels, the Drifter an awl, and they joined their mate in squaring off against the Frenchman. This removed them from the path of the moonlight, which now fell squarely on the figure who was skulking in the stairwell. Sully didn't recognize his face at all, but there was something about the man's strange choice of apparel that rang a distant bell. Though most of his years as a Case Worker were lost to his memory, the Keeper was pretty sure he'd seen the same aviator's helmet and brown bomber's jacket on a statue outside the Big Building.

"Waitamminit!" Sully blurted out loud, though no one on the roof could really understand what he was ranting about. Not until he shoved away the gag with his tongue and shouted at the top of his lungs, "I know who you are!"

"It can't be," thought Becker Drane, seeing exactly the same sight that caused Daniel J. Sullivan to hop up and down on his chair with glee. But it was.

Fixer #7—whose name had been kept on the Duty Roster for over ten years to both honor his accomplishments and the hope that maybe he was still alive—stepped onto the roof deck with a wry grin upon his face and a dusty old Toolmaster 44™ slung over his shoulder. Becker could tell he was somewhat perturbed that Sully had blown his cover, but then again, the direct approach wasn't working out so bad either.

"You're . . . you're . . ." The Wordsmith's voice cracked on its way past his lips.

"Tom Jackal," said Thibadeau, caught between shock and admiration. "Aren't you supposed to be Lost in Time?"

"Rumors of my demise have been greatly exaggerated." The Welshman's eyes burned so brightly that Becker could see them twinkling from across the roof. "I've just been living in a much better place."

The blood had run from the faces of the Wordsmith and Drifter, and Becker's nemesis, the Flavor Miner, was literally quaking in his boots. Only the woman called Lena seemed to keep her cool.

"You're Tom Jackal? Wow . . . you looked so much taller in your photos."

"It's not the size of the man." Jackal stepped out of a divot on the rooftop, and as it turned out, he *was* just as tall as he looked. "It's the magic in him."

"Would you like me to put in a call to the Museum of Natural History?" Lena laughed a little too loudly. "Because it looks like Chiappa's not the only dinosaur on this roof."

Jackal feigned tipping his hat, as if admiring the jibe, then turned to the Fixer in question.

"You're looking fit, Lucien. Ombretta must be feeding you well."

From behind his ropes and gag, Mr. Chiappa shrugged, as if this were all just another day on the job.

"Rest assured, I'll have you back at her dinner table in a matter of—" Jackal stopped, and the fun and games abruptly ended. At this point, the unexpected visitor was close enough to see how badly The Tide had roughed up Becker Drane. Only a few hours ago, the kid from New Jersey had been sharing dinner and white lies with his own children, and the father in Tom Jackal was deeply unamused. "Which one of you did that to the boy?"

The Miner and Wordsmith backed away from Thibadeau so fast, you would have thought he was on fire.

"I beat him fair and square," posited the Frenchman, but his voice sounded defeated. "Ask him yourself."

"I got a better idea, friend." Jackal dropped his Toolkit and helmet to the floor and began to remove his illustrious coat. "How 'bout you and me have ourselves a little fair fight too?"

Strangely enough, as Jackal stretched his neck and loosened his shoulders, Thibadeau didn't even bother to enroll the assistance of his fellow Tide members. Whatever bond they once shared had clearly been poisoned by the night's proceedings.

"Is this really necessary, monsieur?"

"No." Jackal pulled off a thick roll-neck sweater to reveal the white tank top beneath. "But it might be fun."

Thibadeau dropped his head, then fell into the same kiba dachi stance that had confounded Becker Drane since their days in Training. "Then *combattons*!"

His opponent raised his fists, as if he'd been in a few brawls on the mean streets of Cardiff. "After you."

In the movies and on television, when one sees a battle reach its climax, it often appears as a ballet of martial arts; perfectly executed leaps and flying fists of fury. But in the real world, fighting is an ugly, awkward thing. And it was an ugly, awkward thing that Tom Jackal did to Thibadeau Freck, as he pounded the Frenchman into submission.

"As for the rest of you . . ." Jackal cracked his bruised knuckles, then turned to the quickly receding Tide. "Why don't you save me the trouble and turn yourselves in?"

The three remaining male members of the cell actually looked as if they were considering the offer, but Lena would hear none of it.

"I don't know about you, but I have no desire to spend the rest of my life in Seemsberia!" She pulled a fearsome set of Chop Sticks from their hiding place in one of her boots. "We are four against one!"

"Correction." Mr. Chiappa rose from the chair, the ropes that once bound him sliding from his body like wet spaghetti. "Four against two!"

As The Tide stood slack-jawed at the Fixer's Houdini-like escape, Jackal's laughter boomed across the rooftops. "Don't you know anything? If you're gonna tie up a Fixer, better make sure he doesn't have any Elbow Grease™ up his sleeve!"

Chiappa wiped the oily substance from his forearms, then whipped the gag from his mouth. "I could use a Second Wind™, Tomas!"

Jackal tossed his Toolmaster 44 over to his old friend and comrade.

"What's mine is yours."

As the Corsican helped himself, the writing was on the wall, and no one saw it clearer than the Flavor Miner. He had already done a few years in Seemsberia for smuggling Dulce de Leche off Mount Caramel, and as far as he was concerned, if you can't do the time, don't do the crime. But if he was gonna do that time, it wasn't gonna be for kidnapping, or even for aiding and abetting the detonation of a Time Bomb . . .

It would be for tossing that snot-nosed punk off this roof.

"Lookin' for me?"

The Miner wheeled toward the sound of Becker's voice, expecting to see the boy still bound and gagged, but all he saw on the chair was a pile of empty ropes. The Fixer, on the other hand, was crouching by some bags of birdseed, where someone had had the lack of foresight to leave a fully stocked Toolmaster 3001. Due to all the extra Space inside, there were literally dozens of possible weapons that would be perfect for just such an occasion, but #37 had made his selection quite some time ago. He whipped out a fresh Can of Buttwhuppin'™ from its refrigerated pocket, and gently unscrewed the top.

"Told you so."

Even while Fixer Drane was sweeping up the roof with the Flavor Miner, his mind was entirely elsewhere. It was actually in a small cabin in the woods of Greenland, where a beautiful mother and her young children were no doubt clustered about the fire, wondering if their husband and father would ever be coming home. Becker had no idea if those people even existed anymore, given that the owner of that Frozen Moment had left it behind. But whatever it was that caused Tom Jackal to walk away from everything he loved, it had happened just in the nick of time.

"How'd you find us, Tom?" Becker placed the unconscious Miner next to Thibadeau and the others, who were handcuffed and seated in a row. The only female member of the cell had made a slinky exit during the melee—down the fire escape and into the streets of Manhattan—but they had to let her go, because there were bigger fish to fry. "I mean, how'd you even know where we were?"

"You can thank Linus for that." Jackal was of course referring to Sully's cantankerous "roommate," and he quickly recounted the tale of how the craziest trip through the In-Between he'd ever taken had landed him in the disheveled Hall of Records. "By the way, Daniel, I put on a new DVD and cleaned his cage, but you may have some ruffled feathers to smooth over when you get back."

The Keeper raised a hand in the affirmative, but he was too

preoccupied perusing *The Grand Scheme of Things* to care about anything else. Lucien Chiappa, on the other hand, was starting to come to grips that a man whose funeral he had somberly attended had seemingly returned from the grave. The English teacher's eyes welled up with tears and words failed him, so instead he kissed Jackal on both cheeks, per the Corsican tradition.

"It's good to see you too, old friend."

"But . . . how?" was all Chiappa could stammer.

"You can thank that rotten kid." Jackal gave Becker a friendly shove (which almost knocked him off his exhausted feet). "He gave me this whole song and dance about saving The World."

Becker tried to play along with the ribbing, but he couldn't shake the guilty feeling that regardless of how good the cause, it was he who had destroyed a happy, loving family.

"There'll be time to catch up later, kid." Tom could tell that the boy he'd rescued from hypothermia had yet to ask the most pressing of his questions. "Right now, my 7th Sense is shivering me timbers."

Fixer Chiappa concurred. "Briefer Shan and I tracked the Split Second to the Tide's headquarters in Meanwhile." Becker and Jackal were equally taken aback by their fellow Fixer's remark—#37 by the fact that Shan Mei-Lin was still alive, and #7 that Chiappa had lived to tell a tale of Meanwhile. "The only problem is, the Containment Field they're keeping it in is on the verge of falling apart."

"Not to worry, Monsieur Chiappa," said Thibadeau Freck, hands bound behind his back. "I'm sure Big Ben has rectified the situation."

"Wrong," answered the Fixer. "The design itself is fatally flawed."

"How do you know?"

"Because I'm the one who designed it."

Thibadeau's last bit of moxie fell from his eyes—eyes that swiveled upward to Becker Drane. Their relationship was probably shattered beyond repair, and the same could be said for his relationship with fellow Tide members. With nowhere else to turn, the Frenchman turned to himself, and found the decision an easy one.

"There's a modified Skeleton Key around my neck." When Thibadeau leaned to the side, a brown leather cord became exposed. "It will take you straight to Meanwhile."

"Sellout." The defeated Drifter spat in Thibadeau's eye.

As Jackal snapped the Skeleton Key off the cord, Becker pulled out a handkerchief and wiped the spittle off his adversary's face.

"This doesn't change anything."

"I know." Thibadeau looked at Becker one last time. "Just don't let The World be destroyed."

Fixer Drane nodded somberly, then joined his fellows for a meeting of the minds.

"Even if we can get to the Split Second, we still don't know how to Fix it." Becker stared contemptuously at the Time Being, who was attempting to put her garden back in order. "Because *she* doesn't feel like interfering with the unfolding of the Plan."

The owner of the roof deck swept up a few broken flowerpots, upset by neither the day's events nor the tone of Becker's voice. In fact, Sophie seemed as fond of the boy as the moment she'd met him, when they'd shared a cupcake before the madness ensued.

"Didn't I tell you the Plan would provide?" She motioned to Fixer Jackal, as if his coming to the rescue had been part of an intricate Chain of Events she'd been expecting. "And it will continue to do so if you have a little faith."

"Please forgive the lad's temerity." Though Jackal and the Time Being had never met, a moment of respect passed between the living legends. "He's in a New York state of mind."

"The city will do that to you sometimes."

"Never sleeps. Now if you'll just excuse us for a moment . . ."

Jackal tipped his aviator's helmet like a gentleman, then pulled the two Fixers aside.

"Don't sweat it, boys. Whether she helps us or not is beside the point."

"How can you say that?" asked Becker, electrified by the Welshman's confidence, but not even daring to hope. Jackal zippered up his bomber jacket—like he was about to step into the driving snows of Myggebungen—then swung his Toolkit over his shoulder and reached inside.

"Because I got one of these."

12.5 [29]

Some Gave All

Meanwhile, The Seems

"I admire your courage, miss." Big Ben Lum stared in wonder at the young woman inside the Containment Field. "In all the years I've worked in Time, I've never had the privilege of touching raw Essence with my own hands."

"Thank you for the kind words." Briefer Shan blinked away the sweat from her eyes and looked out at the masked figure on the other side of the glass. "But if I could just have a few moments to concentrate . . ."

Shan Mei-Lin was presently standing on a small patch of dirt just large enough to fit her left foot. Her right was positioned against the side of her knee in the yoga pose known as "the tree," for most of the surrounding field was nowhere near

29. Though Superstition, a sub-department of the Department of Everything That Has No Department, is believed to be close to breaking the stranglehold of the number thirteen, usage of the cursed integer is still not recommended.

secure enough to bear her weight. All around her, pinholes of blue light shone up through the floor, the bellow of the In-Between below growing louder with each passing minute.

"My apologies." Big Ben found a stool among the Tide's remaining equipment and sat his ninety-six-inch frame upon it. "Please continue."

For who knows how long, Shan had crouched atop the Containment Field, studying the Split Second through her Hour Glasses. Though it was bouncing off the walls like an invisible superball, Mr. Chiappa's archaic Tool made it appear to move in slow motion, and she soon detected a symmetry to its path. Not only was it reflecting off the same spots again and again, but there appeared to be a space at the center of its pattern that was large enough to fit a person inside. Maybe even two.

Lowering herself through the aperture on the roof was by far the most terrifying experience of the Briefer's life. Her eyes saw a slowly moving projectile through the lenses, but her mind knew the reality of the situation . . . that if any part of her body made contact with that projectile, it would be neatly sliced off. Relying upon a combination of breath control, gymnastics, and Seems Chi, Shan arced her form over, under, and around the Split Second like a contortionist, and against all odds reached the crumbling dirt of the floor in one piece.

"Can you feel it yet?" Ben's hand caressed the glass, as if he was trying to answer his own question. "I'm told the Essence is like a splash of warm water, without any of the wetness . . ."

"That's an apt description." The Briefer flashed back to that terrible moment in Time Square when her hands and hair had been aged into that of an old woman's. "But thankfully, my Sleeve appears to be keeping dry."

"I'm glad to hear it, miss. But you should know . . . sooner or later, your clothing will become saturated. After that, it's just a matter of, well, you know."

"I'll be sure to keep that in mind."

With her life hanging by the slightest of threads, Shan found strange comfort in this conversation. The enormous Minuteman had slipped into Meanwhile only moments after she'd slipped into the field, but instead of trying to sabotage her Mission, he seemed quite enthralled by it.

"As far as I know, the repair of a completely Split Second has never even been attempted." Big Ben crossed his elongated limbs. "May I inquire as to your strategy?"

"The key is to keep this thing from getting into the In-Between. Whoever built this Containment Field clearly had no idea what they were doing."

This comment seemed to hit Ben where it hurt, because he dropped his head in his hands, and something emerged from the other side of his mask that sounded like weeping.

"I know you think this is my fault—*I know you do!* But I swear, I followed his design specifications to a *T*!"

Shan's hand, which had been wriggling toward the flap of her Briefcase, suddenly stopped at her hip. "Whose specifications?"

"I would never have done this if he hadn't promised me it would be safe." Lost in a swirl of emotion, the Minuteman didn't appear to hear her question. "Keeping Time for The World is my only reason to be!"

Ben rose to his feet and slapped the glass in a fit of rage, causing the entire Containment Field to shudder. The Briefer knew that if there was even the slightest deviation to the Split

Second's path, her number was up, so she quickly tried to regain his attention.

"Fortunately, I happen to be in possession of the Second's better half." Shan painstakingly removed the empty silver shell from her Case, and held it tight against her chest. "All I have to do is nab the troublemaker."

"Have you considered a baseball mitt?" asked the Minuteman.

"Yes, but my arm would be torn off." Shan again wriggled a hand inside her Briefcase. "No, I was thinking of using a Catch-All™."

"Yes . . . yes . . . that's brilliant!" Big Ben's desire to make up for the disaster he had helped to create was more than evident. "But what you're suggesting is a two-person job."

"Don't be silly, Ben." Shan's alarm increased as she watched him place two misshapen hands upon the glass ceiling and effortlessly pull himself up. "Without a Sleeve on, you'll be killed before you ever get inside!"

Ben's oversized body was now lying flat across the top of the glass. "I've been working with the Essence ever since I was a child, when my father was a Third Wheel in the Underground Time Zone. It would never hurt me."

"The Essence doesn't care about you, Ben! The Essence just is!"

"That's where you're wrong, miss. And I'm going to show you how wrong you are . . ."

But just as he attempted to lower himself through the membrane, a circle of blue light once again drew itself in the darkness of Meanwhile.

"Thibadeau?" Ben shielded his eyes until the circle was complete. "Is that you?"

"Not exactly," said the voice of a teenaged boy, and Shan felt her heart leap into her throat. Emerging through the Skeleton Key portal were two familiar faces—one from a famous Mission Simulation, and the other she'd last seen at a hospital in a Frozen Moment.

"Fixer Drane!" The Briefer could barely contain her joy. "Thank the Plan!"

"Nice to see you too, Shan." Becker smiled and dropped his Toolkit to the floor. "Sorry it took me so long to find you."

"What you doin' up there, big fella?" The bearded man in the aviator's helmet stepped into the light of the Containment Field and took a gander up at Big Ben.

"It's the only way to make it right," Ben whispered. "The only way."

"He's lost it, sirs." Shan cried. "He's trying to come inside!"

The two Fixers looked at each other, and one took the lead.

"Fixer Jackal and I are here now, Ben, and we've been trained to handle this." Becker could sense the big man's intensity, and tried to keep his voice on an even keel. "So just come on down and let us do our job."

"The kid's right, big guy." Jackal put his foot upon Ben's stool and began to tie his bootlace, as if this were anything but a moment fraught with disaster. "You don't have to do this at all."

With a deep sigh, Big Ben finally reached up and took his mask off, revealing a strangely boyish face for someone so large. His eyes were red, his cheeks streaked with tears . . . and the look in his eyes told both Fixers that it was already too late to stop him.

"Yes, I do."

With a sad smile, Ben reached his right foot through. But Shan was screaming before he ever had the chance to use his left . . .

Time Management, Department of Time, The Seems

Permin Neverlåethe sat alone in his office, numbly staring at the carpet patterns on the floor. All the other desks and cubicles were empty, and the only sound in what was once the hustle and bustle of Time Management was the clicking of a metronome on his mantel. The ancient wind-up device had been a gift from his predecessor, Joan Tissot, who gave it to the new Administrator as a symbol of everything his department should be. Rhythmic. Punctual. And above all, consistent.

Yet here he was, piloting the ship of Time on the day of its sinking. And like that proverbial sea captain, the only satisfaction available was that if it all went down, at least he would go down too. But even that was small comfort, for Permin knew that the destruction of everything he believed in and strived for had not been an accident, like engine failure or an iceberg. Someone had been directly responsible.

Ding!

The Administrator heard the elevator doors outside his office slide open and footsteps gently pad toward him.

"Hello?" he asked, amazed at how weak and pathetic his voice sounded.

"Hello, Permin."

A dead man was standing in his doorway.

"Lu . . . Lucien?" Neverlåethe felt the surge of joy that can only accompany an honest-to-goodness Miracle. "But . . . but . . . how?"

The Administrator jumped from his desk chair and was about to throw his arms around the best friend he had in The World, but—

"Don't, Permin." The exhaustion in his old friend's voice was palpable. But more than that, Fixer Chiappa seemed incredibly sad. "I know everything."

"About what?"

"It was you who helped The Tide steal the Frozen Moments and sneak inside the Gears." Mr. Chiappa sat down on the chair that faced Permin's desk, then swiveled around so he wouldn't have to look the Administrator in the eye. "And it was you who built the Time Bomb."

Neverlåethe's mouth went dry, but he still managed to croak, "But that's . . . that's . . . I've never heard something so crazy!"

"I've been to Meanwhile, Permin. Seen the blueprints and the Time sheets, which could have only come from one place." Though Chiappa didn't raise his voice one iota, Neverlåethe had never heard the Fixer sound so angry. "So please do not dishonor the memory of our friendship by telling me a boldfaced *lie*!"

Tears were already running down the Administrator's face, as at last he could stop running from the shame of his betrayal. "I . . . Lucien, you don't understand. Triton promised we could slow Time down, let people live longer—"

"There'll be time to explain yourself later, when you've

251

resigned your post and turned yourself in to the Powers That Be."

Permin nodded, trying to make Chiappa see that he would do anything to make this right. But the Fixer wasn't finished yet.

"Right now, two Fixers and a Briefer are attempting to repair the Split Second before it destroys The World, and they will probably all lose their lives in the process. If you know of any way—however small—that you can help them on their Mission . . . then now is the time."

"There is no way to help, Lucien." Arguably the most decorated Administrator in all the departments wiped his reddening eyes with a shirtsleeve, then looked again at the metronome above his desk. "Because it can't be done."

Meanwhile, The Seems

"Stay calm, Shan!" shouted Fixer Drane. "Whatever you do, don't move!"

The Briefer stood quivering in place, still in shock from what had just occurred. As soon as Big Ben Lum's massive leg had slipped inside the Containment Field, the boyish giant's entire body had been instantly reduced to ash. His remains had fallen upon Shan's head and accumulated in the fabric of her Sleeve like a terrible gray snow.

"It's how he wanted to go," whispered Becker, and in her heart, Shan knew this to be true. "We should all be so lucky."

"What are you doing in there, by the way?" asked Jackal, hands running over the glass as if testing it for defects. "All by your lonesome?"

"Getting ready to use a Catch-All to nab the Split Second." Shan's legs were starting to cramp, so she cautiously switched their position.

"Good plan. But how were you gonna put the two pieces together?"

"Um, I hadn't really gotten that far," Shan Mei-Lin confessed. "But I was thinking maybe . . . Krazy Glue?"

"Not strong enough." Jackal then reached into his Toolmaster 44. "What you need is something with a little more bite."

Fixer #7 pulled out a section of white nylon that resembled the lacing of a football—except several feet long and without the football itself.

"A Stitch?" Briefer Shan was utterly confused. She knew that Stitches were used by the Department of Fun to keep people in The World from cracking up during fits of Laughter, but she'd never heard of one being used for this purpose before. "How will that help us?"

"It's the strongest cohesive ever made in The Seems. And you know what they say about Stitches in Time[30]?"

The twinkle in Jackal's eye said that even he didn't know it would work, but any doubts Becker and Shan might have had were swept aside by the veteran Fixer's bravado. Not to mention the fact that no one (not even the owner of Rufus the dog) had ever exploded from laughing too hard.

"Ben was right about one thing, though." #37 studied the interior of the Containment Field and ran his own Mission Simulator in his head. "This is a two-person job."

---

30. "A stitch in time saves nine."

The Fixers looked at each other, and it was pretty obvious that both were planning on being that second person inside.

"Ro Sham Bo?" asked the younger of the two.

"It's the only way."

In Becker's life experience, the simple hand game also known as "Rock, Paper, Scissors" had been the most effective means of resolving disputes at school or on the playground. Over the years he had developed a strategy—"play the person, not the hand"—and since Jackal was just about the manliest man he'd ever met, he figured there was no way he was throwing anything but rock. So he chose paper.

"Sorry, Ferdinand." Jackal's right hand cut Becker's paper neatly in two. "I've always been a scissors man myself."

As Becker kicked himself for making the obvious call (and for revealing his dreaded first name), Fixer #7 quickly scaled the wall of the Containment Field. Once he'd reached the top, he rolled up his own Sleeve—dusty and smelling of mothballs but still eminently protective—and pulled the mask over his head.

"Don't you need Hour Glasses, sir?" Shan realized with dismay that tossing hers up to the Fixer would be impossible. "You won't be able to see the Split Second without them."

"The 5th Sense will deceive you, Briefer Shan." Behind the goggles of his Sleeve, Jackal closed his eyes up tight. "But your 7th will always tell the truth."

When Shan Mei-Lin had descended through the deadly obstacle course presented by the Containment Field, it had taken her over ten painstaking, heart-wrenching minutes to reach the safety of the floor. To her and Becker Drane's amazement, Fixer Jackal blindly squeezed through the membrane on the ceiling—which had been designed to let things in but not out—then swung himself against one of the walls, kicked back to the opposite side, did a reverse tumble across the dirt of the floor, and rolled to his feet directly in front of the Briefer. All with his eyes closed. And all without a single scratch.

"Incredible." Shan's and Jackal's faces were now but an inch apart, and she watched him open his crystal blue eyes. "Totally incredible."

"Thanks, Brief." Jackal rotated his right shoulder, as if the tumble had thrown it a little out of whack. "But I'm still a bit rusty."

"Stop showing off in there, Tom." Becker forced his own dumbfounded jaw back into place. "How bad's the floor?"

"It'll hold for another ten minutes, maybe twelve." Tom gave Shan a wink to let her know that Time was on their side. "But my 7th says we got a problem with the Containment Field itself."

"I'm on it."

Becker placed his bare hands against the cold glass, then closed his eyes and extended his own formidable awareness. Instead of being intimidated by the clinic Jackal had just administered, he was utterly inspired to reach farther with his 7th Sense than he ever had before.

"You're right, Tom." Becker's eyes snapped open, and he reached for the flap of his Toolkit. "A big problem."

The young Fixer whipped out his Electric Eye™ and pressed it to the spot where he'd detected that something was amiss. Like a jeweler looking for a flaw in a precious stone, he scanned the core of the transparent wall, and it didn't take him long to find what he was looking for. Spreading like the filaments of a spiderweb or the branches of an oak tree were thin cracks in the glass, which told Becker exactly what he didn't want to hear.

The Containment Field was about to blow.

"Any day now, Drane," cracked Fixer Jackal. "We're not getting any younger in here."

"You're not getting any funnier either," fired back Fixer Drane, struggling to separate the pieces of This, That & The Other Thing.™ The three-part apparatus was designed for jobs involving machines or equipment on the verge of explosion—an unfortunately common occurrence considering the archaic nature of most Seemsian technology—and Becker hurriedly began the installation.

This he wrapped around the five surfaces of the Containment Field like transparent aluminum foil. That he roped around This as if he were binding up a birthday present with twine. And The Other Thing he clamped to the loose ends of That, so he could pull the entire contraption tightly against the glass and keep it from shattering into a million pieces.

"I think we're . . . ," Becker's frostbitten hands screamed in agony as he twisted the Tool with everything he had, ". . . all good."

Jackal nodded, then threw a look of concern at the young woman whose face was pressed against his. "How long have you been in here, Shan?"

"I don't know, maybe fifteen, twenty minutes before you got here."

"Then we don't have any Time to lose." Jackal reached inside Shan's Briefcase to put her plan in motion. The Tool they would rely upon to snare the runaway Split Second looked much like the top of a trampoline—a thin black fabric stretched inside a circular rim—except it worked by the exact opposite principal. Objects that made contact with its elastic face didn't bounce high into the air but had whatever force that propelled them utterly removed. "You do the Catching. I'll do the Stitching."

"Yes, sir."

Shan squeezed the Catch-All tight and focused on the half of the Split Second that ricocheted around them. But since it was moving a whole lot faster than her Hour Glasses suggested, she couldn't imagine how she would time the moment when she reached the Tool into its path.

"Just close your eyes, Shan." The Fixer seemed to know exactly what she was thinking. "Let the 7th Sense do the work for you."

The Briefer did as Jackal suggested, removing her Hour Glasses and shutting her eyes tight. She'd practiced this technique constantly at the IFR, in the Mission Simulators and on the final level of the Stumbling Block, but never had the stakes been so high.

"I don't know if I can do this, sir."

"I do."

"But I'm afraid."

"So am I." Jackal looked his Briefer in the eyes one last time and allowed her to see the truth of his proclamation. "That's what my MIM is for."

In Missions past, Shan Mei-Lin would have said, "I don't have much use for the MIM, sir," as she had done with Fixer Chiappa earlier on this fateful day. But the darkness of Meanwhile had steered her to a different place inside herself, and the utility of the Mission Inside the Mission was quite apparent. As was the identity of hers . . .

257

"Bohai," she whispered aloud, then shut her eyes again and reached out with her 7th Sense. This time, the fear that clouded her awareness disappeared before the love she felt for her long-lost brother, and just as Jackal has suggested, the path became clear. The very tips of the fingers that held the Catch-All seemed to measure the Split Second's loop and knew exactly when would be the right moment to interrupt it . . .

"Sorry . . . to bother you guys . . ." On the roof of the Containment Field, Fixer Drane was struggling with all his might to keep his grip upon This, That & The Other Thing. "But if you're gonna do this, you better do it now!"

Indeed, the cracks in the walls that had once been microscopic were expanding to the size of icy tendrils, and worse, the thin strips of metal that welded the ten-foot squares of glass together had begun to rattle like a radiator. Tom Jackal's eyes fell to the crumbling dirt beneath him, the blue light breaking through it in ever-increasing streaks. In his right hand was half a Second, an exact replica of the one that was about to explode through the floor on its way to the unsuspecting World. Regardless of the danger, it was long past time to Stitch the two together.

"Start your countdown, Shan."

Frozen Moment Channel, The In-Between

"Use your imagination?"

Briefer Harold Carmichael was still suspended in the In-Between, still struggling to weld the uncooperative Q-Turn into the Animal Affairs Tube. Tony the Plumber's idea had been brilliant in theory, but installing a heavy metal pipe inside a transparent-walled, magnetically-powered, electrified Tube wasn't exactly the same proposition as fixing a leaky faucet.

"That's easy for him to—*ooof!*"

All the wind was suddenly and forcibly yanked from the C-Note's lungs, and he didn't need Li Po or any other master of the 7th Sense to tell him that something *very* wrong had just happened in The Seems. His Blinker said the same thing it had for the last half hour or so—"Split Second repair in progress"—but that feeling of being out of breath only got worse when the Receiver on his belt started to blare.

"Briefer #321 here, over."

"*Listen to me, C.*" C-Note immediately recognized the caller as his favorite Fixer from the isle of Staten. "*You need to get yourself outta that Tube RIGHT NOW.*"

"Why, what's the 411?"

"*All's I know's the kid and his team were about to Stitch that crazy thing together, but something must've gone wrong.*" Tony the Plumber's voice had none of its usual swagger. "*'Cause the Essence of Time is coming your way!*"

"How much?"

"*Enough to trash a whole city—let alone you.*"

The med student in Briefer Carmichael recognized that the weak feeling spreading throughout his body was the sympathetic nervous system contacting the chromaffin granula, activating the adrenergic receptors and resulting in a surge of the first messenger hormone commonly known as adrenalin. "How long I got?"

"Less than sixty seconds." Tony didn't beat around the bush. *"Don't try to be a hero, kid."*

"But didn't you say the Essence was gonna take out a whole city?"

"There ain't nothing you can do about that now."

C-Note took five of those less than sixty seconds to listen to the roar of the In-Between and clear his heart and mind.

"We'll see about that," he said, before gently hanging up the phone.

Only a week ago, Harold Carmichael had been at wit's end—convinced that he didn't have what it took to be promoted to "the best job in The World." But a sloppy dollop of clouds painted by a former classmate of his had changed all that, and given C-Note the Confidence to do what he was about do now.

From within his Case, the Briefer removed a long sheet of Time-resistant fiberglass. It had originally been reserved for one of the Powers That Be who wanted spoilers on his car that would never rust.

"Sorry, dogg. I'm gonna have to get you next week—if there is a next week."

C-Note curled the fiberglass into the shape of a funnel, which he then inserted into the mouth of the Q-Turn, which he then connected to a brand-new catalytic converter that he had spit-shined himself. When clamped together, this combination added up to a makeshift version of the same remarkable device he'd seen with his mind's eye . . .

A car engine.

"Hope it takes premium."

"Whoa."

Becker Drane blinked away the stars from his eyes and slowly lugged himself back to his feet. He was amazed to find himself still atop the Containment Field, which, despite the physical trauma of the last few minutes, had managed to stay in one piece. The same could not be said for the inside, however . . .

"You guys okay down there?"

Huddled together in the center of the field were two people dressed from head to toe in the same white fabric. They hugged each other tightly, for only a small patch of dirt remained beneath them, most of the floor having collapsed into the highways and byways of the infinite blueness below.

"I think I'm fine, sir." Briefer Shan looked up at the boy on the glass ceiling above. "Fixer Jackal?"

Tom Jackal's eyes were closed tightly behind the goggles of his Sleeve, and for a second Briefer Shan feared the worst . . . until a weary voice emerged.

"No worries, kids." The Fixer finally opened his eyes. "I take a licking, but I keep on ticking."

Satisfied that his team was okay, Becker took a seat on the edge of the roof, ran a hand through his shag of sweaty hair, and tried to process what had just happened.

On the count of three, Shan had extended the Catch-All into the path of the Split Second, and despite its incredible velocity, it had stuck to the surface like a fly on a paper. The Second itself had been another matter, though. The two halves magnetically repelled each other at first, and when Jackal tried to force their reunion, a large stream of Essence had squeezed out. The Fixer shoved his Briefer out of the way, and though he was soaked from head to toe, his brute strength allowed him to finally Stitch the sphere back into one piece.

"Got a present for you, Drane." Jackal released his grip on Shan to hold up a silvery object that was wedged inside their bear hug. It kind of looked like a basketball, except made of shiny metal and with a single lace that wrapped itself all the way around. "Make sure you stop by the Fun House and thank them in person!"

Becker couldn't believe his eyes—the Stitch had actually worked, and the volatile Second was no longer split. It was just an ordinary rock that could go back to doing its job of helping provide a pleasant rate of Time in The World.

Ring! Ring!

"This had better be good news," Becker thought to himself, as he lifted his Receiver for what seemed like the umpteenth time that day. "#37 here."

"Kid—it's me, T the P."

"Please tell me that Tokyo isn't a dustbowl . . ."

"A dustbowl? Nah, you got it all wrong!" Becker had only heard Tony this giddy one time—five minutes before his beloved New York Jets blew a chance to make it to the Super Bowl. *"Our main man C-Note built himself a Time Machine!"*

"A Time Machine? What the heck is that?"

"It's like a V6 engine, except it don't run on fuel. Runs on Essence of Time—and it sucked up every last bit!"

"Way to go, C!"

"They're sayin' this could be the reusable energy source The World's been looking for!"

"Do me a favor, T." Becker knew from experience what this meant for Briefer Carmichael's career. "Make sure you ask him if he knows how many Fixers there are in The World."

"Done. How we doin' in Meanwhile?"

Becker wanted to shout at the top of his lungs, "We did it! We did it!" but he remembered what one of his mentors Casey Lake used to say at times like this. "We've still gotta cross our I's and dot our T's."

"Roger that, kid. T the P out."

The chief "I" for Becker to cross was getting his people out of that Containment Field, so he rolled up his own Sleeve and pried a hole in the thin, semipermeable membrane. From there, it was quick work to lower a rope down to his two partners . . .

"You first." Jackal gently squeezed Shan's shoulder, and both could feel how heavy the protective fabric had become. "If you don't get out of this thing soon, I'll have to call you Ye Ye."

As she grabbed the rope, the Briefer smiled at the use of the Mandarin term of endearment for grandmother. She asked, *"Ni hue bu hue shuo zhong wen?"*

"Shuo de hen cha." Jackal replied.

Becker lugged Shan out of the Containment Field and back onto the roof, then began to help her out of her Time-drenched Sleeve.

"We need to get you out of this thing and over to the Department of Health for a full checkup. And maybe even some more of that Anti-Aging Cre—"

But when he lifted the mask and goggles away from Shan's face, Becker couldn't hide the shock and horror on his own.

"What is it, sir?"

The Briefer's Sleeve had clearly soaked through, for what was once the face of a nineteen-year-old girl was now a woman in her early thirties. Becker didn't answer her question, only helped her out of her gear and wrapped her in a blanket. But if it had done this to Shan, what had it done to Tom Jackal, who had Stitched the Split Second with his very own hands?

"Tom, you gotta get out of that Sleeve right now."

"It's too late, Becker."

Shan could sense some awful knowledge passing between the two Fixers and she didn't like the way it made her feel. "Too late for what?"

"For an old man who's already lived nine lives."

Tom Jackal took off his Goggles and peeled back his Sleeve so only his head was revealed.

"No," said Becker.

Already, Tom's hair and beard were turning gray, and deep wrinkles were forming around his eyes. His back had also begun to hunch forward, as if it could no longer bear the weight of his body.

"Don't look so glum, people. These are what they call the golden years."

Whereas the effects of Shan's exposure seemed to have run their course, the Essence had not finished wreaking havoc upon Jackal's body. He struggled to remove the rest of the Sleeve, but even shedding himself of the soaked clothing didn't seem to stop the aging process at all.

"Surely there's something we can do . . . ," Shan's eyes asked Becker, but all the Fixer could do was shake his head, while beneath her blanket, the Briefer began to cry. Not for the twelve years that were gone, but for the man who was losing his life because he had saved hers.

"Becker . . ." Jackal willed himself forward and staggered down a thin strip of dirt that led from the center of the Field to the edge of the glass. "Get me my Toolkit."

The old Toolmaster 44, scarred and weathered from a long life of service, sat on the floor outside the Containment Field. As Becker hopped the ten feet down and dragged the leather saddlebag over to the glass, he could not look Shan in the eyes, because he didn't want her to see what was about to pour out of his.

"Bring it over here, boy." Jackal's voice was getting raspy and weak, so Becker had to lean in close to hear him.

"I know you're wondering how I could have left my family, knowing that I would never see them again." Becker shook his head no, but Jackal saw through it. "They wouldn't let me stay—not knowing what would happen to The World and that I had the power to stop it. They forced me through that Door."

With the crooked finger of a ninety-year-old man, Jackal feebly pointed to a pouch on the side of his Toolkit.

"I brought something to show you."

Becker unsnapped the pouch and there was only one item inside. It was a small Polaroid photo of the Jackals—Tom, Rhianna, and their children—piled on top of one another in a heaping mound of snow.

"I told you it was real, Becker." Despite his age, Jackal's eyes burned as brightly as they ever had. "It was all real."

Becker Drane forced a smile because he wanted the last moment of this great man's life to be a happy one.

"Don't feel bad for us, son, because our love will survive anything." The Fixer willed his lungs to draw one final breath. "And I know I'll see them in A Better—"

With that, Tom Jackal leaned his tired head against the side of the glass, and right before Becker's eyes, crumbled into dust.

Frozen Moments

Alton Forest, Caledon, Ontario

Jennifer Kaley stood beneath the fortress of Les Resistance and looked up at the night sky, disappointed. The distinct feeling she'd had ever since a mammoth tree smashed to the forest floor had mysteriously vanished without a trace. It wasn't the most pleasant sensation—a mix of chills, goose bumps, and nausea—but now that it was gone, Jennifer almost missed it. Like hiccups.

"Hello?" No one was allowed in the park after dusk (including JK) but she could've sworn she heard a footstep. "Is anybody out there?"

The woods had seemed almost enchanted when she returned to this spot, but now that magic hour had passed, and with it the promise of something extraordinary, she felt more than a little bit frightened.

"Marco?" The crunching through the leaves seemed to be

getting closer, and judging by the rhythmic "pit-pat," they were not the tracks of a deer or chipmunk. Jennifer waited expectantly for the "Polo" in return, but all that echoed back were footsteps that were growing in frequency and pace.

"C'mon, you guys. This isn't funny."

But then it hit her that none of her fellow club members knew that she was still in Alton. In fact, no one knew that she was—not her parents, not her friends, and not the rangers who had closed up the park for the night. The sounds of the forest rose up like a choir and the night seemed to turn even darker, and Jennifer couldn't take it anymore. She had to make a run for it . . .

Back through the brushes, over the waterfall, and around the rock formations she went. All kinds of terrible images flashed through her head, of other girls she'd seen on the news and stories people always told at school, and this only prompted her to move faster—until suddenly the footsteps stopped in their tracks. For standing in front of her was a boy about her age, with a messenger bag slung over his shoulder and a badge on his chest.

"Jennifer?"

"Yeah?"

"It's me, Becker." The boy stepped farther into the pale moonlight, and even though she'd only seen it once, almost a year ago, Jennifer immediately recognized his face. "Becker Drane."

If Becker was hoping for a soldier's reunion, he didn't quite get it. Not because Jennifer wasn't ecstatic to see him, but because she was convinced this had to be another dream. She looked the soon-to-be eighth grader up and down, his outfit only confirming that this was definitely a night vision or a hallucination from working too hard on the fort and not drinking enough water.

"Are you one of those dream-stalkers I read about in *Omni*?" Jennifer asked, figuring that since she had to be in an alternate reality, she could pretty much say anything she wanted.

"No," Becker returned. "This time it isn't a dream, it's real. Look."

Becker took a few steps closer before he realized the girl was truly scared. But she let him pinch her arm anyway.

"So?" She was still a lot more than doubtful. "I can get pinched in a dream and it's still a dream."

"Here." He threw the girl his Blinker. "Digital clocks don't work in dreams."

Jennifer studied the weird device, which was not exactly a digital clock and not the kind of object one might use to prove that everything is as it should be, but the accurate time and date onscreen at least gave her pause. She looked Becker up and down, then pinched herself one more time.

"Ouch." A little too hard. "So wait—if you're really here"— Jennifer was starting to accept the fact that he was—"then are you telling me that everything that happened last time in my dream was . . . real?"

"Um . . ." It wasn't totally lost on Becker that he was in grave violation of the Rules. Not just the Rule Against Using the In-Between for Personal Transport, not just the Rule of Thumb, not just the Keep Your Mouth Shut Rule, but the granddaddy of 'em all (and the one he'd recently promised not to break)—the Golden Rule. But after all that had happened tonight, he didn't really care.

"Yes."

For the next few minutes Becker spilled the beans and Jennifer picked them up, one by one. The Fixer let her look inside his Toolkit, showed her the Mission Report that explained "the bizarre incident of the falling tree," even led her to the locked and rusty Door on the side of the park ranger's hut, which he had used to make the journey here. By the time the two finally sat down on a hollow log in a patch of ferns, Jennifer was in the state of catatonia that can only come from finding out that everything you thought was real—including the very world in which you lived—was actually not what you thought at all.

"So you're saying that the feeling I've had all day was my 7th Sense?"

"Yeah." Becker nodded. "And if you were feeling it that strongly, you should totally fill out a Seemsian Aptitude Test. I bet they'd accept you at the IFR in a flash."

"Being a Fixer sounds pretty cool." Jennifer thought it over for a second. "But I think I'd rather be one of those people who try to help everyone on their way . . ."

"You mean a Case Worker?"

"Yeah. That seems like a totally sweet job."

"Totally. I'll see if I can put in a good word with Human Resources."

All around them, the crickets chirped in the night.

"There's one more thing I don't understand . . ." Jennifer looked at Becker with whatever suspicion she still had left. "How come you came here?"

"I . . . um . . . I just had a really hard day at work . . ." Becker's thoughts were running together. There was so much he wanted to say—about Tom Jackal, about Thibadeau Freck, about Amy Lannin, even about how he had followed Jennifer's progress against his better judgment. But the moment he tried to talk, the weight of The World that he'd been carrying on his shoulders all day, and perhaps all year, finally broke.

"What is it? What did I say?"

"Nothing," Becker reassured her, beyond embarrassed that he was bawling his eyes out in front of her. "It's me, not you."

Jennifer gave him some space to just be where he was, because she hated it when her mom or dad interrupted her when she just wanted to cry and get it out of her system.

"I wish I had a Toolkit, so I could give *you* something," Jennifer offered, and even though she didn't, it was the thought that counted to the Fixer.

"Back to your question . . ." Becker rubbed his nose on his sleeve and found his composure. "Remember when we had the Dream and hung out at the Point of View and talked about the Plan?"

"Of course I remember." In fact, Jennifer could still feel the wind on her face, hear the seagulls, and see the single sculler who had waved to the two of them as he rowed by on the Stream of Consciousness below.

"Well," Becker continued, "a lot of stuff has happened since then . . . and I'm just not sure if what I told you is true anymore."

"About The Seems?"

"No, not that." Becker knew that certain things were definitely true. "Just that there's a Plan and that everything that happens in it is good. Because I'm starting to think that the Plan—if there even is one—isn't so great."

"I don't know, Becker." Jennifer smiled at the irony of this situation, for it was the Fixer who had first convinced her to look at the glass half full. "After that dream, I woke up the next day and I tried to do what you said—to pretend that The World was a magical place and there was a Plan—and before I knew it, everything started to look different."

This made Becker happy, because he had never really gotten a full report as to whether the Dream he had helped design for Jennifer had actually worked. But that feeling quickly faded.

"A friend of mine died tonight," he confessed. "Somebody I cared a lot about."

"I'm sorry, Becker."

"Me too. And it's really hard for me to believe it was a good thing."

They just sat there for a little bit, looking up at the stars, both of them thinking they should probably say something else but not sure what that something else was. Jennifer finally broke the silence.

"So that's why you came here? To talk about the Plan and stuff?"

"Not really."

Becker didn't want to come off as creepy, but he had already come clean about The Seems, so he went out on a limb.

"Um, I don't think we talked about this in the Dream, but Fixers have this thing called a Mission Inside the Mission. It's kind of like a little story or a person that you keep in your mind when you're Fixing. So you don't get really freaked out about the fact that you're trying to save the whole World . . ."

"That makes sense."

"Well, I . . . after our last . . . meeting . . . I kind of fol-lowed along about how you were doing in your school, just to make sure you were doing okay. And since then, when I go on a job . . . my Mission Inside the Mission, is, um . . . it's you."

Jennifer didn't quite know what to say. She had definitely thought that Becker was cute when he had visited her in the Dream, but back then, she was so wrapped up in her own issues that she had never really thought much about it. (Not to mention she didn't think he was a real person.) Seeing him again tonight, with his shaggy hair and tear-stained face, basically worn down to nothing by the craziness of work, stress, school, family, and other worlds, she couldn't help but move a little bit closer to Becker on the log.

"That's cool. I've never been anybody's Mission Inside their Mission before."

They both laughed nervously, then looked away.

"I, uh, guess we better get going," said Becker.

Jennifer knew that he was right and that it was getting way too late to be out here in the middle of the woods. But before she pedaled home to beat the missing persons report her mom and dad would soon be filing, she decided to do something she'd never done before. Sure, she'd practiced it in the upper reaches of her imagination, and when it happened to girls in the movies, she always wondered if it could possibly be that perfect and romantic in real life.

There was only one way to find out.

Dunhuang, China

The city of Dunhuang was in ancient times the hub of the Silk Road, and was often referred to by the travelers who came through it as "*Sha Zhou*," or "beautiful desert oasis." The traveler who cautiously emerged from a nondescript door behind the Dinzi Lu bus station knew these facts, of course, for she had spent the first seven years of her life in this out-of-the-way place. The date on the local newsstands said it had taken her twelve more years to come back, but to Shan Mei-Lin, it seemed a whole lot more like twenty-five.

After she'd been debriefed by Central Command, the Briefer was given a complete physical by the Department of Health, which determined that she indeed had been transformed into a thirty-two-year old woman by the Essence of Time. But instead of being depressed or weighed down by the loss of her youth, Shan felt lighter than she had in years. Younger, even. Because no longer was she moving forward in her life to escape where she'd come from. No longer did she feel the need to run away.

The afternoon heat forced Shan to remove her denim coat as she made her way though the streets by memory. It was all coming back to her now—the grocery store where she would help her Ye Ye pick out vegetables, the vacant lot where she and Bohai would climb the mound of sand and dirt and declare everything they could see their kingdom, and most of all, the ramshackle three-bedroom house at the end of Lanzhou Street.

It only took Shan one look at the front lawn to confirm that her family still lived there, her brother included—for alongside her mother's favorite crumbly statue of the Buddha and her father's muddy work boots was the same beat-up dirt bike that Bohai bought for himself on his fourteenth birthday, the last the siblings shared together. Now it was she who was the older of the two, and Shan felt one last pang of anxiety, worrying how her family would react when they saw her hair, her hands, her age.

But then she remembered what Mr. Chiappa had said to her, right before they parted ways in Customs. The Fixer confessed that he too had heard a voice in Meanwhile that had guided him toward a light both inside and out. It had left the old English teacher with the feeling that perhaps what had always been interpreted as a warning in "the Manual" was, in actuality, a promise. One that should be savored, for, in regard to both of them, it had undoubtedly been kept.

"Those who enter Meanwhile are never seen again."

Shan Mei-Lin knocked on the door, and when her brother, Bohai, opened it, she was completely unprepared for the smile upon his face.

The Bronx, New York

"No offense, kid." The pretzel vender who worked Macomb's Dam Park rolled his steel cart onto the edge of the grass and threw a few more twists onto the coals. "I'm really not into Hare Krishna."

The bald, barefoot, and red-gi-wearing stranger held up a finger, pleading with the man to hear (or see) him out, and began to splay out a series of ancient tiles on the ground.

"Seriously, buddy—the game's starting in two hours and I don't want you scarin' off my customers."

When he first emerged through the Door into New York

City, the Initiate had dreamed of rescuing the Mission in a blaze of glory. But before he could even hail a cab, the shiverings and quiverings that had racked his body mysteriously stopped. Part of him feared that perhaps Li Po was right—that he was not ready to put his newly minted 7th Sense to the test—until his Blinker had flashed the good news: "Split Second Fixed." But even though The World had been saved and his friend Becker Drane had been the one to save it, the lanky Seemsian had to admit he was a little depressed about showing up late.

The Initiate had proceeded to wander the streets of New York for fourteen straight hours, stopping at coffee shops, warming his hands over a fire in the Bowery, even standing behind the glass at a twenty-four-hour car wash and watching the shiny rides go through. Yet again, his hopes of becoming the first one in his family to make it to Fixer would have to wait. To make matters worse, the subway ride he thought would take him back to Central Park had dropped him off here—and his Vow of Silence made it nearly impossible to ask for directions.

"If you wanna play Scrabble, be my guest." The pretzel guy angrily lifted up his cart and began to look for a new place to set up shop. "Some of us gotta make a living!"

As the vendor disappeared into the New York afternoon, the Initiate slumped his shoulders and sat silently on the curb. For six months he had yet to say a single word, but now, feeling more like a failure than he ever had in life, he couldn't take it anymore. He picked up his Receiver and dialed "Crestview 1-2-2."

"Hello?"

"Grandpa, it's me!"

"Simly?" Milton Frye was arguably the greatest Briefer who

ever lived, but he'd been retired for many years now and didn't hear as well as he used to—which is why he was shouting into his grandson's ear. *"What's wrong?"*

"I'm lost, Grandpa!" Briefer #356, also known as Simly Alomonus Frye, may have been dejected, but he couldn't believe how good it felt to use his vocal chords again. "I'm somewhere in New York City."

"I thought you were at that yoga retreat."

"I am. I mean, I was. I mean, I need your help!"

In a flurry of words, Simly related how a terrible premonition had led him literally across The World to the corner of East 161st Street and Ruppert Place. But by the time he was done, he was practically in tears.

"Easy, Simly, take it easy . . ." His grandfather's raspy voice had always been a source of comfort to Briefer Frye. *"I want you to turn around."*

"Okay."

"Do you see a big building in front of you?"

"Yeah! It says 'Yankee Stadium' on the front and there's all these people going in."

"Good. Now go up to the ticket window and ask for Jimmy the Usher. Tell him you're Milton Frye's grandkid and you need two front-row tickets for tonight's game."

Simly's face lit up—he had always dreamed of seeing the fabled New York Yankees play in person. His grandpa had met Mickey Mantle once, even watched The Babe play, and when he wasn't Briefing on historic Missions, he spent many a day perusing box-scores or sneaking off through the In-Between to catch a matinee.

"But, Grandpa, why two tickets? Who else is coming with me?"

"Who do you think's coming, ya numbskull?"

Though they often spoke on the phone, the two hadn't seen each other in forever, because the retired Briefer rarely left his house anymore. But Milton wasn't going to miss his only daughter's only son's first baseball game . . .

"And make sure you get me a bag of peanuts and a Coke!"

Cape Cod, Massachusetts

Five hours to the north of Yankee Stadium, straight up Interstate 95 and across the Bourne Rotary, Becker and Benjamin Drane were walking down a stretch of white sand beach. The Fixer had snuck into Shanty Town under the cover of darkness, and since his bedroom was stashed away in the basement, it was an easy trick to swap places with his Me-2. But getting back in good graces with his little brother was another story.

"So, Me told me you were feeling a little bummed out while I was gone?"

Benjamin's only response was a half-hearted shrug.

"Listen, I know that we haven't spent that much QT together, and it sucked to find out that a lot of the times when you thought you were doing something with me, it was actually Me-2. But I hope you realize how much you mean to me . . ."

Benjamin continued punishing him with the silent treatment.

"It's why I told you all those stories about The Seems—stories I never told anyone but you—and it's why I got permission to do something that's only been done a handful of times in the history of The World."

That at least got the boy to turn away from the ocean and look in Becker's direction.

"You know how you always said you wanted to be a Sunset Painter?" Benjamin nodded, and Becker pointed about a hundred yards in front of them where a man with a smock and a plastic beak on his nose quietly painted on an easel not ten feet from the shore. "Well, there's someone I want you to meet."

A soon as they approached, the stranger with the thin handlebar mustache was full of smiles.

"Zere he is. Ze man, ze myth, ze legend." The Maestro was truly thrilled to see his young friend again, and bent down to talk to the younger of the boys. "You know, your brother is a great man!"

Benjamin shyly smiled, as if to say, "Yeah, right."

"Figarro Mastrioni, Master of the Sunset Strip . . ." Becker said "Sunset Strip" with extra emphasis, because he knew the Maestro was a bit of a showman. "I would like you to meet my brother and aspiring artist, Benjamin T. Drane."

As soon as Benjamin realized he was meeting a real Sunset Painter and not another Bob Ross knockoff like the kinds he'd seen in the Catskills, his own vow of silence dissipated in a flash.

"Cool."

"Maestro, I know you don't normally give lessons. But I want you to show Benjamin everything."

Figarro bowed and, judging by the glorious Sunset over the Atlantic Ocean that was already half-completed on the canvas in front of them, Benjamin could tell he'd been left in good hands.

"Okay, dude. I guess I forgive you." The little boy extended a hand, and his older brother shook it. "But don't let it happen again."

With Benjamin getting his first taste of real Impressionism, Becker finally had a few minutes to be alone, and what better place to have them. He took a few deep breaths and the ocean air filled his lungs. To his left was a salt-water taffy shop with kids who loitered out front, eating cotton candy and popping wheelies on their dirt bikes. He was jealous that they didn't have to grow up ahead of time, while he felt like he'd aged twice his own thirteen years in one day. Much like the Briefer who had served so valiantly by his side.

Fixer #37 pulled a fresh Slim Jim from his back pocket and reflected upon what was by far the roughest Mission of his career. He knew that even though it had come to a successful conclusion, there would be a lot to answer for. Which is why he'd left a letter in the office of his former instructor before making his way back to Cape Cod.

Dear Fixer Blaque,

I'm sure you'll be getting a memo from Central Command, but I wanted you to hear it from me first: I broke the Golden Rule again tonight . . . and maybe some others. I take full responsibility for my actions

and apologize if this has caused any embarrass-
ment. I also look forward to telling you my side of the
story . . .

> *Yours Truly,*
> *F. Becker Drane (#37)*

P.S. Tom would have wanted you to have this.

He had included the old photograph of the Jackal family, because he knew how close the two legends had been. Fixer Blaque would undoubtedly take the second death of his best friend just as hard as the first, and Becker hoped the sight of Tom in such a happy place would ease the sadness. His own emotions were another matter.

As the waves splashed over his bare feet, Becker thought back to his conversation with Sully at the café. The Keeper of the Records had insisted that something was behind the Plan, but he had never said what it was. And after the crazy path this day had taken—from the disaster in Time Square to reuniting with Amy Lannin to Thibadeau Freck being shipped off to Seemsberia—it was hard to tell whether those A's, B's, and C's had led to D's, E's, and F's, if anywhere at all . . .

The one thing he did know was what happened in Alton Forest, and the simple memory of it brought a big smile to his face. He wasn't about to put it on his Post-Mission Report, but he was pretty sure that back in the Department of Time, a cube had recently arrived in the slush fund of the Daylight Savings Bank. It was no doubt already in his private tray, to be withdrawn and savored sometime in the future. But that didn't mean he couldn't savor it now . . .

Fixer Drane had been way too much of a wimp to make the first move with Jennifer Kaley, but thankfully she wasn't. His (and her) first kiss didn't last very long, maybe a second or two, but as Sophie Temporale had so aptly put it, "Time is relative." As Becker bent over and picked up an old seashell, he played over the memory again, and again, and again . . . and it only got better. Whatever the consequences of his actions on this Mission, he would think about that tomorrow. Today, he was just happy to be alive, and he chucked the shell into the ocean with a shout.

It skipped three times, then fell beneath the waves.

Epilogue

Thought Track #3, The End of the Line

"Last stop, End of the Line!"

The Conductor of the Trans-Seemsberian Express hopped off the train and into the cloud of steam that was forming around its giant steel wheels. Only seconds ago his brakeman had pulled the lever that made those wheels screech, bringing the locomotive to a halt in the remotest destination in The Seems. But much to the Conductor's surprise, not a single passenger was getting off.

"Last stop! End of the Line!"

The man in the blue hat and red tie scanned the platform one last time, then pulled a pocketwatch from inside his blazer. "24:59." Oh well. Time to turn the old girl around . . .

"All aboard the Trans-Seemsberian Express! This train will make the following station stops: Seemsberia, Obscurity, the Outskirts, and Beyond! All aboard!"

A few tired workers shambled off the wooden benches and dragged their heavy bags up the steps. Most the Conductor recognized as Thought Chippers—those who toiled in the unforgiving heat of Contemplation—but he was quite sure that the old guy in the dust-covered hat and beard was a Hope prospector. By the despairing look on his face, today's dig hadn't gone so well.

"That's all of 'em, Tommy." The Conductor gave his engineer the nod, then hopped on the bottom stair. "Let's move her out!"

Like some ancient lumbering beast, the last remaining steam-powered train in The Seems dragged itself into motion. Smoke belched from its stacks, pistons and coupling rods squealed, and with a final blow of the whistle, the Trans-Seemsberian Express slowly vanished into the night . . .

Leaving seemingly no one behind.

"That was nifty." A man's voice harshly split the silence, emanating from a dark alcove beside an out-of-order vending machine. "But totally unnecessary."

There was no response but the moan of a distant desert wind.

"I assure you, we are quite alone."

"None of us is alone," replied the voice of a woman, from the other side of the tracks. "Least of all out here."

Someone dressed in a hooded cowl emerged from behind a rusty handcar and began to make her way across the rails. The man she was approaching slipped from the safety of the shadows and lowered a sturdy hand to help her up to the platform.

"I should've known it would be you," said Sophie Temporale, pulling back the hood to reveal her flowing gray hair. "In my heart, I think I already did."

"Was I that obvious?" asked the man who now called himself Triton. Gone was the digital mask that had kept him shrouded during their previous conversation, replaced by a face and voice that the Time Being knew all too well.

"All this cloak-and-dagger stuff is right out of your playbook," she said. "Not to mention the backroom politics."

"When you are the hunted, you make do with whatever room you can find . . . be it attic, basement, or rooftop garden."

Triton led her to the westernmost portion of the station, where the Tracks ended in huge rubber stoppers that kept the Trains of Thought from careening off-rails. Unlike Sophie, he was dressed in jeans, hiking boots, and a warm hunting jacket to protect him from the winds that howled across the desert. The desert he hoped she would enter with him tonight.

"Have you given any more thought to my offer?" he asked.

"I have."

"And?"

"I've decided to accept."

The leader of The Tide clenched a fist to suppress any visible signs of excitement. Now that the Time Being was on board, the others would follow suit, and there was literally nothing to stop his plan from coming to fruition.

"Excellent."

Triton smiled and pointed to the Middle of Nowhere, where things like Time, Nature, and Reality quickly lost their meaning. Way, way out there in the shifting sands, just barely visible beneath the starless sky, was the glow of what could only be a campfire . . .

"Then follow me."

Glossary of Terms

Agents of L.U.C.K.: Members of a covert team charged with spreading the life-changing substance to its appropriate Sectors in The World.

A Better Place: Where people of The World go when they die.

California Cheeseburger: A cheeseburger with lettuce, tomato, mayonnaise, and raw onion.

Court of Public Opinion: The judicial branch of The Seems, interpreting and enforcing the Rules and Regulations.

Crestview: An exclusive gated community on the cliffs of the Stream of Consciousness.

Daily Plan: The leading newspaper in The Seems.

Daylight Savings Bank (FDIC): The Savings & Loan inside which The World's Frozen Moments are stored.

Day That Time Stood Still, the: November 5, 1997.

Dead Man's Hill: The lower half of South 5th Avenue, Highland Park, New Jersey.

End of the Line: The last stop of the Trans-Seemsberian Railroad—just on the edge of the Middle of Nowhere.

Essence of Time: The potent extract responsible for keeping The World on schedule.

Firsts, Seconds, and Thirds: The three naturally occurring geological phenomena from which the Essence of Time is distilled.

Frozen Moments: Pristine moments of human experience preserved in cubes of ice.

Fun House: The R&D wing of the Department of Fun.

Glitch: A small but lethal nuisance that can wreak havoc in The Seems and hence cause mass destruction in The World.

Grand Scheme of Things, The: The original design document used to build The World.

Highland Pizza: The inconspicuous Italian chalet on the corner of North Sixth and Raritan avenues in Highland Park, New Jersey. Also, Becker Drane's second-favorite restaurant.

Institute for Fixing & Repair (IFR): The state-of-the-art facility in The Seems responsible for training all Briefers and Fixers.

Irie: A Rastafarian exclamation celebrating anything that is good.

Jinx Gnomes: A popular comic strip turned hit TV show in The Seems.

Knockout Punch: A mix of 100% juice (not from concentrate) known to render those who drink it temporarily indisposed.

Manual (aka *The Compendium of Malfunction & Repair*): The technical volume containing "everything you need to know to Fix."

Marco Polo: 1. The Venetian trader and explorer who gained notoriety for his worldwide travels. 2. A form of tag, usually played in a swimming pool.

Meanwhile: A bleak and lightless nether region of The Seems.

Memory Bank: The fortresslike institution in which the Memories of The World are kept.

Metrocard: The reloadable laminate affording one access to the New York City subway system.

Middle of Nowhere: The only location in The Seems that is off-limits to everyone, regardless of Clearance.

Mischievous Imp: A former employee of the Department of Thought & Emotion who was sentenced to Seemsberia for sending unauthorized impulses and desires to the people of The World.

Most Amazing Thing of All: The most amazing thing of all.

Mother of All Glitches: The mother of all Glitches.

Obscurity: The retreat and wellness colony in The Seems attended by those who need a little time away.

Rock, Paper, Scissors (aka "Ro Sham Bo"): A game of simple hand gestures used in conflict resolution. (Note: Paper covers rock. Rock breaks scissors. Scissors cut paper.)

SBC (Seemsian Broadcasting Company): The top-rated drama and reality channel in The Seems.

Second Hand Store: A Time Square antiquary packed with tchotchkes from back in the Day. Prices negotiable.

Second in Command: The highest-ranking official in The Seems.

Seemsberia: A vast expanse of frozen tundra on the far reaches of The Seems.

SeemsBurger: A startup franchise attempting (with little success) to replicate Worldly "fast food."

Seems Chi: A "boundless first" form of calisthenics aligning mind and body before or after a long day of World-building.

Seemsiana Purchase: The windfall transaction in which private landowners sold a tract of property to the Powers That Be, with the stipulation that it be used for the construction of a new Customs terminal.

Silly Putty: An inorganic polymer invented by the Department of Fun in 1943 (WT) and leaked to General Electric in the hopes of bringing a little enjoyment to The World.

SNN (Seemsian News Network): The 25/7 breaking news source of The Seems.

Stumbling Block: A multitiered obstacle course designed to test the physical, emotional, and spiritual limits of Candidates at the IFR.

Sunset Strip: The back lot in the Department of Public Works where Sunset Painters prepare their daily masterworks for display.

Tastee Subs: With two convenient locations, the "tastiest" hero this side of Mickey's. Also, Becker Drane's third-favorite restaurant.

Thin Air: A Bermuda Triangle–like corner of The Seems where people inexplicably vanish, often never to be seen again.

Ticky: A member of the IT staff of the Department of Time.

Time Bomb: A volatile explosive activated by the Splitting of a Second.

Time in Memoriam: The downtown bakery responsible for such delectable treats as Déjà Vus, Hour D'oeuvres, and Linzer Tortes.

Time Square: The historic downtown center of the Department of Time.

Time Zone: One of three areas where Firsts, Seconds, and Thirds are found—Mountain, Lake, and Underground.

WDOZ: A radio station in the Department of Sleep broadcasting the sweet sounds of slumber to listeners in The World.

Wedgie: The always-traumatic experience of having one's full body weight lifted off the ground by the waistband of his/her skivvies.

Well of Emotion: A hollow or pit from which feelings are dredged.

White Rose System: The 24/7 fast-food mecca on Wood-bridge Avenue, Highland Park. Also, Becker Drane's favorite restaurant.

Zeppole: Italian for doughnut.

Time Is of the Essence

The production of Time in The Seems is a dangerous and intricate process. It relies primarily upon the mining of a series of minerals infused with an energy or "Essence" that causes things around them to age at a specific rate. These minerals are referred to as: Firsts, Seconds, and Thirds.

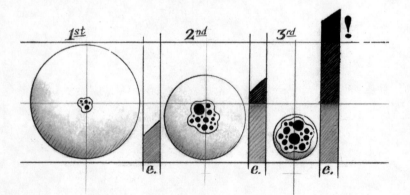

The shells of Firsts are soft and hold very little Essence, while Thirds are nearly indestructible and, should the surface be cracked, contain enough to obliterate both The World and The Seems. Once these orbs are harvested, they are encased in Time-resistant glass and flooded with water from the Stream of Consciousness to safely extract the Essence.

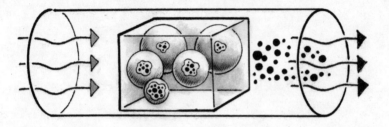

This infused liquid is then pumped via pipeline to the Department of Reality, where it is sprayed directly onto the Fabric as it is woven into The World.

The sum of the Firsts (1 tickogram), Seconds (2tg), and Thirds (3tg) is referred to as the "Multiple" and accounts for the rate at which Time moves. A Multiple of 9 (traditionally two Firsts, two Seconds, and a Third) equates to the "normal" pace of life in The World. During periods of stress or peak performance, however, Time can appear to slow to a crawl of 6, while if having fun, it may seem to fly by at 12.

Tools of the Trade

Selected Tools from "The Split Second."
(*Note:* Reprinted from *The Catalog*, copyright © Seemsbury Press, MCGBVIII, The Seems.)

Tool Name: Connective Tissue™
Use: Personal attachment. When Buddhist philosophy won't cut it, neither will anything else! (*Good to 5,546 lbs of breaking strength.*)
Designer: Al Penske

Tool Name: Can of Buttwhuppin'™
Use: Left your Fists of Fury™ on the kitchen table? No worries—open up a Can of Buttwhuppin' instead! Comes w/8-oz. reusable can.
(*Buttwhuppin' refills avail while supplies last.*)
Designer: Klaus van Barrelhaus

Tool Name: Elbow Grease™
Use: Get yourself out of any jam with the slipperiest substance known to man! Makes WD-40 look like peanut butter!
Designer: Al Penske

Tool Name: Sticky Feet™
Use: Keep yourself firmly planted on the ground with this all-star addition to your Fixer footlocker! Runs bigger than Speed Demons and Concrete Galoshes. *(Available in sizes 3–15, A-EEE.)*
Designer: The Handyman

Tool Name: Skeleton Key™
Use: Seems-World travel. A quantum Leap from the antiquated Door system! One per Fixer. DO NOT COPY.
Designer: Al Penske

Tool Name: Toolmaster 44™ *(Discontinued)*
Use: Distressed leather, handstitching, and deep saddlebags—seasoned Fixers only. *(Individually numbered/ Limited edition.)*
Designer: Morton Penske

Tool Name: Fallout Shelter™
Use: Catastrophe management. When you wish you didn't have to, you'll be happy you did. A must for anyone in the top thirty-eight.
Designer: Al Penske

Tool Name: Water Wings™
Use: High Tide is no match for these high flyers. Elevation to ten feet. Puncture resistant. *(Not to be combined with Hovercraft HG™ models or Turf Board XL™.)*
Designer: Al Penske Jr.

Tool Name: Q-turn™
Use: Re-routing, re-piping, re-directing, re-organizing, re-bounding, re-versing, re-gurgitating. Nothing is impossible with a little "QT!"
Designer: Al Penske Jr.

Tool Name: Oven Mitts™
Use: Sick of getting burned on the job? Protect the hands that feed you with these fluffy power-paws! *(Fireproof to Brimstone/cold-resistant to –273°K!)*
Designer: The Handyman

Tool Name: Catch-All™
Use: Falling Sky on your docket again? Whatever's coming at you, slow it down and rein it in with this golden glove hopeful! *(Available in velvet and everyday suede.)*
Designer: Al Penske Jr.

Tool Name: Flash in the Pan™
Use: Put the Iron Chef to shame with this fabulous flambé! Sheds polarized light for eight-plus minutes! Also good for frying an egg *(not recommended)*.
Designer: Al Penske Jr.

Tool Name: Hot Potato™
Use: Low carb diets draggin' you down? Come in from the cold with these toasty orbs sure to heat up your trip through the In-Between! *(Order now—they're flying off the shelves like . . . well, you know.)*
Designer: Chef LaRobierre

Tool Name: Hour Glasses™ *(Discontinued)*
Use: With hand-ground lenses and sleek North Seemsany design, these trifocals can literally make Time stand still! (Or speed up.) *Originally used by Reality Checkers back in the Day and available in* The Catalog *for the first time!*
Designer: Morton Penske

Tool Name: This, That & The Other Thing™
Use: Things falling apart again? Hold it all together until you can apply the perfect Fix! *(Some assembly required.)*
Designer: The Handyman

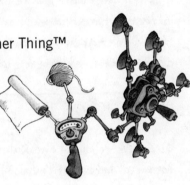

Tool Name: Sticks & Stones™
Use: Will break *their* bones—when names are not enough to harm a flea. Fighting is never recommended, but if attacked, make them pay! *(Pressure-treated Stick. Stone that would level a Philistine.)* Not responsible for bodily injury resulting from use of Tool.

*For more information on Tools, arcana, and Seemsian *détritus en général*, please visit the Fixer's Lounge area of theseems.com. [Password: **LTF-FTL**]

Form #**1030**
Post-Mission Report

Mission: The Split Second [037009]
Filed by: F. Becker Drane

Summary:

This was a very challenging Mission. I've had some personal things going on and unfortunately, it's kind of spilled over into my professional life. On the other hand, I believe great strides were made into understanding the infrastructure and methods of The Tide and I hope this will be taken into consideration. Regardless, I am confident this experience will serve me well in the future.

Areas for Improvement:

Obviously, following the Rules has been a major problem for me of late. But I'm also looking forward to improving in several other key areas, including hand-to-hand combat, maintaining my composure during frustrating moments, and strategy regarding Rock, Paper, Scissors.

Rate Your Briefer (1–12): <u>11</u>

Shan Mei-Lin basically put on a Briefing clinic today. Not only did she shake off the initial blast in Time Square to continue serving on the Mission, but she also showed great initiative and courage when she was separated from not one but two Fixers. Most of all, she was prepared to make the ultimate sacrifice for The World. With a little work on the MIM (work that may already be done), I recommend her without reservation for Fixer.

Suggestions Box:

Just an idea, but perhaps on "cataclysmic"-level Missions like this, it may be worth calling in a team of Fixers, multiple specialists whose talents could mesh into a cohesive unit, and thereby maximize safety for The World. That and combining the Receiver into the next series of Blinkers. It's a pain to carry both.

____✓____ Check here if you wish to donate used or outdated equipment for the IFR's "Tools for Tots" program.

_____F. Becker Drane_____ Signature

FIXER AND MRS. JELANI BLAQUE
& THE POWERS THAT BE
CORDIALLY INVITE YOU AND A GUEST TO

A RETIREMENT CELEBRATION FOR

FIXER LUCIEN CHIAPPA (#12)!

WHEN: MIDSUMMER NIGHT'S EVE
WHERE: THE FLIP SIDE, THE SEEMS
RSVP: BECKERDRANE@GMAIL.COM

Kindly indicate your choice of entrée when RSVPing:
Corsican Chicken Casserole
Blackened Compliment with Medley of Seasonal Squash
In-Between Burger & Fries

Music By:
The Procrastinators, The Musical Genius & More!

NO GIFTS, PLEASE.
JUST BRING YOUR BEST MR. CHIAPPA STORY TO SHARE!

Admits one plus guest. Original invitation required at door.

SEEMS CROSSWORD

*For solved puzzle, please visit www.theseems.com > Fixer's Lounge

Across

1. He only got a C+, but it sure came in handy
5. They're usually in Alton Woods (if you know where to look)
8. "A _____ in Time Saves Nine"
12. Connects The Seems and The World
13. 2400 is perfect
14. Loves to watch Jinx Gnomes (or from Charlie Brown)
16. Rachel Adler Bat-Mitzvah, in a manor of speaking
17. Jennifer Kaley's Case Worker
18. Their "'Tom Sawyer" rocked both sides in the 80s
20. Simly's grandpa Milton's favorite baseball team
22. Last sighted near Tatoosh
23. 12th Sense
24. Fixer #1 meditates here
25. Casey tried to surf these (you shouldn't)
26. He can be found flipping burgers at this side
27. National holiday in The Seems

Down

2. Sweeter than a blackberry or a boysenberry :-)
3. Simly _____ Frye
4. Little Unplanned Changes of _____
6. The Glitch and Permin live there now
7. Sleep ingredient--not Refreshment, not Snooze
9. Comes in regular and messenger bag styles
10. "_____ to Fix, Fix to _____"
11. The Institute for Fixing & _____
13. "You can't be twenty on _____ mountain, though you're thinking that you're leaving there too soon"
15. Easier way in than a Door
17. Freck family winter chalet
19. Only place to get a newspaper (or Soft Drink) in the In-Between [Hint: BeckerBlog]
21. Becker's friend Connell Hutkin's mother's second husband

Deleted Scenes from *The Split Second*

In every Seems book (and all books, really) there are many scenes that end up on the cutting-room floor. But in this book, dear reader, you are in luck! We have decided to release two never-before-seen deleted scenes from *The Split Second*. Read on and enjoy.

Deleted Scene #1:
"Stanton & Rivington"

This scene was part of a larger subplot involving Fixer #11, also known as Lisa Simms. In her "real life," Lisa is first violinist for the London Philharmonic Orchestra, but she is famous in The Seems for being one of the three Fixers who took part in the Mission known as "Hope Springs Eternal." This thread was meant to explore the complicated relationship between Fixers Simms, Jelani Blaque, and Tom Jackal, who broke Lisa's heart long before he "died" on The Day That Time Stood Still. In the end, the authors decided to save that story (and the fate of escaped Tide operative Lena) until The Lost Train of Thought.

———————

Corners of Rivington and Stanton, New York, New York

"Simms to Central Command, come in." Lisa Simms ducked into the shadows of a construction scaffold and whispered into her Receiver. "I've got her."

In an apartment across the street and three stories up, Fixer #11 could just detect the slender outline of a woman nervously pacing and smoking a cigarette.

"Where is she now?" came back the Dispatcher.

"Appears to be a Tide safehouse." She upped the magnification of her Trinoculars™ and took a closer look through the gauzy white blinds. "I think she's alone, but I can't be sure."

Lisa had just arrived at 274 West 12th Street to investigate the loss of radio contact with Becker Drane when she had spotted a female dressed in black scaling down the fire escape and making the final ten-foot jump to the sidewalk. The fugitive matched exactly the description of the Tide operative named Lena. She was listed as "at large" in the most recent Mission Update, and the Fixer had immediately given chase through the streets of the West Village, below Washington Square Park, across Broadway, and finally to here, at the corner of Stanton and Rivington.

"Should I take her down?" The violinist knew that her classical training applied not only to Beethoven and Rachmaninoff, but to the art of Fixing, and if she needed to extract Lena from New York City, she wasn't afraid.

"*Negative.*" The Dispatcher's voice was hoarse beyond recognition from the longest day of his career. "*Maintain surveillance until further orders or ground situation changes.*"

"But, sir, I was hoping to assist Drane with the Fix." Lisa snuck a quick peek at the Blinker on her belt. "Mission Update says '*Split Second repair in progress.*'"

"That's a double negative, #11." The Dispatcher's tone left no room for argument. "*This is the best chance we've ever had to observe the Tide's World based operations. Besides, #37 is already being assisted by Fixer Jackal.*"

In her twenty-plus years as a Fixer, Lisa Simms had experienced more surprises than she cared to remember, and she felt quite confident in her ability to roll with the punches. But nothing could have prepared her for the words that she'd just heard in the ear-piece of her Receiver . . . or what it felt like to hear them.

"Fixer who?"

Deleted Scene #2:
"The Small Blue Envelope"

Cutting this scene from the book definitely hurt, because the authors wanted to return to the place where the story began. It was removed from the last chapter in the interest of pacing, but hopefully readers will enjoy finding out what happened to the people we met there . . .

Los Angeles, California

A tall, skinny kid in hospital scrubs took off his headphones and stepped beneath the overhang of a weather-beaten bus stop. The noontime sun was high in the sky, and since most of the commuters who used this stop were still at work, the bench sat unoccupied. Which was all good as far as Harold "C-Note" Carmichael was concerned.

This had probably been the craziest week of his life. He'd gone from down to up to up to down so many times, he didn't know which end was which anymore. But when Tony the Plumber had slapped him on the back and told him the one thing that every Briefer longs to hear— "I think I'm looking at #39!"— C-Note thought he'd finally, FINALLY, arrived at the top. And then he came back to The World . . .

There, tucked into his mail slot at USC Medical School was a small blue envelope, which he knew meant only one thing: the score on his dreaded surgical exam was in. Two weeks ago, C-Note was pretty sure he'd shanked the thing, which would pretty much end his notion of becoming Dr. Harold Carmichael. Or at least the kind of doctor that his mother always dreamed he could be.

As he sat upon the bench and tried to work up the courage to open the same blue envelope, two people he recognized as regulars on this bus line stepped in from out of the sun. It was that nice but shy young Mexican girl and that really NOT nice guy in a business suit who C-Note usually did everything he could to avoid. But what he couldn't figure out was why they were holding hands . . .

"*Hola,*" said Albie Kellar, noticing the Briefer's stares. "How you doing over there?"

"I'll tell you in about thirty seconds."

Albie whispered something in the ear of Anna Morales, and she smiled, as if some secret were passing between them. Together, they watched as the student/pizza delivery driver/car detailer who would in two weeks be promoted to the ranks of Fixer opened up the envelope in his lap and read the score that was printed on the page. Interestingly, his face had no reaction whatsoever—not until he picked up his cell phone and chose one of the numbers programmed into speed-dial. At that point, it was pretty clear to Albie and Anna exactly how C-Note was doing over there . . .

"Hey, Ma . . . guess what!"

READ ON FOR A SNEAK PEEK AT
BECKER'S NEXT MISSION IN

Can Becker Drane get this Mission back on track?

the seems
the lost train of thought

John Hulme and Michael Wexler

Eve Hightower stepped to the front of the executive suite, having exchanged her judge's robes for the business casual attire of her office. But there was nothing informal about the way she cleared her throat and began to address the four others who'd been asked to join this classified briefing.

"I know you probably expected the administrator of T&E to run this meeting, but as you'll soon see, Dr. Thinkenfeld's absence is not a coincidence."

The Second in Command grimly turned to the first page of the Mission Report and continued.

"Yesterday morning at exactly 07:35 a.m., a train loaded with all The World's Thought for the next six weeks departed on schedule from the End of the Line. Unfortunately, it failed to reach the next station stop in Seemsberia—let alone deliver its precious cargo back to this department."

The gasp that slipped from Becker Drane's mouth wasn't the only one in the room.

"When all attempts to reach conductor or crew proved futile, the decision was made to assemble a team of Fixers whose combined skills made them uniquely qualified to locate and retrieve the missing train."

Eve Hightower pressed the intercom button at the head of the table.

"Kevin?"

As the AV Mechanic dimmed the lights, Eve swiveled her chair around to face a flat-screen display.

"Central Command received the following transmission early this afternoon."

The images that flashed onscreen shook like a home movie— barely focusing on a flip-flopped foot, a mound of sand, and the bright blue sky above before tumbling crazily toward something new. But whoever was operating the camera soon got her bearings, and a wide and barren landscape finally came into view.

"I hope you guys are getting this."

Becker immediately recognized the Australian accent of Casey Lake, and deduced that the footage had been shot via the wireless Seeing-Eye attachment available on all the Toolshed's latest optics.

"We lost radio contact with Central Command approximately one hour ago, but we'll continue broadcasting just in case." A gust of wind caused Casey's microphone to pop and skip, but the audio quickly recovered. *"Update is as follows."*

The camera began to march slowly up the rise of a sand dune.

"Away team arrived End of the Line to find station staff absent and no visible sign of the missing train. Initial sweep yielded no evidence of theft or intrusion, but following a hunch, Fixer Simms uncovered a set of tracks leading directly into the Middle of Nowhere—"

Becker was stunned to be looking at actual footage of that forbidden wasteland on the very edge of The Seems—especially when Casey crested the hill and peered down upon the other side.

"This is what we found when we followed those tracks."

Stashed in the valley formed by a ring of towering dunes was a rusty red caboose, half-buried in the sand. The train it had once been attached to was nowhere in sight, nor were the rails it must've ridden to get there. In fact, the only other things visible onscreen were the sweeping sands and two figures scrambling around the car, both wearing Extremely Cool Outfits™ to protect themselves from the heat.

"How in the name of the Plan did it get there?" asked the white-haired old woman who was sitting directly to Becker's right. "I don't see any train tracks."

"Please hold your questions until we reach the end of the clip, Sylvia," answered a voice with a thick African accent.

"Sorry, Jelani."

Becker bit his own tongue and refocused his attention onscreen, where a massive figure was poking his head from beneath the abandoned caboose.

"Locking clamp snapped like twig." As usual, the Sprechene-infaches™ struggled to translate the Fixer known as Greg the Journeyman's obscure Yakutsk dialect. *"What could do such thing?"*

"Smell that Scratch?" Casey sniffed the air, and the Journeyman did the same. *"It's London to a brick that a Brainstorm came through there."*

Fixer Lake tilted her eyes (and the camera) up to the roof, where the third member of the away team was sitting in the lotus position, eyes closed, arms extended.

"Po, you picking up anything?"

The inscrutable Li Po, #1 on the Duty Roster, silently shook his head no.

"Me neither." Casey spat with frustration, then spoke directly to whoever might be listening to her broadcast. *"If you're getting this back home, we're pretty much flying blind out here when it comes to the 7th Sense. Can only assume that stories about Middle of Nowhere are true, and will compensate accordingly—"*

"Cassiopeia!"

The voice of an Englishwoman called out, and Casey turned the camera toward where the caboose would be heading if it were still attached to a train. A slender figure was emerging from a path that cut between the dunes.

"No more tracks, as far as my Trinoculars™ can see," said Fixer #11, Lisa Simms. *"But I do see puffs of smoke in the direction of the mountains."*

"Then that where we must go," said Greg, and despite the shadow that came over Fixer Simms's face, she agreed.

It was easy to see why the Powers That Be had assigned this particular group of Fixers. Casey was a no-brainer for team leader, and if there was any chance of 7th Sensing where the missing train might be, Li Po would be the one to feel it. Greg the Journeyman's physical strength was the stuff of legend, while Lisa Simms was the only active Fixer to have entered the Middle of Nowhere and lived to tell the tale. With such a mighty collection of talent, Becker couldn't fathom what went wrong.

He was about to find out.

"All right, mates." Onscreen, Casey Lake was pulling a hand-painted Turf Board™ out of her Toolkit. *"Let's get after these whackers . . ."*

But their departure was interrupted by the sight of Fixer #1 rising to his feet atop the caboose and extending a finger off toward the horizon.

"What's wrong, Po?"

Casey and the others turned in the direction he was pointing to see a strange light emanating from somewhere on the other side of the dunes. Whatever the source, it was almost as bright as the sun shining over their heads.

"It is . . . *werry beautiful*," whispered Greg the Journeyman, and when he turned to the increasingly shaky camera, there were tears rolling down his bearded cheeks. As if to confirm his opinion, Casey turned her gaze back toward the light, which was so bright now that it hurt to look at even in the screening room.

"Cover your eyes, people!" The broadcast was starting to flicker and skip. "Cover your eyes!"

Greg directly ignored her order, stumbling even closer to the source of the eerie illumination, while Lisa Simms had switched over to Night Shades™ and was desperately flipping to the darkest setting.

"Cassiopeia, I think we should—"

But the woman who was the first violinist for the London Philharmonic in her "real job" could not muster the strength to finish the sentence. Fixer Simms collapsed to the ground with her hands over her eyes and rolled into a little ball. And the light got brighter still.

"What is it, Po?" Fixer Lake shouted, and for the first time since they'd met three years ago, Becker heard fear in her voice. "What's happening?"

On the roof of the caboose, Li Po was also wiping streaks from his eyes, but from the smile on his face, he appeared to be laughing, not crying. Then the unquestioned master of the 7th Sense turned toward the camera and did something he hadn't done in almost thirty years.

He spoke.

"The Most Amazing Thing of All."

The last thing Becker saw was Casey Lake digging a hole in the sand beneath her feet—as if she might claw her way to some refuge from the unbearable brightness. And then, in a flash . . .

. . . the video went white.

JOHN HULME AND MICHAEL WEXLER are also the authors of *The Seems: The Glitch in Sleep* and *The Seems: The Lost Train of Thought*. They accidentally stumbled upon the existence of The Seems after opening an unlocked Door in Wilmington, North Carolina, during the summer of 1995. From that moment on, they were obsessed with the curious realm and sought to pen a book series based on their discovery. Though the project was held up in administrative Red Tape for nearly eleven years, the Powers That Be finally signed off on its release, resulting in the text you now hold.

Hulme lives with his wife, Jennifer, and his children, Jack and Madeline, in a small New Jersey town with crookety sidewalks and tree-lined streets.

Wexler was recently spotted near Tatoosh, Washington. The sighting was never confirmed.

www.theseems.com